P9-CQA-554

7651 00060 6290

√

2/07

MYSTERY

Sykes, Jerry
Lose this skin

Crestwood Public
Library District
4955 W. 135th Street
Crestwood, IL 60445

Lose This Skin

Jerry Sykes

FIVE STAR
An imprint of Thomson Gale, a part of The Thomson Corporation

Crestwood Public
Library District
4955 W. 135th Street
Crestwood, IL 60445

THOMSON

GALE

Detroit • New York • San Francisco • New Haven, Conn. • Waterville, Maine • London

SYK

THOMSON

GALE

™

Copyright © 2007 by Jerry Sykes.

Thomson Gale is part of The Thomson Corporation.

Thomson and Star Logo and Five Star are trademarks and Gale is a registered trademark used herein under license.

ALL RIGHTS RESERVED

This novel is a work of fiction. Names, characters, places, and incidents are either the product of the author's imagination, or, if real, used fictitiously.

No part of this book may be reproduced or transmitted in any form or by any electronic or mechanical means, including photocopying, recording or by any information storage and retrieval system, without the express written permission of the publisher, except where permitted by law.

Set in 11 pt. Plantin.

LIBRARY OF CONGRESS CATALOGING-IN-PUBLICATION DATA

Sykes, Jerry.
   Lose this skin / Jerry Sykes.—1st ed.
     p. cm.
   ISBN-13: 978-1-59414-537-7 (alk. paper)
   ISBN-10: 1-59414-537-7 (alk. paper)
    1. Police—England—London—Fiction. 2. Children—Death—Fiction.
  3. Criminal investigation—Fiction. 4. London (England)—Fiction. I. Title.
  PR6119.Y535L67 2007
  823'.92—dc22   2006029979

First Edition. First Printing: February 2007.

Published in 2007 in conjunction with Tekno Books and Ed Gorman.

Printed in the United States of America on permanent paper
10 9 8 7 6 5 4 3 2 1

For Dixie

PROLOGUE

"Go on, Karl, give your Gran a kiss." Rhiannon Burns's tone was gentle but insistent.

Her son hesitated at the foot of his grandmother's bed, a little afraid. Looking at her crinkled leather face under the light and shade of the bedside lamp, he sought out some hint of emotion in her solid pupils, but it was as if she had fallen asleep with her lids open. The folds of skin in her neck looked like damp old newspapers stacked in a cupboard, and great knots of bone were turning her fingers into petrified claws.

It's all right, you won't catch her arthritis, Rhiannon wanted to tell him, but she too found it difficult to accept the picture of her mother fast becoming a housebound skeleton.

"Come on, you've got school in the morning," she said instead, putting her hands on Karl's shoulders and gently pushing him towards the bed. At first he seemed to resist the momentum, but then all of a sudden he darted forward with his arms outstretched, falling headfirst onto the bed and planting a kiss on the shadow on the bedclothes cast by his grandmother's head. "Bye, Gran," he squealed before running out of the bedroom.

The old woman placed her hand on the spot that Karl had kissed and smiled. "He's a good boy," she said.

"Most of the time," smiled Rhiannon. From out in the hall she could hear Karl opening the front door, a burst of voices and music echoing in the stairwell. "I'll call you soon, Mum."

Rhiannon stepped up to the bed and kissed her mother on the cheek. "Bye," she said, and then turned and left the bedroom.

Karl was waiting for her on the communal landing. Impatient to get away, he started down the stairs as soon as she stepped out of the flat and pulled the door closed behind her, calling out a final farewell as she did so. On the ground floor, Karl pushed open the front door of the building and stepped out onto the short path that led up to a broken gate and the street.

Curdled screams caught his attention, and he looked over towards the pavement to see a man and woman with their faces inches apart, arguing. He could not make out what they were saying, the cries and strangled sentences, the grunts and broken words, but from the fractured rhythms of their body language it looked like it was not the first time that they had been at each others' throats. A group of people was standing on the pavement a few feet away, watching with amusement. Outside the pub on the corner to his left, another group of people was also watching the argument. And to his right, Karl saw a third group laughing and pointing at the couple fighting.

Karl thought the people watching were having a good time, and he wanted to run up to the gate and get a closer look, join in the fun. He glanced over his shoulder to see where his mother was and, on hearing the clack of her feet on the first floor landing, turned back to the action.

He saw that red temper had flared in the man's face, and in the short breaks in the traffic on Brecknock Road, he heard a hard rumble of abuse pouring from his contorted lips.

The object of his anger, a small brunette in a sleeveless black blouse and khaki shorts, tried to stand proud and firm, but her head and shoulders shuddered under the constant pounding of his dark assault. She shuffled around on her feet, turning her head from side to side as if attempting to deflect his rage.

Karl felt a curious sense of fascination in the pit of his

stomach, a secret thrill at the terrible compulsion of it all.

"What's all that noise?" said Rhiannon, stepping out onto the path. "What on earth's going on out there?"

"It's a fight," replied Karl, tearing his gleeful attention from the couple for a second.

Rhiannon scoped out the scene in silence: the couple fighting out on the pavement, blocking their route, the small groups of people watching in childish fascination, and, standing in front of a car stuck in the middle of the street, two men who regarded the spectacle with an attitude of superior detachment.

Karl started to drift up the path.

Rhiannon watched the couple argue in grim remembrance, echoes of her own marriage breakdown in the to and fro of anger.

The man slapped the brunette across the face, snapping her head to the side, and a thin stream of blood and spittle shot out of her mouth. She stumbled and reached out a blind hand as a burst of startled breath and laughter jumped from the audience.

"He just smacked her across the face," gasped Rhiannon, feeling a queasiness start in her stomach.

Red let the brunette regain her balance, ten feet to the right of the gate, and then he stepped up to her again.

Rhiannon noticed that Karl was now almost at the gate.

"Karl, come back here," she called out to him, but her words fell on deaf ears and so she started walking up the path.

On reaching Karl at the gate, she heard the sound of a police siren from the direction of Tufnell Park tube station. The feuding couple seemed not to have heard, their language and hand gestures as hard as ever, but the audience sensed that the fun would soon be over and started to drift from the scene.

Rhiannon glanced up the street. Seconds later she saw the police car appear and, almost at once, start to slow down. She reached out and put her hands on Karl's shoulders.

The siren was getting louder, the police car closer.

Sensing his final chance, Red stepped up close to the brunette. He raised a hand smeared in blood, and slapped her hard across the face, causing her to fall to the kerb like a stone, scraping her knees as she hit the ground. Stunned, she shook her head a couple of times and then, taking a deep breath, lifted her head to let the man see that she was not beaten.

In the latest scuffle, Red and the brunette had rolled out of his line of sight, and so Karl wriggled from under his mother's hands, opened the gate, and ran out onto the pavement, taking up a position on the edge of the kerb. Rhiannon took a step forward and made a grab for him, but then something changed her mind and she glanced up the street to see where the police car had got to, knowing that it would soon all be over. She watched it approach and slow down, the siren still piercing the cool night air, but then to her astonishment it appeared to speed up again as it neared the car parked out in the street. The two men standing in front of the car had to jump out of its path as the police car cut in too close to them, the driver appearing to lose control for a second. The car shuddered and jerked from side to side before the driver managed to regain control, a loud screech tearing out from underneath the protesting metal, but he seemed to be having trouble with the brakes.

Refreshed by the sounds of the police car, the brunette climbed to her feet and lurched at Red in a final stab at righteous retaliation. Crashing into him, she started to pummel his face and chest with her fists. Red took a step backwards, flailing his arms in the air, and tried to deflect her blows. But the force of her rage caused him to lose his balance and, finding himself falling, he spun around in a last gasp attempt to remain on his feet. In the ensuing tumble of limbs, he knocked Karl into the road just as the police car scraped against the kerb.

Silence echoed in the street, and then the hoarse cries of Rhiannon Burns ripped through the scene as her son was hit square on the right hip and tossed into the air. Spiralling across the front of the car, cracking the windshield, he bounced on the roof and the boot before crashing down onto the road. A pool of blood spread around his head and shoulders.

1

Thursday, 21 October

Seven months after the event, Frank Roscoe still had no clear recollection of the precise moment that he had been shot.

He could remember the blue flash of a gun in the open rear window of the car that pulled up in front of him, and he could remember the moment he crashed to the street in a sudden burst of blinding pain, but the fraction of a second in which the gun flared and a bullet shattered his left heel still held no memories for him at all.

Since the incident he had spent much of his time in silent concentration, attempting to reconstruct the sequence of events in his mind, running the moments before and after the shooting into one another to recreate the entire scene. But even after all this time, he had come no closer to seeing the truth. It was as if the moment had been cut from his bank of memories in order to spare him future flashback trauma, and it disturbed him to think that such an important moment had all but disappeared from his life. His subconscious, too, seemed to have buried the incident deep in his dreams. The nights he came close to seeing something, he would wake from the depths of sleep with a jolt and find himself stretched out on the bed in a cold skin limbo.

"There's still some scar tissue around the base of the tendon," said the doctor, running her fingers across the raised pink scars that snaked around his ankle.

Her hands felt cool and hard to the touch, almost inhuman,

more like pieces of timber than flesh and bone, but Roscoe knew Dr. Ellen Jenkins to be all too human. A doctor of considerable skill and compassion, she had been the surgeon who had looked after him from the start, performing the operation to rebuild his ankle from the splintered pieces of bone and torn muscle that the bullet had left behind. And then, despite her tremendous schedule, making the time to see him on a regular basis afterward, easing his fears and making him feel like he was the sole patient on her list that mattered.

"I can feel it," said Roscoe. "It's like there's something in my shoe all the time, a pebble or something."

The bullet had clipped the top of his heel and torn from the bone part of the sheath that housed the Achilles tendon. The tear had been repaired, but some scar tissue still remained in the base of the sheath and it was preventing the tendon from moving unobstructed.

"That should feel better in time," said Ellen.

Roscoe felt short little snaps of pain in his foot as she massaged the base of the tendon. "You sure about that?"

"Well, there'll always be some scar tissue. The bullet did a lot of damage, but the more you help it, the harder the body'll work to overcome it."

"I try and walk a couple of miles every day," said Roscoe.

"That all helps," said Ellen. "But the main thing at the moment is to keep seeing the physio. While the body's still healing itself. You are still seeing him, aren't you?"

"Twice a week," said Roscoe, grimacing under her touch.

"Don't worry, he'll have you back at work in no time," said Ellen, and then paused to look at him from under the crooked fringe of her bangs. "That is what you want, isn't it?"

Roscoe hiked his shoulders. "I'm still thinking about it," he said, avoiding her gaze.

Ellen changed tack. "Is your father still helping you out at home?" she asked casually, recalling the elderly man who had sat in accusing silence beside his son's bedside each visiting time, leaving on the dot as soon as his allocated time was up.

"No, he . . ." Roscoe corrected himself. "We were never that close, and his visits were just too . . ." His forehead creased as he sought a suitable word. "I don't know, I guess too painful for both of us. In the end, it was easier for me to hire one of the neighbors to run errands for me." He offered her a brief smile.

Ellen captured the haunted look in his eyes behind his smile and felt the muscles in his calf tense, the fractured light, the pain that lurked deep inside. She remembered that when she had first spoken to him after the operation, it had been a physical pain that had kept him awake at night. But as the foot had gradually healed, the physical pain had been replaced by a desperate need to understand what had happened to him and the mental anguish that accompanied such a frustration. She massaged his ankle some more, and then flicked her finger across the tips of his toes and said, "Okay, you can put your shoe back on now."

Roscoe had been shot as he had stepped out of the Echo Barn, one of his favorite bars on Chalk Farm Road, the main road that led from Camden Town up to Hampstead and all points north. He had decided to call in for a drink and a spot of lunch before heading off to see his father down in Camden Town. It had been a warm afternoon and, like most of the other bars and cafés on the street, the Echo Barn had tables in front of the premises to catch the lunch trade. But Roscoe had gone inside where the bar had been quiet, and he had spent the time chatting to the barman, a student at UCL who thumped the drums in a band that rehearsed in the basement, about the bands he had seen at the Borderline the night before. Roscoe had eaten a plate of pasta and drunk a couple of beers to help ease the tension that always appeared in his shoulders whenever he planned to visit his old man. Just before one o'clock he had drained the last of his beer and stepped out onto the pavement, pulling up short at the sudden flash of brilliant sunshine that bounced from the side of the Roundhouse across the street. He had raised a hand to shield his eyes, and that's when the blue Metro had cut out from the line of traffic in front of him and screeched to a halt at the kerb. He had not reacted at first, but then a white face and a gun had been thrust out of the back window, and on blind instinct he had tried to turn and run back into the bar. But the shooter had fired before his limbs could react, and the bullet had punched a hole through his ankle, dropping him to the ground as sure as if it had pierced his heart. Three more shots had been fired in rapid succession, but the gunman had panicked after the first one and the bullets had ended up buried in the stone front of the building beside the Echo Barn.

Three detectives from Camden Town CID had been put on the case as soon as the call came into the station, and within a couple of hours one of them had come up with a piece of CCTV footage from outside a bar fifty yards up the street from where the shooting had taken place. The tape had been of poor quality. One of the barmen explained that although the tapes were rotated on a weekly basis, the same tapes had been in use for almost three years. Most of the faces had been little more than monochrome sketches, but later, from the brittle depths of sedation in his hospital bed, Roscoe had been able to make out the shooter's car as it had parked outside the bar and a man in a baseball cap had climbed into the back seat. He could not be sure about the slice of face on the tape, but the profile was familiar. The clock in the top corner of the screen read 12:43 p.m., ten minutes before the incident. The boffins had been able to unscramble the tape and make out the registration number, but it turned out the car had been reported stolen from an office block in Harlesden earlier that morning and was found burned out in a car park at the back of Euston Station later the same night.

After the operation, Roscoe had spent two weeks flat on his back in the hospital, another two months up to his knee in plaster, housebound, and then a further three months on crutches. It had been just two weeks since he had been able to put aside the crutches and walk unaided, albeit with a strong limp, and he still felt the occasional shot of pain and a stiffness in his ankle. It had been a difficult time for him, and back at home he had become more and more withdrawn. As a natural loner, the close friendships of his twenties and thirties had long since foundered as those friends had drifted into marriage and parenthood, their hours and habits at odds with a single man working strange shifts that cut across the hours of darkness and light. It had been some time since he had been in a relationship, and all that remained of his blood relations was his father, Jack Roscoe, and an elder brother, Phil, who came and went on an unpredictable tide. Roscoe had never been able to work out the reason his father felt the need to keep everyone at arm's length, but he had always been that way, even with his own family, and his lukewarm response to the attack on his son had done nothing to bridge that gap.

When the small squad turned up no other significant leads, and the last of the three detectives had been taken off the case a month after the incident, the Chief Constable had sent out a car and called Roscoe into his office. Told him that he could no longer authorise the use of personnel, but if Roscoe had the strength and the inclination, he could continue to look into the case himself and make use of all the facilities he needed. And so Roscoe had sat at the scarred oak table he had purchased in Camden Market, his plaster-encased foot balanced on a mountain of cushions, and put in serious time on old paper files, computer disks, and his own personal notebooks. He had asked a couple of his colleagues at the station, Sam Fletcher and Brian Dineen, to help out and, despite an initial reluctance on their part, in the end both had provided valuable and discreet legwork on his behalf. He had been grateful for their help, but he had not seen either of them for a few weeks apart from the time Fletcher had called and asked him for his help on a case he was working—a drug dealer who had been pushed from the roof of a building on the Castle Estate—and he was starting to feel isolated. And so far each lead that had been unearthed turned out to be no more than another dead end.

His instincts told him that he would find his assailant buried in the files stacked beside the TV in his front room; he just had to take the time and look deeper into it. Or perhaps he just needed to take a break and then come back to it fresh. But the fact that he had so far come up blank filled Roscoe with a deep sense of fear and apprehension. The shooting had altered him, made him more focused, less patient. In the past, he had lived for the most part in some emotional place buried deep inside himself, but now he lived out there on his skin, susceptible to all the vibrations that London had to offer. He could see the difference, too, and most of the time he was able to keep it in check. But in his darkest hours he knew that a fundamental part of him had been destroyed, and to balance the equation he needed to destroy a part of someone else.

Roscoe left the hospital and stepped out onto the street, headed up past the car park to Haverstock Hill. Dark clouds had bunched in from across the heath, and he could smell rain on the air. He turned up his collar and pushed his hands deep into the pockets of his jacket. The rumble of dance music leaked from a dark red Taurus stuck in the traffic on the far side of the street, and the crackle of talk show DJs that streamed from the open windows of black cabs sounded like a roomful of drunken strangers.

Roscoe looked around as he strolled down the hill, past the restaurants and the print shop, Starbucks and the florists, and found himself projecting the blurred mask of his assailant onto the faces of the people that he passed: a tall black kid in a hooded anorak; a bloated drunk on a bench, a can of cider clenched in his fist; a kid in a denim jacket and jeans that chafed around his knees, fat trainers that trailed black laces.

On the far side of the street stood the old Hampstead Town Hall. Long abandoned, it had now been restored into an arts centre. He remembered an occasion before the restoration when he had been called to the rear of the building after the corpse of a woman in her late forties had been found there. She had been beaten about the head and her left hand had been hacked off. After the killer had been tracked to a flat in the cheap end of Highgate, Roscoe had been sent out to pick him up, and the man had threatened to hack his balls off with a kitchen knife. The man had repeated the threat when he was sentenced to ten to fifteen in Belmarsh. Roscoe strode on, nearing the tube station, and crossed the path that led to a small council estate, a pair of tennis courts, and the reclaimed nature reserve that backed onto the Isokon flats on Lawn Road. Some summers back, a charred corpse had been found dumped in the long grass on the reserve. A couple of teenagers had robbed a man of his cash and credit cards as he had stepped out of the tube station one afternoon, and when he had threatened to call the police, the kids had forced him into the shadows at the side of the station, knocked him unconscious, pulled him into the woods, and set him on fire.

Roscoe had suffered these flashes of past violence a thousand times since he had first joined the force, and for the most part they had never bothered him in the slightest. But since his shooting, he had started to look at them afresh, almost as if they had become premonitions of his own violent end, as if his own death could be just as random, pointless, and premature.

Any one of these, he told himself as he looked once more into the faces of the people that he passed. Any one of these.

Since he had been discharged from hospital, it had become his habit to have lunch in the Echo Barn at least once or twice a week. He told himself that he came into the bar just to be out of the flat, back in the rush of the streets. But in truth he knew that he sat at the bar in the hope that his continued presence might provoke memories of the shooting. Seven months later, the bar still held its secrets.

Roscoe pushed open the front door and took a seat at the end of the counter. Music from an old Josh Rouse album, *Under Cold Blue Stars*, bounced from the four speakers set high on the walls, the track "Nothing Gives Me Pleasure." He picked up the lunch menu from the bar and checked the specials on the piece of paper clipped inside the laminated folder. It had just turned noon and he had skipped breakfast, but he still had no appetite. He dropped the menu back on the bar and pushed it to one side. He was the sole customer in the place, and as the track faded into silence, a man in a blue cotton shirt and black cords came out of the kitchen. He spotted Roscoe and halted in his tracks. He pointed at the chill cabinet and tilted his head in question.

Roscoe hesitated for a second too long, and then smiled and shook his head. "Just coffee for the moment, thanks."

2

DC Rob Spencer looked across at DS Marnie Stone in the passenger seat. "He just came into the station and handed the earrings back to you just like that?"

"I know, unbelievable," replied Marnie. "Told me that I must've left them on the bedside table by mistake, and then dropped them into my hand. I'd only been in the office for about ten minutes when Dobie rang and told me there was a man in reception that wanted to see me." She stared out of the window at the street as they headed up through Chalk Farm.

"Had you been seeing him long?"

"I don't know," said Marnie, lifting her shoulders. "About a month or so, I suppose."

"And you didn't notice that he was a borderline head case before that? You didn't pick up on any clues, *detective?*"

"It takes a little time for a man to revert to type," said Marnie with an air of hard-earned knowledge. "Especially after he's just been through the lengthy process of reinventing himself for a new relationship. But you're right, I should have picked up on something earlier. Like the time he broke away from me to hang up his chinos the first time we started to roll around on the sofa." She smiled to herself at the recollection. "I'd worked up quite a head of steam by then, but by the time he'd finished hanging up his clothes, I was just about ready to call a cab."

Spencer shook his head, surprised once more at her candour and her deadpan manner. He took a quick appraising look at her across the seats: mid-thirties, light brown hair cut short, an oval face and lids that hooded her warm brown eyes as if she had just woken up, making him think of erotic adventures in the dark. At work she often wore loose clothes, and he used to think that she did this to offset the creep of time, but then he had seen her out running on Parliament Hill one morning in her shorts and a tight T-shirt and he had been surprised at her shapeliness, the muscle tone, and the firmness of her bumps and curves.

"Just dropped them in my hand, kissed me on the cheek, and then said that he'd call me later. I didn't know what to say, what with Dobie looking at me like I'd just been caught sleeping with my old headmaster or something."

Spencer cut another look across at her face, noticed the sparkle of amusement in her eyes.

"Anyway, the next time I was round at his place I left a pair of panties in the bed, on the side he usually slept on. Just stuffed them down under the duvet, right down near the bottom. Less than an hour later, I saw his name pop up on my mobile. I knew that he'd found them and that's what he was ringing about, but I let it go. Sure enough, he was back on the line ten minutes later. I let that one go as well, and the one after that, and the one after that. . . . After I let the fourth one go, he didn't call me for another week, and I never did see those panties again."

"I bet he came in and handed them to Dobie and Dobie took them home," said Spencer. "He's probably wearing them right now."

Marnie laughed and then shook her head, trying to rid her mind of that particular image.

Spencer drove in silence for a short time, and Marnie continued to look out the window. She saw an old man standing at the side of the road, waiting to cross. Rake thin, he had jaundiced skin and a shopping bag clasped tight to his chest. Too crooked and choked on old smoke to make it to the traffic lights, he looked like he'd been there for some time, waiting for a Samaritan to come along and help him to cross. In this part of the world that could be forever, thought Marnie.

"Another time we were round at his place watching a bit of TV, playing CDs, stuff like that. Chatting about our histories. I picked out some music to play, stuff that I liked—not easy, by the way, he had terrible taste, his CD collection looked like the collection of someone that doesn't actually like music, like he bought all his stuff from a supermarket—and the next time I was round there I noticed that he'd made them up into this neat little stack for me, right in front of the rest of his CDs. He even put them in alphabetical order."

"Sounds like a solicitor," said Spencer, chuckling once more.

"I bet that's not too far from the truth," said Marnie. "His bedroom, honest, it was like having sex at a crime scene—don't touch this, don't put your foot there. Jesus, what is it with you men, what turns you into such control freaks?"

Spencer smiled and shook his head.

He turned onto Prince of Wales Road, and the pair lapsed into a comfortable silence. Spencer noticed that Marnie had turned her attention back to the street, and he glanced at her once more, trying to make her out. One of the other DCs who had worked with her before—she had been transferred to Kentish Town from Kilburn less than three months earlier—had told him that she had a dark sense of humour which she often turned on herself, and he had wondered what he had meant. The first couple of weeks they had worked together, she had displayed precious little emotion at all, but as he had spent more time with her, she had loosened up and he had started to understand her character. His colleague had been right about that sense of humour, but he still had no idea what led her to it.

The car passed the junction of Malden Road. On the far corner, under a streetlamp that leaked its broken bulb on a noose of electrical cord, Marnie saw an old couple on their way up to the lido on Parliament Hill, rolled towels tucked under their arms. The man wore sandals and his toes looked like walnuts. She smiled to herself and then turned to speak to Spencer, but as she did so, something across the street caught her attention and she tapped Spencer on the arm. "Quick, pull over," she said under her breath. "And don't make a fuss about it, all right?"

Spencer eased his foot down on the brake pedal and steered the car into the kerb. Marnie nodded across the street.

Spencer scanned the area, and then turned back to Marnie. He nodded once to let her know that he had seen the black kid framed in the door of the small supermarket, and then both of them looked back across the street.

Eighteen at the most, the kid sported a Nike jacket over a striped baseball shirt, loose jeans, and black trainers. He had scooped cheeks and large stained front teeth which looked like the turrets on a model castle. He punched a thumbnail into the foil cap of a bottle of banana milk and then sucked hard on the bottle like he had been taken from the teat too soon. Drops of the milk spilled on his shirt. He broke for air, took another pull and then let out a satisfied sigh. Wiping the back of his hand across his mouth, he turned and headed for the entrance to the estate that backed up to the store.

"Do you recognise him?" said Marnie.

Spencer narrowed his eyes and shook his head.

"You remember that Dutch tourist who was robbed at the cashpoint on Haverstock Hill a couple of nights ago, had a Stanley knife whipped across his cheeks when he tried to fight back? I think we've just found our master craftsman."

"Are you sure?" said Spencer. "Are you sure it's him?"

Marnie made no response, concentrating on tracking the kid with her eyes. She waited for him to turn off Prince of Wales Road into the narrow side road that led back around to the estate and then jumped out of the car and ran across the street.

Spencer locked the car and ran after her.

Marnie reached the entrance to the estate in time to see the kid walking past a children's roundabout tilted on its side. There was also a set of swings and a couple of benches on a concrete mound. Tall blocks of brick flats overlooked the area on three sides, the back of the supermarket and a launderette bordering the square on the fourth. In the far corner of the square, a darkened stairwell led to the upper floors of the flats. An archway at the foot of the stairwell led through to a car park and Malden Road. On the concrete to her left, Marnie could make out the perfect afterimage of a burned out car.

Marnie looked around for Spencer, found him nowhere to be seen. When she looked up ahead again, the kid had taken a seat on one of the benches. He was still drinking, and as he lowered the bottle, he spotted Marnie watching him. He took her for police at once, and his mouth fell open spilling banana milk down his shirt. Dropping the bottle on the ground, he leapt to his feet and ran off in the direction of the car park and Malden Road.

"Wait," shouted Marnie, taking chase.

Just then Spencer stepped out from behind the stairwell. He stood in the walkway with his feet apart and his arms floating out at his sides like a gunslinger. Perspiration clouded his face and his shoulders rose and fell in rhythm with his breathing.

The kid tottered around for a brief moment, his limbs jangling like electric cables that had just been cut. He angled his head and searched all the balconies that surrounded them. Then he looked across at Spencer and back at Marnie.

In the sudden flash of hatred that passed across his face,

Marnie knew at once that he had just pinned her as the weak link in the chain. His first and last mistake.

The kid turned his back on Spencer. He slid a Stanley knife out of his coat and started to walk fast towards Marnie.

Marnie stepped towards him, keeping her eyes on the knife.

Sudden noise broke from a flat on one of the upper floors, the blast of a TV and then the slam of a door.

The kid came closer, his face a hard mask of anger and corruption.

Marnie matched him step for step.

Pulling out his radio, Spencer called out for her to stand back and wait for back-up. The radio crackled, but before he could raise a response, Marnie had jumped up close to the kid and landed a surprise punch on the side of his neck that shook him like a storm. He tried to slash at her hands as he stumbled, but she danced out of his reach, and then stepped back in and hit him again, felling him to his knees, a splash of blood on his cheek, his buck teeth painted crimson. The kid stretched out his hands as he crashed to the floor and the knife skidded out of reach.

Marnie stepped back and stared at him spread out on the concrete, searching his eyes for just a trace of the fear that his victim must have felt, but came up clean.

Spencer stuffed his radio back into his jacket pocket and pulled his handcuffs from the back of his belt. He jumped astride the kid, turned him around, and snapped the handcuffs around his wrists. He left him on the ground as he took a handkerchief from his own pocket, folded it around the handle, and picked up the knife. He raised it up to his face and peered at it. There were flecks of dried blood where the hilt met the blade.

"I think we'll find that's Dutch blood," said Marnie.

Spencer looked into her face, surprised at the casualness of her tone, and had the distinct feeling that if she had not been in full view of at least a hundred flats, she would have taken great pleasure in being far more brutal with their suspect.

Back at the station, Spencer booked the knifeman in at the desk and then led him to one of the interview rooms in the basement. Marnie headed up to the canteen to fetch Spencer and herself some coffee and a can of Coke for the kid. At the top of the stairs she ran into DCI Belmont as he stepped out of the CID room. "Ah, Marnie," he said, sounding pleased with himself. "Just the person I was looking for. What've you got on at the moment?"

The DCI was a short man, as thick around the middle as he was around the shoulders. He had brittle black hair that stuck out from his head like he had just been electrocuted and permanent red cheeks, a combination that took more than a decade off his face. But ever since he had made it into a desk job, he felt that his boyish looks somehow diminished the hard effort he had put in on the street, making him seem like one of those fast-track graduates the rank and file despised so much, and so he took every effort to counter their effect. Towards this end, on the last Friday of each month, he stopped in at the Italian barber on Parkway and asked him to shave his head clean. Today, a week before the end of the month, his hair had almost grown back to an electroshock position.

Marnie stopped in her tracks beside him, told him about the kid that she and Spencer had just picked up.

"Let Spencer deal with that," said Belmont.

"Why, what's up?"

"You remember Paul Ballard, the man who was pushed from the roof of the Castle Estate last month?"

"Yeah, I remember him," said Marnie, nodding. "A street dealer who used to work out of the booths on Kentish Town

Road. The usual tale if I remember: a suspect and no witnesses."

Belmont cracked a mirthless smile. "Aren't they all," he said, matter-of-fact. "Anyway, the family thinks that there must be at least one person out there who saw what happened that night. They just put up a reward of ten thousand pounds."

"Ten grand," said Marnie, surprised. "Where did they find that kind of money? The father was an electrician's mate, wasn't he? A labourer, worked for the council or something."

Belmont hitched his trousers up over his stomach and shook his head. "Maybe they took out a loan or remortgaged the house. . . . I don't know. . . . Whatever, the point is, they want answers."

"But it was Fletcher's case," pleaded Marnie, knowing what was coming.

"Fletcher's on leave this weekend," replied Belmont. "Taking the kids up to Center Parcs, or one of those other open prisons for adults they call holiday centres. But as it was you who helped him run the house-to-house enquiries, you're the one best placed to pick up the baton."

"Can't it wait until he gets back?"

"The story's going to be in the *Journal* tomorrow."

Marnie rested her hands on her hips and let out a great sigh. "So what are you telling me, sir? That you want me to follow up on every crackerjack lead that comes into the station?"

"Get yourself over to the estate this afternoon," replied Belmont, nodding his head. "Check out the place before the calls start to come in. Give yourself some ammunition against all the nutters that'll never have even been to the place. And lighten up, Marnie, don't look so worried. There's not that many people out there who'd put their lives on the line for ten grand."

3

Roscoe drained the last of his coffee and looked around the room at all the people who had started to bunch around the tables. He had been sitting at the bar for close to an hour, listening to the music and chatting to the barman, and he had seen a number of familiar faces come through the door, some who had been in the bar at the time he had been shot. Lunchtimes, the Echo Barn catered to the same crowd of IT and media people who worked in the numerous offices and studios that proliferated around Camden Lock. He had spoken to all of them in detail at one time or another since the shooting, and not one of them had been able to tell him much more than the colour of the car that had ferried the shooter. Roscoe had been on the force long enough to know there was little chance that that would now change.

"You need a refill, Frank?" called the barman.

"Thanks," replied Roscoe. He shook a cigarette out of the pack on the bar and put a match to it.

The barman refilled the cup and then dipped back into the kitchen.

"Hello, Frank."

Roscoe turned in his seat to see Rhiannon Burns standing beside him. She smiled at him and older memories flooded out the more recent ones. Rhiannon had been married to an old friend of his, Charlie, and back in the late eighties the three of them had been part of a loose bunch of people that had hung around Camden Town together. But when Rhiannon got pregnant, the couple had decided to move to Brighton to raise the large brood of kids they planned to have. Things had not worked out, however, and after a few years Rhiannon had returned to London, moving into her mother's flat. Charlie had remained in Brighton, more or less cutting himself off from his old friends, and gradually Roscoe had lost touch with him. They had been close for a long time, the kind of friends that can only be made in your twenties when you have finally lost the crushing self-consciousness of your teens but before real life gets in the way. But Roscoe knew that once those kinds of friendships had faded, then the raw materials needed to rebuild them would also have been lost forever. He had bumped into Rhiannon a number of times since her return, less so since she had left her mother's place and moved out to Maida Vale, but times had changed and the conversation had been strained, friendly but strained.

She had her auburn hair bundled up on top of her head, held back under a blue bandana, a style that pitched the sadness etched in her face out at the world. She looked like she had been crying for days, the skin around her eyes bleached red from tears, and the eyes themselves seemed to be focused on something beyond the physical. She was dressed in a pair of loose jeans torn at the knee, a crumpled suede jacket over a pale blue blouse, and a scuffed pair of Doc Martens.

"Hi, Rhee, how's it going?" Roscoe reached out and took hold of her hand. Karl, her ten-year-old son had been killed by a police car responding to a domestic violence incident a little over five months earlier. The boy had been trying to sneak past a couple as they had fought on the pavement and been knocked into the road just as the patrol car screeched to a halt at the kerb. Roscoe had read about the result of the inquest in the local paper, the police driver being cleared of all charges.

Roscoe had still been in plaster at the time of the accident, but Rhiannon had been to see him after the funeral and it had broken his heart to see the look of desolation on her face, her spirit ripped out and tossed aside. Physically, she seemed to have shrunk, her skin cold and loose on her bones.

Rhiannon took the stool beside Roscoe and rested her arms on the bar. "It's still hard, you know?" she said, shaking her head. Roscoe tried to catch her eye, but she was staring straight ahead. Picturing her son alive, he knew. It was a look he had come to recognise over the years. "But it's getting easier, if something like this could ever be said to become easier. Less hard, I suppose. Yeah, that's more like how it feels. Less hard."

"He was a great kid," said Roscoe, his words wrapped in smoke. "It can't have been easy for him, you and Charlie splitting up like that. And that's a credit to you, both of you, something to remember him by."

"It did make him grow up pretty quickly," she said, her eyes still locked on the middle distance. "But he seemed to have come through it all right. When we came back to London, he decided that he wanted to be my equal, not my child anymore."

"I remember," said Roscoe, smiling. And then, embarrassed at the fresh spill of emotion: "What can I get you to drink?"

"I'll have a Budweiser, thanks," replied Rhiannon.

Roscoe raised his hand in the direction of the barman, and motioned for two Buds, pushing aside the fresh coffee. The music had changed on the house stereo and an old Guided by Voices album crackled from the speakers, *Do the Collapse*. Roscoe had a couple of their albums, but the production on this one smothered the lo-fi charm that had made their earlier stuff so memorable.

"How's Charlie getting on? Has he been up to see you lately?"

"He was up here last week for the inquest," she said, cradling one hand in the other. "I thought we might be able to give each other a bit of support, but after the verdict went against us we fell back into arguing again just like old times. I know that he was desperately hurt by what happened to Karl, but sometimes I think we've drifted so far apart it's like we were never together in the first place." A sad smile flitted across her face. "I don't know, maybe I shouldn't be so hard on him. At least it helped take my mind off it all for a few hours."

"I think I saw him," said Roscoe. "Down in Camden Town one morning. He looked a little confused, didn't seem to know where he was going."

"You spoke to him?"

"No, he was just heading into the tube station," Roscoe lied. The truth was, Charlie had been walking straight towards him, but Roscoe had felt a tightening in his chest at the sight of his old friend, and not being sure of what to say to him or how to deal with the grief that coated his friend like a second skin, he had dipped into the health food store until Charlie had passed.

"He hadn't seen Karl for a couple of months when he died, and I think that sort of made him feel like he'd abandoned him," said Rhiannon. She paused for a moment, her lips open a fraction, thinking. "He never blamed me for the accident, but I could see that he felt he had to blame someone, and he had real trouble holding that back."

"I suppose that's one of the curses of the modern family," said Roscoe. "That time apart, the loss of communication . . ."

"Sometimes I think of Charlie as one of those old men sitting in their deck chairs on the front in Brighton, muttering to themselves. Saying all the things he wanted to tell Karl in life but never got the chance."

Rhiannon smiled a little, then watched the barman approach and put their drinks in front of them. Roscoe handed the barman a ten and then poured some beer from the bottle into his glass. Rhiannon did the same, took a little sip, then put the glass back down. "Look, Frank," she said, leaning a little further into the bar. "I'm sorry to drop this on you like this, after your own troubles and all, but I need your help."

"Sure," said Roscoe. "What can I help you with?"

"A week before the inquest, Ian Cahill—you remember Ian Cahill, the man who saw what happened the night Karl was killed—a week before the inquest, he walked into Kentish Town police station and withdrew his statement. Told them he must've made a mistake, he couldn't remember that much about the accident."

Roscoe felt his heart sink in his chest. Rhiannon had first mentioned her suspicions to him when she had come to call on him at home, a captive audience. She had told him that she was certain it had been no regular accident. From what she could recall, the police car had speeded up as it had approached the scene and appeared to be aiming for someone in the crowd that was packed around the arguing couple. And it was travelling so fast that the driver was unable to stop when Karl was knocked into his path. At the time, Roscoe had reasoned her suspicions had been aroused from grief, the desperate outpourings of a mother attempting to find a reason for the death of her child. But after five months he expected Rhiannon to have accepted Karl's death as the tragic accident it so clearly was.

"I remember you told me something about this before," said Roscoe, stubbing out his cigarette.

"It means I was right, doesn't it?"

"I don't know," said Roscoe. He wanted to tell her that she was still in mourning, that it wasn't just Charlie who needed someone to blame. "It's tragic, I know, but these things happen."

"Do you have any idea how many people were killed in police car chases last year?" asked Rhiannon.

"Rhiannon, please—"

"More than forty, and another seven from other stuff, including two from cars responding to emergencies."

"Looks like you did your research," said Roscoe.

"Two, Frank. Two people killed by police cars responding to emergencies. Put aside the fact that a couple fighting in the street could be called an emergency, and what've you got? What are the chances of it being an accident? You know Brecknock Road, Frank. Hook a left out of the tube station and it's a straight road all the way down to the Hilldrop Estate, fifty yards past where Karl was killed. It was a clear night, the driver must've been able to see what was happening for at least a hundred yards. The couple was fighting on the pavement, for Christ's sake. You want me to believe that the driver didn't think about that, that they could've fallen into the road? In normal circumstances, he's not going to go anywhere near them. So how come he ends up hitting a ten-year-old boy who fell into the road—fell into the *gutter*, Frank, not even the road, the gutter—fell into the gutter just three feet from where they were fighting?"

Roscoe nodded and then took a sip of beer. He turned to look out the front door, blinked, and took in the people out on the street, the traffic backed up at the lights. A man in a cream linen suit was standing on the spot where Roscoe had been shot, oblivious to the pavement's recent history. He held a fat paperback in his hand, his thumb stuck down inside the pages. He kept reading a couple of sentences and then looking up the street towards the Lock, waiting for someone. The autumn sun reflected from the chrome bumper of an old Capri that idled at the kerb, making Roscoe think of that moment seven months earlier when he himself had become a statistic. He considered the statistics Rhiannon had just unloaded on him, the numbers that people used to prop up their lives, to justify their actions.

"What did your solicitor say?" he said at last.

"On the record? It's too late."

"And off the record?"

"Off the record, that someone took a trip out to see Cahill and warned him off the case." She took a mouthful of beer, and then ran the back of her hand across her mouth.

"So now he wants me to go and talk to him for you?"

Rhiannon shook her head. "It wasn't like that, Frank. Well, yeah, all right, I suppose it was. I told him that I knew you, that we were old friends, and he mentioned that maybe you could try and talk to Cahill for us, find out what happened."

"I don't know, Rhee," said Roscoe. "I don't want to put a black mark on another copper if there's no reason to."

"But I know what I saw, Frank."

Silence fell on the scene, creating a gulf between them.

"I just had time to take hold of his hand before he died," said Rhiannon at last, her mind shifting to another place. "Did I tell you that, about holding his hand? He never wanted me to before, but this time he let me hold his hand. He couldn't talk, but I could tell that he wanted me to hold his hand. He must have known he was going to die." She leaned forward and held her left hand in her right. "Tight, like this," she said. "The way I used to when he'd just started at school. He looked so alone, even in the middle of that crowd. It must be terrible to have to die like that, in front of a lot of strangers. Karl was scared to death and all I could do was hold his hand." Tears fell from her cheek onto the bar. "I might as well have not been there."

"I don't know, Rhee. . . ."

"All you have to do is go and talk to him," said Rhiannon. "Tell me you'll do this one thing for me, Frank." She took out a pen and a small notebook from her rucksack, flipped it open and scribbled a name and address on a fresh page. She ripped out the page, put it on the bar, and pushed it in his direction.

Roscoe looked at it but did not pick it up.

"What about the rest of the people who were out there that night?" he said. "Were there no other witnesses?"

Rhiannon shook her head, no.

Roscoe felt a surge of dark heat flood his heart, the familiar truth that people did not want to know about crimes that happened right in front of them.

He picked up the scrap of paper from the bar, glanced at it, and then stuffed it in his pocket. He looked into Rhiannon's face and put his hand over hers. "I can't tell you that I know how you feel because I'd be lying," he said. "But I do understand your frustration that everything is out of your hands."

Flickers of light illuminated her pupils.

Roscoe tried to tell himself that he was going to help her because of their friendship, their shared past, his real and heartfelt affection for Karl himself, but in truth he suspected that he did not operate on such an altruistic level. The lack of progress in his own case had warned him that he might have lost his instincts as a detective, that his senses had hardened as if scar tissue had formed over his mind as well as his foot. Perhaps if he helped Rhiannon, stepped outside his own situation and acted once more on a pure police level, then perhaps he could recover his instincts and return to his own case refreshed.

"I'll talk to your witness for you," he said.

Rhiannon's face cracked into a smile, a smile tainted with loss and burned innocence, but a smile nonetheless, and she reached out and gave him a brief awkward hug, light as a feather.

Roscoe noticed that the Guided by Voices' CD had reached "Hold on Hope," one of the few tracks on the album he liked.

4

Pulled up at a red light at the foot of Haverstock Hill, Con O'Brien looked across at the students behind the front fence of Haverstock School. Lunchtime and most of them were out: the older ones leaning against the chain link fence in attitudes still under development, while the smaller children chased a football around. Beside the locked front gate a large black woman squatted on her haunches and pushed a box of KFC underneath the fence. On the other side of the fence, a girl picked out a piece of chicken from the box and took a bite. The woman couldn't lift the fence high enough to push the cup of Coke underneath and so the girl drank it through a straw poked through the fence.

"Look at that," said O'Brien. "A couple of more years and that girl is going to be in the same state as her mother."

"Check out the outfit," said his partner, Sean Dillon. The woman wore a black Calvin Klein tracksuit with blue stripes down the limbs. "You think Calvin had someone like that in mind when he designed that outfit? You think he knows his sweatshops are making clothes for people the size of a fuckin' house?"

"If he uses twice the amount of material, then maybe he can charge them twice the price," O'Brien deadpanned.

"Looks more like three times in her case," replied Dillon.

"Probably a fake anyway, bought on Inverness Street."

The light changed and O'Brien pulled away.

Dillon continued to watch as the girl stuffed a piece of chicken skin into her mouth, and then sucked the grease from her fingers. He felt his stomach contract and turned to face the road up ahead, reminded once more that people disgusted him.

As the car reached the top of the parade of shops on Chalk Farm Road, a short man in a pale blue suit ran out into the road and started to flap his arms around.

"What's this dandified little fucker want?" said Dillon.

O'Brien steered the car into the kerb. He cut the engine and then climbed out of the car and adjusted his belt.

"This way," said the man. He turned and hurried across the pavement, gesturing for them to follow. "Follow me."

O'Brien started after him, Dillon slow on his heels.

The man led them up a narrow alley between an antique furniture store and a Moroccan café that opened onto a courtyard at the rear of the parade. There were large aluminum bins behind each building, and on the far side of the courtyard a high wooden fence was covered in graffiti. Behind the antique store, O'Brien spotted a pair of trainer-clad feet sticking out from behind the bin and his heart jumped in his chest. The man who flagged them down strode up to the side of the bin. O'Brien called out and told him to keep back, but his words fell on deaf ears.

The man stopped close to the feet and pointed down at a pair of broken trainers, a look of indignation on his face.

Seconds later, O'Brien stopped beside him and took a quick look at the man on the floor. "You think he's dead?"

"No such luck," sulked the man, and kicked one of the feet.

"Hey, there's no need for that," said O'Brien, reaching out a hand to hold the man back. He heard a brief sound erupt from behind him, and glanced back to see Dillon hiding a tired smirk.

O'Brien lowered himself to his haunches. Discarded needles and thick flakes of burnt aluminum foil littered the earth around him. He rested a hand on the bin and leaned in for a closer look at the face: scarred from drugs and bleached of all colour, black stubble spread across the chin and cheeks.

"So what're you going to do about him?" said the man.

"Just leave it with us," said Dillon, stepping up. "I think we can take it from here."

O'Brien held the palm of his hand up to the prone man's mouth for a second, felt the faint moist air of life. He nodded and then turned the man's head from side to side, checking for blood, but both the back of the head and the ground were clear. There were dried bubbles of spittle on the cracked lips. He thumbed back a lid, noticed the pupils rolled back in the head.

Dillon rested his hands on his hips and looked around the courtyard, taking in the rear of the buildings. "Are you the manager of one of these shops or something?"

"The owner," replied the man. "I own the antique pine furniture store."

"Okay, the owner. And what's your name?"

"Crane," replied the man. "Noel Crane."

"And you just found him lying back here like this?"

"I was in the office at the back of the shop. I heard someone out near the bins." He clenched his teeth and shook his head. "But there's always someone back here," he continued, and gestured at the debris scattered across the hard earth. "Fucking junkies, they're going to put us all out of business."

O'Brien slapped the crackhead across the face. "Come on," he said. "Wakey, wakey, time to go home."

"What did you think was going to happen when you chased them all out of King's Cross?" said Crane indignantly. "Where did you think they were all going to go? It's like you don't want to do anything about them except keep moving them around like a herd of poisonous fucking cattle or something, wherever the grass is greenest. I lost almost fifteen grand last year."

Dillon looked at the ground beneath his feet, took in the discarded needles, the empty crack vials. He recognised the red tops scattered in the dirt near the fence as Bar Code product. Bar Code was one of the top drug suppliers in Camden Town. "So this is not the first time this has happened?" he said, boredom and contempt edging his words. "It's happened before?"

Crane held up his hands in frustration, fists loose. "Only practically every fucking day," he said, his tone rising with his indignation. "Don't you people talk to each other? If it's not me, then it's one of the other owners here on the street."

"Sometimes we have other priorities," said Dillon.

"I don't give a shit about your other priorities," Crane said and then kicked the man on the ground again. Neither of the policemen made a move to stop him. "Right now, all I want to know is what you're going to do about this piece of shit."

The man on the floor let out a short groan and his head rolled to the side a fraction.

Dillon looked at the man on the floor, back at Crane.

"Looks to me like he's not going anywhere under his own steam for the time being," he said, pretending to stifle a yawn. "So other than dragging him down to the station and letting him sleep it off, there's not much more we can do."

"But I just told you that he's been losing me business."

"You mean he's been stealing?" asked Dillon.

Crane leaned into Dillon, his forefinger raised in front of him. "Last week one of my customers had her bag snatched from right in front of the store. She was going to buy a couple of wardrobes. I don't think she'll be coming back, do you?"

"And you think it was this man here?" asked Dillon, motioning to the man on the floor with his foot.

"Well, no, but . . ."

"So he hasn't been stealing?"

"Well, no, but that's not the point—"

"It *is* the point," said Dillon, hard and firm, pinning Crane to the earth under his stare.

Sean Dillon had a scar across the top of his left cheek. He told people he had sustained it at the brutal hands of his father when he was just nine years old. In truth, he had inflicted the scar himself with a cheap plastic comb as soon as he had made the decision to join the police force at fifteen. He had been bullied at school and hated people to think that he could not take care of himself. The scar told them otherwise.

Crane held his stare for a moment, and then blinked and turned his face aside.

O'Brien lifted the crackhead into a sitting position and rested his head against the side of the aluminum bin. He pushed some hair, thick with grease, out of the crackhead's face, and behind the dirt noticed that it had regained some of its colour. Fresh bubbles of spittle popped in the corners of his mouth.

"Like I said, unless he's been stealing, then there's not much more we can do," said Dillon. "We get twelve, fifteen calls an hour about people taking drugs outside their premises. If we responded to all of them, took them all into the station, then there'd be no time left to deal with the serious stuff."

"If this was Primrose Hill you'd do something about it," said Crane, a last stab at righteous anger.

The main line out of Euston Station cut across Camden Town to the south, and then ran parallel with Chalk Farm Road before heading out of London to all points north. Primrose Hill, home to film stars and other kinds of rich people, sat on the far side of the tracks. Such was the difference between the affluent village-like neighbourhood of Primrose Hill and the rundown stretch of Chalk Farm Road north of Camden Lock, that the footbridge which spanned the railway tracks behind Chalk Farm tube station had been dubbed Checkpoint Charlie.

"I heard the folk on the Hill have hired their own police force," said Dillon, no longer bothering to hide his indifference. "Seems like they didn't think much of our service, either."

Crane shook his head and stared into the policeman's face again for a second, the crooked smile that mocked his entire life, and then turned on his heel and stomped off down the alley.

Dillon watched him go, grinning, and then followed his path back to the car.

"So are we just going to leave him here?" said O'Brien, gesturing towards the crackhead.

Dillon ignored him and kept on walking.

5

Marnie left the car on a meter in front of the Verge on Kentish Town Road, a late-night indie venue painted marine blue that used to be a pub called the Castle. Beside the club stood the old South Kentish Town tube station. The station was closed in 1924, the lift shaft and stairwell boarded up, the ticket hall converted into shops soon after. Marnie recalled hearing a strange tale about the station on the radio, broadcast by the late poet laureate Sir John Betjeman, if she remembered correctly. Some months after the station closed, a bank clerk who normally disembarked at Kentish Town, the next station on the line, had been so engrossed in his newspaper that he had stepped off the train in error when it had stopped at South Kentish Town one night. Stranded in the dark and unable to attract the attention of a passing train, he had taken a chance and climbed the three hundred stairs to the surface to find his escape blocked by the solid floor of the new shops. He had then walked back down the stairs and with some difficulty climbed the lift shaft, only to find that escape route blocked as well. Tired and frustrated, he had returned to the platform and after further fruitless attempts to flag down a passing train, had lain down on the platform and gone to sleep. Betjeman had left the tale there, and in Marnie's view that was the way it should have been. For the people condemned to live on the Castle Estate some decades later, there was no comfortable ending for them either.

She passed a parade of rundown shops, a launderette with

strips of silver gaffer tape stretched across the cracked front window, and a shop that sold nothing but international phone cards. Young people looked at her with old eyes. The old looked at her and saw nothing at all. On a corner beside a pub with boarded-up windows and doors, thick clumps of weeds sprouted from a line of hanging baskets out front. She turned into the wide paved alley that led to the Castle Estate. On the left of the alley, ten feet in from the main road, stood a four-pack of phone booths, the call centre for the drug trade on the estate. One kid in a hooded top sat on the wall behind the booths, munching on a rolled cuff. Marnie paused for a second, stamped her foot on the ground and the kid jumped in the air, whipped his head around to face down the noise. She shot him a hard smile and he pulled the hood down across his face and scooted off behind the nearest building.

The sun had fallen behind a string of clouds and Marnie felt specks of rain on her face. She slid her hands into her pockets and hurried across the estate to one of the small blocks that bordered Castle Road on the far side.

She pressed a numbered button on the metal grid set into the brick wall beside the front entrance and then stood back, looking around. Moments later a voice said, "Yes?" and Marnie replied, "It's Detective Sergeant Stone from Kentish Town. Marnie Stone."

The door clicked open and Marnie pushed on through into the lobby.

On the second floor she was met by a light-skinned black woman. Lucille Hook had braided hair pulled back under a patterned headscarf and a smooth face that belied her age. She wore a dark blue tracksuit, Adidas stripes on the arms and lower legs, and a pair of tan leather sandals on her feet.

She ushered Marnie into the front room and then headed into the kitchen. Marnie heard her fill the kettle and took a seat on the edge of the sofa. She looked around at the African prints on the walls, the dark wood sculptures incongruous in the midst of brittle IKEA furniture. In the centre of the mantelpiece stood a framed photograph of her eldest son, a snapshot that had been enlarged in the absence of another more formal portrait. Marnie guessed that he had never been in a position to have a formal portrait taken: a school that had not cared or ever had enough cash, a college graduation he had not lived to see.

Richard Hook had been shot and killed outside a nightclub in Camden Town some fifteen months earlier. The killer had been caught, but Lucille still did not understand the reasons behind his death, and she had tried to make sense of it by helping other people in the same situation. Together with another woman on the estate, whose son had been beaten to death for his mobile phone, she had formed a pressure group, MAD. Mothers Against Drugs lobbied local politicians and the police to take action on the drug menace facing the people of Camden Town. Ten months earlier, their efforts had started to bear fruit: the council had brought forward their plans to relandscape the Castle Estate, making it less user-friendly for the scores of drug users that crept across its broken, barren surface each day. Lucille Hook commanded a lot of respect in the area, and a great number of local people tended to confide their fears to her, as if she were some kind of community priest. Marnie had met her on a couple of occasions and respected her success.

Lucille carried a couple of mismatched mugs of coffee into the front room and placed them on the table in front of the sofa. She fetched a jug of semi-skimmed milk, a bowl of sugar, a teaspoon. "Help yourself to milk and sugar," she said, as she lowered herself into a threadbare armchair.

"This is fine, thanks," said Marnie.

The pair chatted around the real issue for a couple of minutes, the conversation getting weaker and weaker, and then

Lucille leaned forward in her seat and let out a sigh. "Is there anything in particular I can help you with?"

Marnie felt the heat rise in her throat at the accusation that she never came down to the estate unless it was for business. She knew it was the truth but let it pass. "Do you remember Paul Ballard, the man who was pushed from the roof here last month?" she said, pointing in the general direction of the roof. "His father just put up a reward for information leading to an arrest. It's going to be in the *Journal* tomorrow, so over the weekend we're going to be following up on any new leads that might come into the station. I just thought I'd drop by and see if you'd heard anything more since we last looked into it."

Lucille shook her head. "I ain't heard nothin' about that."

"It was a warm evening, nine o'clock, there must've been someone around."

"People round here like to mind their own business," said Lucille. "Make it through the day in one piece."

"But this is their business," replied Marnie. "And if you didn't believe that then you wouldn't be out there helping them."

"There's not many people in this world who know what it's like to bury your own child," said Lucille, a hard set to her face belying the emotion in her voice. "Every night, even after all this time, I still cry myself to sleep. Old Father Time playing his cruel tricks on me like that, switching me for my boy right in front of the gates of St Peter. No, if I do this for anyone, I do it for me and my boy."

"I don't believe that's the only reason."

Lucille shuffled in her seat, looked deep into Marnie's eyes. "If you can make it safe for these people, then you know that they will talk to you. You have the problem, not the people around here. You blame us, but we are the ones at risk."

"I hear what you're saying," said Marnie. "But all I can do is work with what I'm given, and that includes any information I get from you."

"If you want to see what's going on down here, then you got to put your eyes down here," said Lucille.

Marnie left Lucille ten minutes later and headed over to another building on the estate that overlooked Castle Road. The rain had stopped, and as she approached the block, she saw a fresh bunch of flowers tied to the railing that surrounded the building. Beside it were another couple of bunches, for the most part crumbled to dust now, just a few colourless stalks tied up in string. She stopped and looked at the flowers for a moment and then tilted her head back and looked up at the roof.

Four weeks earlier, Paul Ballard had been found dead at the foot of the building, spread across the path that ran in front of the railing. From his injuries it was clear that he had either fallen or been pushed from the roof of the four-storey building. Ballard had been a known small-time crack dealer who operated from the phone booths on the far side of the estate, and the police soon had a suspect in custody—a man seen arguing with the dead man in a nightclub two days earlier—but as there had been no witnesses to the murder and precious little forensic evidence, the police had no choice but to release him.

And now Paul's father had put up a reward of ten thousand pounds for information leading to an arrest and a conviction.

Marnie walked across to the battered front door, pulled on the handle, and found it unlocked. She heard a quiet hum as the door opened, the final breath of the lock. The lobby smelled of cider-piss and charred food. Fast food cartons and broken glass spread across the floor like a loose mosaic, and shit and graffiti smeared the walls. She held her breath and stepped across to the stairs and started to climb, no use in attempting to use the lift. On the first floor she heard a TV turned up loud and the thick thump of a bass rattled the door at the far end of the corridor. She took another breath and climbed on.

Marnie climbed until she reached the roof, and pushing the door open, she stepped out into an open space that chilled her to the bone. She checked over her shoulder and then propped the door open with a broken piece of brick. She looked around at the crack debris, broken pieces of furniture, scraps of clothes, the dried curls of human faeces. She stepped across to the front of the building that looked out over the square and all the way up to Camden Lock, edging along to the spot above where the body had been found, to the small garden situated there, no more than four feet square. The garden was built inside a brick wall, about ten inches tall, and the plants were arranged in some sort of abstract pattern. It had been a long time since the pattern had been there, and only stumps of life now remained, apart from one yellow flame of flower that burned despite the damage. Used syringes and needles, roaches and torn cigarette packets, balls of aluminum foil, and homemade crack pipes littered the hard soil. The wall had been broken in parts, and some of the soil spilled onto the roof in a loose arc across the buckled asphalt.

Marnie looked across the estate. The updraft of air from the front of the building ruffled her hair, cooled her lips. The block sat on the north side of a courtyard bordered to the east and the south by identical blocks of flats and to the west by Castle Road. The courtyard was overlooked by more than two hundred flats. It seemed unlikely that on a warm September evening there had been no one around, that no one had seen anything. And she was not sure that the posting of a reward would cause someone to come forward. On the far side of the estate she could see a grey-haired man sitting on a stalled exercise bike, a cigarette in his mouth, staring in through his kitchen window at a small television. Near the back entrance to the estate she saw a couple of kids with the rapid head snaps of drug runners heckle some smaller kids that passed in front of them. She tracked the runners into a café on the far side of the street. They looked no more than thirteen or fourteen, and Marnie shook her head at the cycle of history that had crushed them in its path.

She heard the harsh tone of her mobile and she pulled it out of her pocket, checked the name on the screen: Spencer. She clicked the button. "Spencer?"

"Hey, Boss. What happened to you?"

"Belmont tripped me on the stairs," said Marnie. "Listen, can you pull out the Ballard file for me and make up a timeline for the twenty-four hours leading up to when the body was found? Include everyone we spoke to, everyone who made a statement, even those who only had a walk-on part. On one side of the sheet make a note of all the stuff we released to the press, and on the other side all the stuff that was held back."

"What's this all about?"

"The family just put up a reward."

"Oh shit," said Spencer. "How much are they offering?"

"Ten thousand quid."

Marnie heard a brief humourless laugh on the other end of the line. "That's not too bad, I suppose," said Spencer. "At least we know for sure that anything we get'll just be bullshit."

Marnie felt a grim smile crease her face.

6

Roscoe took the notebook page that Rhiannon had scribbled down the address on out of his pocket and matched it to the number on the door in front of him. The house sat in the centre of a red brick terrace just off Camden Road, hidden from the main street behind a secondhand car dealership and a Greek restaurant. Like a lot of streets in the area, this particular street had an air of entrenched shabbiness about it; most of the houses were sunk on their foundations, as if tired of the hard life that filled their brittle interiors. Rain speckled the scene, and the embattled colours of nature peeked out from beneath the flattened patch of earth at the base of the chain link fence that bordered the forecourt of the dealership. Kids in mismatched tracksuits kicked a football around in the middle of the road, bouncing the ball off the cars parked at the kerb.

The house looked no different from the others on the street. Paint peeled from distressed timber and some of the bricks to the left of the front door had started to work loose, the crumbling mortar sprinkled on the concrete path. Roscoe could hear a radio from the office of the dealership, an old tune made up to sound like a dance track, the original song just out of reach behind the fractious beat. On the far side of the street, a man in an old raincoat shuffled past the back of the restaurant, peered into the open kitchen door, took a deep breath, and then strolled on. A man in a smock smeared with blood came out of the door and called after him in Greek, then lifted a filterless cigarette to his lips. Thick ropes of blue smoke drifted out of his mouth and into the restaurant's kitchen.

Roscoe stepped up to the door and rapped on the frame. Stepping back again, he scanned the front of the house and, after a short time, sensed motion to his left, a shift of the cheap bamboo blind that fell crooked on the sill. Moments later he heard the dull echo of feet in the hall.

The door opened on a man in his late thirties dressed in black jeans and a checked shirt, thin hair scraped back in a threadbare ponytail. He looked tired, his pupils little more than pinpricks in scratched blue irises. His hands rested on either side of the door frame, his stance the natural barrier of someone with shadiness in their blood.

"Ian Cahill?" asked Roscoe, and flashed his warrant card.

The man looked at the card for a second, blinked and then focused on something else. In that sequence Roscoe glimpsed the pair of dice behind the man's eyes that he rolled each time he came upon a difficult situation. This time he must've thrown a lucky number, for he soon nodded in response.

"Detective Inspector Frank Roscoe, Kentish Town CID," Roscoe said and then folded the card back into his jacket. "You mind if I come in for a minute and ask you a few questions?"

Cahill dropped his hands to his sides and let out a deep breath.

"Sounds like you were expecting me," said Roscoe.

Cahill offered him a nervous smile, then shook his head. "I should've known there'd be more to it than just coming into the station and . . . well, you know," he said, and his eyes jumped from Roscoe's face to a point in the middle distance and back again. "But look, to be honest, there's nothing more I can—"

Roscoe raised the flat of his hand, palm outwards, to cut him off. "I'm not here to ask you to reconsider your decision."

"You're not?"

"No, stuff like this happens all the time," said Roscoe, bristling with camaraderie. "There's no need to break your balls about it. And besides, it's too late."

"Yeah, I heard," said Cahill, shaking his head. "So, what do you want to talk to me about then?"

"Well, it is still about the accident," said Roscoe.

Cahill regarded the stone set of Roscoe's features and tried to pick up on the emotions that burned beneath the surface.

"It'll only take a couple of minutes," said Roscoe.

Cahill hesitated for a second, rolled the dice once more, shrugged, and then turned and headed back down the hall.

Roscoe stepped into the house, closed the door behind him, and trailed Cahill into the front room.

The room looked like it had not been cleaned in some time. Dust coated all the available flat surfaces, and saucers and plates were covered in rocks of cigarette ash. Piles of CDs and DVDs were stacked about the floor like plastic stalagmites, and in a far corner of the room behind a battered armchair, Roscoe could see blocks of old albums and videos pushed aside like relics from a distant era. The smell of cheap meat floated on the air like a fine mist, and stale alcohol seemed to puff from the carpet with each step he took. On a black Formica cabinet, a TV flickered on one of the confessional talk shows that saturated the afternoon schedules. On the screen an old black man dressed like a seventies pimp fallen on hard times spoke in quiet benediction to a son that he had not seen in a decade, asking him to understand the reasons for his abandonment.

Cahill crossed the room and lowered himself into an armchair opposite the television. He picked up the remote and pointed it at the TV, hit the mute button. Distracted, he stared at the old black man on the screen for a moment, the old man's bald head glowing like a light bulb under the studio lights.

Roscoe took a seat on the sofa.

Cahill stroked his thumb across the mute button on the remote, waiting.

"Like I said, I'm not here to ask you to change your mind about your statement," said Roscoe. "That's between you and your conscience now. No, all I want is for you to tell me, off the record, what happened outside the Linton Tree that night. Basically, all the stuff that was in your original statement."

"How do you mean, off the record?"

"It stays in this room," Roscoe reassured him.

"And how do I know you're telling the truth?"

"The last time you were interviewed, how many officers were there?"

Cahill frowned for a second, thought back. "Two, I think."

"Two," repeated Roscoe. "The reason for that is so that one can corroborate the other. I'm on my own, so nothing you say can be used in evidence. Everything you say is off the record."

Cahill blinked and rolled the dice once more, hesitated, then nodded more to himself than to Roscoe.

"Okay, thanks," said Roscoe. "Do you want to start by telling me where you were standing?"

"In front of the pub, right by the front door."

"On Brecknock Road?"

"Yeah. On Brecknock Road."

"Okay. And you were on your own?"

"Yeah. I was waiting on a friend."

"Did you talk to anyone while you were waiting?"

"No."

"You were just standing there on your own the whole time?"

"Yeah."

"Okay," said Roscoe, nodding, taking it in. "How long had you been out there before the accident happened?"

Cahill shrugged his shoulders, eased back into his seat. "I don't know. About ten minutes or so, fifteen."

"You want to tell me what you saw, what happened?"

Cahill puffed out his cheeks, gathered his thoughts. "The fight started in the pub just as I was getting served. It was quite loud and ferocious, but most of the other people in the place just looked on like it was some kind of cabaret, like it happened all the time." He raised his hand and pointed at the TV, as if a similar scene were currently unfolding on the screen. "But the barman must've soon got sick of it because he kicked them out about two minutes or so after I stepped outside."

"You heard the barman kick them out?"

Cahill nodded. "Well, I heard him shouting after them just after they went outside. The door was open."

Cahill paused, ran a hand across his scalp.

"So what happened then, what happened to the couple after that?"

"I heard them moving off towards the tube station, still arguing."

"How soon after that did the police car arrive?"

"I don't know," replied Cahill, his voice soft. "I heard the siren, but I didn't think that it was coming after them . . ."

"Do you think the couple heard the siren?"

Cahill frowned, uncertain.

"What about the other people who were out there, the ones who were standing closer to where it happened?"

"I don't know, I couldn't see that much. There were about four or five people standing on the corner right in front of me."

"This is good," said Roscoe, nodding. He took a pack of cigarettes out of his pocket. "You don't mind if I smoke?"

"No, go ahead," replied Cahill.

Roscoe shook a cigarette out of the pack and put a match to it, blew smoke out of his mouth. "Right, so what happened then?"

Cahill shifted around in his seat, leaned forward and looked at a point on the carpet a couple of inches in front of his feet. He took a moment to gather his thoughts. "I heard the screech of the wheels on the road, and then . . . and then this . . . and then this horrible loud noise. That must have been when the car hit the kid, I suppose. And then the crowd just kind of splintered in all directions, disappeared, and all of a sudden there was no one there and all I could see was the kid right there in the road. Then his mother—I think it was his mother, it must've been his mother—it took a second for her to realise what had happened. . . . Then she just walked over to him in this sort of trance, took hold of his hand. One of his feet was all twisted around, facing the wrong way."

"You didn't see the police car before that?"

"No," said Cahill, shaking his head.

"What about the driver, what'd he do then?"

"I saw him climb out of the car, but then he didn't seem to know what to do after that. He was just looking around, he didn't seem to be all that interested in what had happened."

"What was he looking at?" asked Roscoe, tapping ash.

"I don't know," said Cahill, shrugging. "He just seemed to be looking around. I don't know what he was looking at."

"Like he was looking for someone in the crowd?"

Roscoe caught the flare in Cahill's pupils for a second, and in that gesture he knew for certain that Rhiannon had been right in her suspicions.

"It was such a tangle out there," said Cahill, sounding dislocated. He dropped his chin and stared at the TV, tapped the end of the remote on the arm of the chair, rotated it and then tapped the other end on the arm, continued to rotate and tap.

Roscoe let him breathe.

"You remember who else was outside the pub that night?"

Cahill shook his head, no.

Roscoe took a deep breath and looked out at the street. He knew that he would get no more from Cahill this time around. The Greek chef was still standing in the open back door of the restaurant, a cigarette in one hand and the knife in the other.

"All right, thanks," said Roscoe, climbing from the sofa. He stubbed out his cigarette on an overflowing plate, thanked Cahill once more, and then let himself out of the house.

Roscoe crossed the street and stood on the opposite side. He took a final look back at the house and saw Cahill framed in the open door, his forehead creased in confusion.

7

Back at the station Marnie collected a cup of coffee from the canteen and headed up to the CID room. She stopped in front of Spencer's desk and asked him about the kid they pulled in earlier.

"He's still down in the basement," said Spencer. "I checked up on him an hour ago, but his lip's still all buttoned up."

"Leave him to rot down there for the time being," said Marnie. "Let's concentrate on the Ballard case for now, get up to speed before the calls start to come in tomorrow, give ourselves a chance to weed out some of the cranks before we waste too much time. Did you manage to make up a timeline for me?"

Spencer took a sheet of A4 paper from his desk and handed it to Marnie.

Marnie glanced at it for a second. "This looks great, Spencer, thanks." She rolled it up into a tube and held it in her hands. "Did you manage to dig out the case file as well?"

"On your desk, Boss," said Spencer.

"Thanks," said Marnie, then turned to walk away.

"So what happened with Lucille Hook?" Spencer called after her. "What did she have to say for herself?"

"Not much," said Marnie as she turned to face him again. "She more or less told me to piss off, said she wasn't going to do my job for me."

"I thought she was supposed to be on our side?"

"She is. . . . Well, most of the time, anyway. Or at least on the side of the angels, the innocent victims."

"So what'd you say to her to make her react like that?"

Marnie shook her head, dismissed the question. "While I was there I took a climb up onto the roof, the spot where Ballard was pushed from. It's like a bone orchard up there, all this debris of the dead around. And I spoke to the caretaker, too. He told me the lock on that building was always getting busted. The roof up there's a particular favourite of the crackheads, apparently. Must be the south facing aspect or something. Anyway, the last time the lock was fixed was two weeks before Ballard died."

Spencer nodded, raised his chin. "I saw that in the file."

"The point is that most of the time the traffic on that stairwell is close to gridlocked, and so any crackhead not face down in his own puke is going to be on that phone tomorrow spinning us a tale about how they saw what happened to Ballard while also trying to convince us that they're not Roald Dahl."

Spencer sniggered, looked around the room.

"So despite the fact that most of the time these things turn to shit, it's more than likely that tomorrow we'll get some kind of a real lead. It won't be a complete waste of time. But the good stuff is going to be buried in among all the bullshit, and it's going to be of the 'I Saw Mommie Kissing Santa Claus' variety. . . . So I want you to go through everything that comes in with a fine tooth comb, all right? Don't dismiss anything."

Spencer opened his mouth to speak, but Marnie had already started across the room.

In her office, little more than a chipboard cubicle in the corner of the room furthest from the door, Marnie pulled up her chair to the scratched metal desk and sat down. She glanced out the window at the primary school across the street, and a slice of Kentish Town Road at the end of Holmes Road in the distance, a hardware store and a bookies on the two corners. She put the timeline on the left hand side of the desk and opened the file.

Two weeks before his death, Paul Ballard had been seen in a raised-fists discussion with a man named Lee Rooker outside Subterranean, a hardcore dance club near the tube station in Camden Town. Three nights later the pair were again spotted at each other's throats in Cotton's, a Jamaican rum bar on Chalk Farm Road, the tussle once more over the charms of a fifteen-year-old blonde who had offered herself up to both men and then sat back to watch the sparks fly.

Statements from both the blonde, Jenna Barnes, and her friend, Shona Kilpatrick, later confirmed Rooker's claim that he had been in a pub near the flat that Barnes shared with her stepfather at the time of Ballard's death. Rooker's brief also included a statement to the same effect from one of the barmen from the pub. On the surface the alibi looked rock solid, and Marnie doubted that so long after the event she would be able to make it bounce.

She flicked through the rest of the file, the usual raft of statements and reports, until she came across a couple of handwritten sheets of paper. Dated a week after Ballard had been found, the note looked as if Fletcher had requested some background information on Rooker from another detective in the station, one DI Frank Roscoe. She had not met Roscoe but understood him to be on sick leave after being shot some months earlier. She flattened the sheets of paper on her desk and started to read the notes Roscoe had left for Fletcher.

Rooker had a reputation as a firecracker that stretched back to the age of fourteen, when he had broken a chair across the back of his math teacher's head after the teacher had dared to question Rooker's arithmetic capabilities. The act had not been the first to be fired from his quick blood, but it had been the one to cast him on a dark trajectory with the authorities, and after a couple of jolts in Borstal, he had spent time in both Belmarsh and Pentonville. It had been almost fifteen months since his last stint, and of late he had been manning the door at a number of bars and clubs around Kilburn and Camden Town. Rumour had it that he also carried out the occasional hit for one of North London's drug barons, but Rooker maintained that this was standard PR put out by the clubs he doored in order to intimidate potential troublemakers. But still the rumours persisted, and just four months earlier he had been linked to the death of a man whose corpse had been found buried under a pile of rubble from a house restoration in a skip on a quiet street in Primrose Hill. Street talk painted Rooker as the killer, but there had been no evidence to link him to the murder and no witnesses had come forward. He also had an alibi for the time of the murder: a woman had taken a shine to him at one of the clubs he worked, and he had spent the following twenty-four hours in her company, rocked on cocaine and supple limbs. The obvious conclusion was that there was a parallel between the two murders, a similar MO if not to the murder then to the setting up of an alibi, but Roscoe had told the lead officer that Rooker was not their man.

Marnie read through the notes once more and then climbed out from her desk and stuck her head out into the main office. "Yo, Spencer."

Spencer looked up from his computer, glanced across.

"You know a DI Frank Roscoe?"

Spencer raised his brows. "You mean the same DI Frank Roscoe who used to work here?"

"That's the one," said Marnie. "You know him?"

"Yeah, he was. . . . He was wounded earlier this year in a drive-by shooting down in Chalk Farm. I think he's just come out of hospital, still on crutches."

"I don't suppose you've got a number for him, have you?"

"I'm sure I can find one," said Spencer, and he started to get up from his desk.

"Thanks," said Marnie, stepping back into her office. She sat behind her desk and copied the last known addresses for Jenna Barnes, Shona Kilpatrick, and Lee Rooker into her notebook, and the name of the club that Rooker had been manning the door for on the night of Ballard's death. She flipped through the rest of the file but came across nothing more of interest. She turned back to the front of the file, found the number for Ballard's parents.

She pulled the phone across the desk and lifted the handset to her ear, punched the number into the grid.

Moments later she heard someone pick up on the other end of the line.

"Is that Mr. Ballard?"

"Speaking."

"Detective Sergeant Marnie Stone, Kentish Town CID. I just wondered if I could have a word with you about the reward."

In her mind, she had the Ballards painted as proud working-class people, bewildered as to how their child could have fallen to such a desperate place. To them, the death of their son would have become more about their failure to offer him a decent home in his lifetime than the trauma of how his life ended. Some people might have called it a natural defence mechanism, and in part that was true, but Marnie knew there was more to it than that. She had come across people like the Ballards before, people who were often blind to the truth about their children, but this time she sensed that it went much deeper. She imagined the mother as a pinched brunette who torqued her limbs into hard knots as some kind of subconscious penitence, and rushed to the end of her sentences on a single breath as if she was not used to talking. Like most blue-collar men of his generation, she imagined the father communicating for the most part in facial tics and basic sounds. And like a lot of couples in a similar situation, she imagined the Ballards led isolated lives and that their sole education came from TV and the shouted headlines of the gutter press. She doubted that the couple had friends close enough to turn to in their time of need.

She could hear the sound of laboured breathing on the line. "I already told you all you need to know," said Ballard at last.

"For the press release, yes," said Marnie. "But there are still a couple of points I need to clear up for the investigation." She paused and listened as Ballard fell silent, then pressed on. "Like why the reward, and why now?"

She heard Ballard take a deep breath, sensed him stand back from the phone and glance at his wife for support. His tone had softened when he came back on the line. "No one'd been in touch with us for about a fortnight or so, and when I called the police station to ask why, I was told that it was because no fresh information had come in. You seemed to have lost interest in the case . . . in our son," he added, almost as an afterthought.

Marnie could hear the accusation in his voice, the accusation that the investigation had been sidelined because his son had been a known crack dealer. The thought crossed her mind that maybe they had come across some of their son's drug money and used it to put up the reward. She knew that the family were not poor, but even so, ten thousand pounds would have been a substantial amount for them. "Are you serious about this? Are you sure that you can afford it? I just need to be sure . . ."

Marnie heard Ballard take a quick breath. "I hear what you're telling me," he said. "But you've no need to worry on that score. The money's not coming from us. No, a man who heard about our situation, I don't know from where, he didn't say, came to see us at the weekend, and said that he'd like to help us. His own son was murdered about two years ago. The murderer was never found and he said that he knew how we must be suffering. He offered to put up the reward for us. Said it was too late for his own son but that he could still afford to help others, he wanted to help others. I didn't want to listen to him at first, but Meg said that if it was the only way to find out what happened to Paul then we had no choice."

"Who was this man?" said Marnie. "What was his name?"

"I'm sorry, I can't tell you that," said Ballard. "One of the conditions was that we kept his name out of the papers."

"Are you sure about that? You can't tell me his name?"

Ballard hesitated. "He was pretty clear about it," he said. "I'd better call him and see if it's okay to let you know. I can call you back."

"Okay, thanks," said Marnie, and took a deep breath. "Look, Mr. Ballard, I must tell you that putting up a reward is not the best way forward. Once the idea is out there, it may divert precious resources away from the real chase and make it even more difficult for us."

"I understand," said Ballard. "But with respect, you haven't got very far so far, have you?"

Marnie felt a rueful smile break on her face. "That's true," she said, but her words echoed back from a dead line.

There was a rap on the door and Spencer stuck his head inside, held up a scrap of paper. "The number you wanted?"

8

Barney Price stepped off the bus at the foot of Camden Road, checked the traffic, and crossed at the lights, then cut through the tube station and came out on the High Street. Thick knots of people blocked his path—tourists looking for a cheap slice of decadence, dope and coke dealers on the whisper—and he shuffled around their static bodies and headed over to Inverness Street and the street market. On one of the stalls selling replica football shirts, he recognised someone from his class who had not been in school since the previous summer. Barney hitched up his collar, turned his head away, and hurried on.

Shake Records stood in the centre of the street, bracketed between a tapas bar and an Italian café. Barney climbed the stone steps, pushed the door open, and stepped inside.

Rock music that he did not recognise bounced from the speakers mounted high in the four corners, and the walls were covered with posters of old rock stars that for the most part he also did not recognise. Apart from Kurt Cobain, the only face he had seen before was Van Morrison, and that was only because his mother had a couple of his albums. Racks of old vinyl albums lined the wall to his left, and to his right, smaller racks held CDs and seven-inch singles. Glass cases above the racks on both sides held the rarer records and CDs, box sets and promos. Faded blue lino tiles peeled from the floor and nicotine stained the ceiling, a reminder of the store's history as a coffee shop.

In front of one of the CD racks, a tall man in a faded and stained blue brushed denim suit flicked through the titles. He had long black hair that shook in a single sheet as his head jerked back and forth, out of time to the music in the shop. The man behind the counter stood and stared at him, his arms folded across his chest.

Barney stepped up to the counter. "Hi, Archie," he said. "Is Mel around?" His stepsister worked part-time in the store, Saturdays and a couple of evenings a week after school.

Archie looked at Barney for a second and then blinked. The kid had told him that he was fifteen, Mel had told him, too, but Archie still thought he looked about ten or eleven. He didn't know why Mel knocked about with him, stepbrother or not. He turned back to the man in denim. He unfolded his arms and rested his knuckles on the counter, and his mouth fell open to speak.

Barney turned to see what had distracted him and saw that the man in denim had pulled out a CD and was reading the back.

"Hey, Skelton," Archie called out across the store. "No Led Zep, remember. Anything else, but no more Led Zeppelin."

"What's happening?" said Barney.

The man in denim—Skelton—brought the CD up to the counter.

Archie took the CD from him and put it on the counter, left it there. "You know you're not supposed to have any Led Zeppelin."

"How much is that?" said Skelton, and took a thin roll of notes out of the front pocket of his jeans.

"You can have anything else you want, but you know I can't sell you Led Zep any more."

Skelton peeled a ten from his roll, picked the CD up from the counter, and tried to hand both of them across to Archie.

"The last time I sold you some Led Zeppelin you woke up the whole fucking dorm in the middle of the night," said Archie. "Did it again and again, every night of the fucking week, until one of the other men came around here and tried to tear my heart out." Archie folded his arms across his chest, shook his head. "He wanted to put a brick through the window."

"If I want to buy this CD then you have to sell it to me, that's the rules," said Skelton. His lips trembled and a fine thread of spittle linked the top lip to the bottom, as if a spider had been interrupted in the middle of its job.

Barney could see the broken veins around his pupils, the cheeks that looked like a faded map of the Underground. His suit had not been cleaned in some time and alcohol steamed from his breath. The blackheads that peppered the skin at the corners of his eyes matched his stubble and gave him the look of a werewolf. Barney had no doubt that he had come from the huge Victorian hostel around the corner on Arlington Road, home to over four hundred men, most of them mad, bad, and alcoholic, doomed to ghost the streets of Camden Town forever.

"If I sell you this then you know he'll only come back, and this time he won't take no excuses. What about Boston or something more laidback like that? Toto or Foreigner."

Skelton put the CD and the ten on the counter and pushed them in Archie's direction. "Someone must've stolen my other copy."

"No," said Archie, shaking his head.

Skelton glared into Archie's face, his fists curling and uncurling in front of his thighs. The record on the deck came to the end of the track and a crackling silence filled the room. Barney could hear the shouts of the traders in the market outside the store. Seconds later, the chime of a guitar sounded from the deck, the thump of a bass drum.

The standoff made Barney feel a little afraid, tightened the knot that burned in his stomach, and he had felt a desperate need to fill the silence. "Why don't you just let him buy the CD, Archie?"

"Just keep the fuck out of it, all right?" snapped Archie.

Barney felt his heart shrink in his chest, and looked from Archie to Skelton and back again. "But I don't understand," he croaked.

"But I don't understand," mimicked Skelton, pitching at a little girl voice and falling short.

All of a sudden Archie snatched the ten off the counter, stuffed it into Skelton's top pocket, and then pushed him hard on the front of his shoulders with a snap of his hands. Skelton jerked backwards, reaching out behind himself and grabbing hold of the album racks to keep his balance. His face took on a mask of disbelief, all wide eyes and slack lips. Archie stepped around the counter and pushed him on the chest once more, took hold of his shoulder and spun him around, pushing him again in the direction of the door. "Just fuck off and don't come back," he said, his face up close to the back of Skelton's head.

Stunned, Skelton shuffled forward, his hands spread out before him as if he knew that he was about to fall.

"And you can tell that to your scummy mates as well. Always coming in here out of the fucking rain, stinking the place up but never fucking buying anything."

Skelton shuffled around and pointed at the CD on the counter.

"No, just fuck off," snapped Archie, hard and fast. "No more records, no more CDs, no more Led fucking Zeppelin, no more nothing." He stepped up to Skelton once more, face to face. The other man held his ground for a second, and then turned and left the shop, slamming the door behind him. The door hit the jamb and bounced open again, and then Archie followed him out and called out to him from the doorstep: "And if there's ever any damage to the shop then I'll know where to come looking, all right?"

Skelton stared back at him from out in the street for a second, eyes burning with anger and humiliation, then spat on the earth and disappeared into the scrum of the market.

Archie closed the door and headed back behind the counter, then started to sort through a pile of old albums. Barney watched him for a couple of minutes, until he thought the pressure had left the store, and then he said, "What was all that about?"

"I thought I told you to fuck off."

Back in the autumn of 1978, Sarah Price (Sarah Crowther, she was then) had left the family home in Southampton and headed up to Manchester University to study history. She had kept her head down for most of her first year, bundled up inside a duffel coat and a college scarf, and lived in an all-female hall of residence, but in her second year she had loosened up and started to put out feelers to the world. Tired of the restrictions of the hall, she moved into a shared terrace house in Rusholme with a couple of other girls from her course. But soon after, she had drifted from her old friends and started to hang around with a new crowd, spending most of her time out at the Factory in Hulme. Seeing the bands from London and New York that had roared through the city on a musical revolution, and the local bands that had come up in the wake of the success of local heroes, the Buzzcocks. Saturdays she would spend most of the day in Hulme, a film at the Aaben in the afternoon, across to the Grants Arms for the latch at five-thirty, and then on to the Factory in time to catch the support band. Besides the drinking there had been other stuff around too, speed and marijuana, a little acid, magic mushrooms in season, and Sarah had spent most of her time on a permanent rattle. When the chance came to take over a council flat near the club, she hustled a couple of her friends together, dumped all her clothes into a bin liner, her books and records into a tea chest, and rushed across to the flat before some other squatters had a chance to stake their claim. The flat was on the top floor of John Nash Crescent, one of the four monolithic slabs of concrete in the centre of Hulme named after famous British architects. The Crescents had been built in the mid-sixties, after the slums that had been on the site since the thirties had been torn down, but barely twenty years later the flats had fallen into chronic disrepair. Families had refused to live in them, and students and the disaffected had all but colonised the area. The flats still housed some of the most desperate people in the region, those whose drug problems made Sarah and her friends' amphetamine antics look like the random clumsiness of sugar-rush kids. But despite all this, neither Sarah nor her friends had felt threatened, and in spite of their differences there had been some kind of outcast camaraderie between the different peoples living there. There was none of the warfare that characterised the adjacent neighbourhood of Moss Side.

Sarah had been content with her life, and it had not affected her studies much; she had still come out with a decent degree at the end of it all. But in the last couple of years she had started to believe that the dark fruit she was reaping had come from seeds planted in that glorious time in Manchester.

These thoughts occupied her mind as she walked up Kentish Town Road, her shoulders slumped under the burdens of the past and the present, the future an abstract notion that she had little time for.

As she approached the entrance to the Castle Estate, she heard the rips and shouts of the druggies who hung around the phone booths. The kids used the booths as a centre for their dealing, and each morning the debris of drug-taking could be seen spread across the estate like a hellish mosaic. The same debris awaited her every morning outside her own flat, on the stairs, and in the lobby on the ground floor. She reached the corner and saw three kids standing there in dark hoods and jeans which ballooned out from their hips and scraped on the earth at the heel. One of the kids clocked her on the walk past, and grinning, he cocked a thumb and pointed a finger at her like a pistol.

Sarah dropped her head and pushed on, but as she reached her block she turned to take a look back and saw that the kid was still watching her, the pistol still pointing at her back.

9

Sean Dillon forked a piece of lamb chop into his mouth and looked across at Con O'Brien on the other side of the chipped Formica table. The pair were sitting in the canteen on the ground floor of Kentish Town police station at the end of their shift. Out of the window they could see the feet of people walking by on their way home, some taking the stone steps up to the station's main entrance. "What about one of those school liaison jobs," he said, chewing. "That must be a pretty easy ride out to retirement."

O'Brien looked up from his steak pie and chips, shot Dillon a look that questioned his judgment. "You're kidding, right?"

"Well, how hard can it be?" said Dillon, affronted. "Keeping a pack of bored and—let's face it—stoned kids in line all day?"

"If that's all that you think it is. . . ."

"C'mon, Con. All the bad guys are out on the street, hanging around the Lock. You know that. The only ones still at school are the ones too scared to talk back to their parents."

"Are you talking about yourself now, Sean?"

"I had my moments," said Dillon, and forked another piece of lamb chop into his mouth.

"I bet you gave your old man a hard time when you were a kid," said O'Brien, smiling across at his partner.

Dillon looked off across the room, flattened his lips.

"How old was he when he died?" asked O'Brien.

"I don't know," said Dillon. "Sixty-two, sixty-three . . . I know he didn't live long enough to collect his pension."

"So what, you made his life a misery and pushed him into an early grave?"

"There's no need to be like that," protested Dillon, that familiar heat starting to rise in his throat.

"Hey, you know I'm only kidding, Sean," said O'Brien. "But no matter how bad you were, try and imagine what it'd be like to have to deal with a thousand kids just like you every day of your working life. And not be allowed to even clip them around the ear or give them the cane or anything like that, lock them up."

Dillon smiled to himself, recalling the times he had come across that idea in his jumbled adolescent mind himself. Looking around the canteen he saw Rob Spencer, one of the fresh faces from CID, at a table in the far corner, hunched over his coffee.

"But that must be the teacher's job," he said. "You only need to jump in if it starts to get out of hand."

Dillon smiled and shifted on his seat. "Some kid gets burned on a deal and punches out the dealer behind the bike sheds, stuff like that."

"Believe me, that'd be a quiet afternoon," said O'Brien, then took a sip of water. He put his knife and fork down on his plate, rested his elbows on the table and folded his hands in front of his mouth. He poked at a morsel of food stuck in his teeth with his tongue, and looked across at Dillon. "If you think some of the estates around here are bad, then you want to see what goes on in some of these schools. This friend of mine, he used to knock about with my sister back when the Forum was still the Town and Country Club, must be about ten years ago now. He used to be a carpenter for the council until he broke his hand in a car accident and couldn't use his tools. . . ."

Dillon let a smirk cross his face at that last remark.

"Hey, what's so funny about that?" said O'Brien.

"This must be a joke, right?" said Dillon, leaning back, his hands spread wide. "The carpenter who couldn't use his tool."

"Remind me to mention that to Ronnie the next time I go and see him up in Golders Green Crematorium."

Dillon bit his bottom lip, felt like letting rip. He hated this shit, the immediate demand for respect from his elders. Fuck, out on the street that kind of respect had to be earned. And it wasn't like he had any illusions about that respect/fear argument, either way it had to be earned. This attitude was something his former partner, Hooper, had struggled to understand, and in the end he had just backed away and left Dillon to his own views. And now after less than a week back on the streets, he was still not allowed back behind the wheel, and he had to put up with some numbskull just out to keep his hands clean until he could collect his gold watch. He would be glad when his probation period was over and he could get back in the driving seat and dump O'Brien back in his garden shed where he belonged. "I didn't mean anything . . . Okay, I'm sorry, all right," he muttered and pushed his half-eaten lunch aside.

He shook his head and glanced across at Spencer once more.

"Anyway," said O'Brien, accepting the apology with a heavy heart. "After he broke his hand, the council gave him a job helping out the caretaker at this school in Kilburn. His first day in the job, he saw this blood on the floor in the main hall and traced it to one of the kids' lockers. He found the right locker, popped it open, and there was this Bowie knife stuffed inside a duffel bag. Blood and some fine blonde hair stuck to the blade. Turns out this kid'd used the knife on his girlfriend's face after she lent her English homework to some other kid in her class." He passed a finger across the sides of his mouth. "Slashed her lips and made her smile just that little bit wider."

Dillon blinked and rewarded O'Brien with a grim smile, but his attention had returned to Spencer on the other side of the room. The detective had pushed back his chair and was now heading towards the door behind them.

"But that's just a footnote," continued O'Brien. "The real tale happened about three months later, right after the school closed up for the summer. . . . Hey, what's going on?"

Dillon had snagged Spencer's arm as the detective passed their table.

"What's all this about a reward on the Ballard case?" said Dillon to Spencer, leaning back in his chair.

Spencer shook his arm loose and narrowed his eyes at Dillon. "Where'd you hear that from?"

Dillon pointed at the ceiling, the general direction of the front desk. "Dobie told me just now when I came in the building," he said. "Some friend of the family put up a reward and now we all have to dance to their tune."

"You know that's not how it works," replied Spencer.

"That's not what I heard," said Dillon. "I heard we have to chase up any lead that comes into the station, however stupid."

"Well, you heard it wrong," replied Spencer, an edge in his voice. "But if the family wants to put up a reward to try and help us do our job, then who are we to deny them that opportunity?"

Dillon looked across the room for a moment. "Yeah, all right, point taken," he said, and tried to look scolded.

"Wait until morning prayers," said Spencer, walking out of the canteen. "I'm sure it'll all become clear then."

Marnie spent the remainder of the afternoon in a fruitless search for Jenna Barnes. She knocked at the address that was listed in the file, but when Jenna's stepfather, a man named Jacks, opened the door he told Marnie that Jenna left weeks ago and he had no idea where she was.

"And I take it you reported her missing," said Marnie.

The man looked back at her with unsentimental eyes.

"She's fifteen," said Marnie, incredulous. "Did it never occur to you that maybe she should be at home?"

Jacks pursed his lips and shook his head, shifted his bulk from foot to foot. "She'll be back when she's ready," he said. "It's not like it's the first time she's run away. She's been in and out of here all summer long. She can take care of herself."

"So you've no idea where she might be—"

"No," said Jacks, the skin around his eyes tightening.

"—or who she might be with?"

Jacks shook his head again.

"Did she ever mention a man named Lee Rooker?"

"She never tells me much about who she sees," replied Jacks.

"What about her mother, then, her friends. You think they might know where she is?"

"Maybe," he said, and his head tilted to the side in a cartoon attempt at concern.

"All right, that's a start," said Marnie, undiluted disdain in her voice. "You do care after all. Or maybe you just need someone to clean up your shit for you afterwards."

"There's no need to be like that," grumbled Jacks.

"Oh, so you do have a sensitive side," said Marnie. "Let's see if we can build on that, shall we? How about we start by you telling me where Jenna's mother lives."

Jacks shot her a look of loathing and then ducked back inside the flat. The door started to ease shut. Marnie stepped forward, reached out a hand to hold it open, and felt the smell of a life bereft of purpose or direction hit the back of her throat. It triggered some kind of sense memories, but when it hit her heart it bounced right back. She had no time for misplaced concern.

Jacks returned and handed her a piece of paper, an address

in Kilburn scratched on it in black ink. She pushed it deep into her jacket pocket. "Do you want me to let you know if I find her?" she said, but when she looked up she faced chipped wood.

Jenna Barnes's mother lived alone in a basement flat just around the corner from Kilburn Park tube station. She had shown a little more concern for her daughter's welfare than her husband, but not enough to warrant praise. She had not heard from Jenna in three months and had no idea where she might be. And no, she had never heard of Lee Rooker either. Marnie thanked her and walked away, brutalised once more by the impression that Jenna Barnes might just as well have disappeared down a crack in the earth for all the concern her parents had shown over her whereabouts.

10

Roscoe threaded a path up through the back streets of Tufnell Park, thinking about what Ian Cahill had told him, lost in thought. His reverie was broken as he stepped across the broken pavement slabs and traffic bumps behind the prison, sensing an eerie silence in the air, as if a thick cushion had been erected around its brick walls to keep out the sounds of freedom.

He came out on Tufnell Park Road opposite the Tufnell Park Tavern, now painted battleship grey and renamed progressbar. He could hear the hard beat of dance music from behind the painted-over windows. He glanced up the hill towards the tube station at the junction of Brecknock Road, the junction from which the car that had killed Karl Burns had emerged, and a picture of the child's parents, his old friends Charlie and Rhiannon, popped into his head. The last time he had seen them truly happy together: Charlie behind the counter of the frame store in Brighton, his thin wrists poking loose from the cuffs of his fisherman's smock, at home in his new role, a contented smile on his face, a glimpse of Rhiannon in the back room as she chased an infant Karl around the stacks of frames, trailing squeals of delight, blue paint slapping from a thick paintbrush held up in his little fist. The sound of smiles high on the atmosphere. He blinked and turned the mental picture around to look at it seven years down the line, and felt a touch of anger that after the funeral Charlie had not stayed on in London to support Rhiannon, but decamped back to Brighton as soon as he had been able. There had been just the one visit for the inquest since, the time Roscoe had seen him down near the tube station, disjointed and with his head in another place. Roscoe had seen that kind of dejection all too often, the brittleness of the father-and-son bond revealed at the point of tragedy, but he had thought that Charlie would be different.

Roscoe waited for a break in the traffic and then crossed the street, headed for the terrace of brick houses that faced the ULU sports ground. He let himself in the front door of the end house, picked up his mail from the side table in the hall, and climbed the stairs to his third-floor flat. His bad foot thumped the front of each step like a piece of rock tied to his ankle.

He dropped his jacket on the sofa and headed into the bathroom. He opened the glass cabinet and took out a bottle of painkillers. He shook out a couple of the tablets into his hand, ran a glass of water, and sluiced the tablets down his throat.

In the kitchen he rustled up a couple of pieces of bread and filled them with slices of roast beef and fresh spinach. He poured himself a glass of cranberry juice, diluted it under the cold tap, and then carried it all into the front room.

Pushing aside a pile of magazines, *Uncut, Mojo,* and the *Police Review,* Roscoe put the glass and plate down on the coffee table. He crossed to the racks of CDs that lined one wall and ran a finger along the titles, at last pulling out Nick Cave's *Abattoir Blues* and sliding it into the stereo. He tipped the volume up a notch, all the better to lose himself in the dark crashing waves of the opening track, and turned back to the sofa.

Noticing the red light on the ansaphone, he made a detour across the room and hit the play button. A crackle on the tape faded into a woman's voice: "It's DS Marnie Stone at Kentish Town station here, Frank. I need to talk to you about Lee Rooker. You spoke to DI Fletcher about him last month, remember, the suspect in the Paul Ballard case. Can you give me a call, please? I'll be at the station until about seven, or you can catch me later on my mobile." She left a number and then hung up.

Roscoe turned the stereo right back down again and carried the cordless phone over to the sofa, lifting his feet and stretching them out on the coffee table. He punched in the number for the CID room in KT, and when someone picked up—a voice that he did not recognise—he said, "DS Stone, please."

He heard a couple of clicks and then: "Stone, CID."

"It's Frank Roscoe."

"Hello, Frank. Thanks for calling back."

"That's all right. I just got in."

"How are you getting along, anyway, Frank?" asked Marnie. "I heard about the drive-by shooting. Is the foot any better?"

Roscoe was taken aback at her directness. He had never met Marnie Stone before, in fact had never even heard of her until a couple of minutes earlier, and here she was asking him personal questions that even his most long-standing colleagues had trouble asking him. He felt his cheeks flush with embarrassment and his tongue hide at the back of his mouth. In the ensuing silence he could hear her breathing fill the open spaces, the sound of "Get Ready for Love" on the stereo far off in the distance.

"It's getting there," he said at last, grinning.

"That's good to hear," replied Marnie. Then she surprised him further: "What about your head? Where's that at right now?"

"Jesus, I don't know," replied Roscoe, still grinning. "I haven't really thought about it. Heading towards bored and frustrated, I must think. I must have read every book and watched every video on my shelves, even the ones I don't remember buying. There's nothing left to do. Still, I shouldn't complain too much. I must be one of the lucky ones. You know the statistics, most drive-bys end up being scraped up off the street. Anyway, what can I do for you? You said you wanted to know about Lee Rooker."

"Yeah, if you can help me that'd be great," said Marnie.

"No problem," said Roscoe.

"Okay, thanks," said Marnie, reaching for her notebook. "Right, let's see. Do you remember the case? The dealer who was pushed from the roof of the Castle Estate last month?"

"Yeah, I remember it," replied Roscoe, laughter and something else edging his words. "The bullet went through my foot not my head, remember. It was a kid called Paul Ballard, right?"

"That's the one," said Marnie, and then all of a sudden a strange feeling possessed her. Something about the way in which Roscoe had responded to her asking him whether he remembered the Ballard case. She hadn't intended to question his mental state, but there was a certain pride behind his laughter that made her empathise with his isolation. "Look, why don't we meet for a drink or something, talk it over," she found herself saying.

"Yeah, okay, sure," said Roscoe after a second, taken aback once more. "Where did you have in mind?"

"I don't know. Where are you right now? I could come over your way." Marnie felt a smile start to rise on her face.

"Tufnell Park Road," said Roscoe, and the image of the battleship grey progressbar popped into his head, the thumping dance music in the middle of the afternoon. "But there's not much around here. How about the Magdala? Do you know the Magdala?"

"Parliament Hill? Sure, I know the Magdala. Seven-thirty?"

"Seven-thirty's fine," said Roscoe, and then said goodbye and ended the call. He held the phone in his lap for a moment, staring at the numbers on the grid and wondering what had just happened. Then he shook his head clear of all the images scrolling past the back of his lids and punched in Rhiannon's number.

It rang a couple of times, then the ansaphone kicked in, and he cut the line. He wanted to tell her about what Cahill had revealed, but he wanted to tell her in person, not via the machine. He also wanted to ask her about Charlie, ask her where he was in her time of need, and he needed to do that in person, too.

11

Barney heard his mother open and close the front door, and then a ten-second slice of street sounds broke into the flat behind her. She scrambled around in the hall for a couple of seconds, hanging up her denim jacket, and then stepped into the kitchen and took a seat at the table opposite him. She folded her arms on the table and leaned into them. Her face looked tired and pale, out of sorts, but an animal quickness lit her pupils. "Hey, Barney," she said. "How'd you get on at school today?"

He bit into a piece of toast, took another bite before he spoke. "All right," he said, and crumbs rolled from his lips onto his shirt. He lifted a hand to his chest and brushed the crumbs onto his lap, brushed them from his lap onto the floor.

"Anything interesting happen?" Sarah offered him a tired smile and leaned back in her chair, pushing her hands up into her hair and anchoring them there for a moment.

Barney felt his heart tick over, fast. He knew that it was only natural for his mother to be interested in his day, and just as natural for him to hold out on her, one of those rules that families understood on instinct. But ever since his brother Luke had died two years ago, he felt that every question of hers held the same motive, to find out how close he was to following Luke down to the lowest circle of hell. He knew that a mother's instinct to protect her child was behind it all, but he was fifteen now, almost a man, and he didn't need all that smother love anymore. He could cope on his own. He *was* coping on his own. "Same old," he said on a leaden sigh.

Sarah offered him another smile, but her attention had shifted to a place outside the room. "That's good," she muttered, and then turned and reached for the kettle on the counter behind her. She lifted it in her hand, shook it and, finding it full, set it back down on the counter and clicked it on.

Mother and son sat and listened to the kettle boil, communicating their unease at being in each others' presence in the depth of their breathing, the cold direction of their glances. It had been like this since Luke had died, the seismic shift in their relationship difficult for both of them to bear.

"Do you mind if I invite Ralph over tonight?" said Sarah at last. Her voice sounded distant and a little confused, as if it belonged to the caller on the far end of an abandoned telephone line and not to her. She had been seeing Ralph Burke, the manager of an organic food store just off Tottenham Court Road, for a little more than two months. He was the first man she had been out with since her husband had abandoned her three years earlier. Barney had been introduced to Ralph a couple of weeks back, the three of them going out for a meal at the Giraffe in Hampstead, and had found him pleasant enough.

Barney popped the last corner of toast into his mouth, shrugged his shoulders. "You have to get on with your life."

"So you don't mind, then?"

"Why should I?" said Barney. "I can always go out."

"There's no need for you to do that, Barney."

"You don't want me getting in the way."

"You won't be getting in the way, love."

"Ralph, he won't want me sitting right there beside him when he's pitching woo."

Sarah let out a short laugh, blushed a little. "Ralph's not like that. You met him. You know he's not like that."

Barney chewed on his toast, kept silent.

"I can always ask him to come over some other time. Maybe we can all go out to lunch together this weekend or something."

"It's okay, Mum," said Barney, pushing his plate aside. "I don't mind. Honest. Tell him to come over if you like."

Sarah reached out and put her hand on top of Barney's, held it tight. "You're sure about that?"

"Jesus, Mum," he groaned. "Can't you hear me or something?"

"I just don't want you to feel pushed out, that's all."

"I don't feel pushed out," said Barney through gritted teeth.

"You know that I'd never put—"

"Look, it doesn't matter, Mum. If you want him to come over then go and ask him. It's not a problem, honest."

Sarah could feel the heat coming off his face.

The kettle clicked off just then. She climbed up from her chair, turning her back on him, and took out a jar of Nescafé from the cupboard. She lifted a mug from the draining board, shook the water from a teaspoon, and spooned instant coffee and sugar into the mug.

Barney sensed that she had fallen silent only to come back at him once more after she had reloaded her guns, and pushed on. "And don't keep treating me like a kid all the time," he said. "Why can't you understand that? I don't need looking after, you asking me if everything's all right all the time. You're not the only one who needs to be getting on with their life."

No response.

Barney narrowed his eyes and stared at the back of his mother's head, the fall of her hair as it reached her shoulders. He tried to picture her face, came up with her nose and mouth, a stranger's eyes. The shock made his tongue turn sharp, as if into a knife.

"And don't keep treating me like I'm Luke either," he

snapped, on a roll now, the tips of his fingers tingling. "Thinking you can still save him through me. It's too late for that, it was always too late for that. He's dead and he'll still be dead tomorrow. And the day after that, and the day after that, and the day after that. . . . He's dead forever. Get over it."

He noticed her shoulders start to shake first, sudden jerks of her neck, and then he heard the first sob break from her chest, a deep troubling sound that felt like it had been torn from the most secret and precious chambers of her heart.

He felt disgust thicken his throat, and he rested his hands on the table, pushed back his chair and left the room in silence.

12

The Magdala Tavern sat at the foot of South Hill Park, the road that led from South End Green in Hampstead to Parliament Hill fields. The place had been a traditional pub for as long as Roscoe could remember, a large main bar to the left and a smaller tap room on the right, but about eighteen months earlier it had undergone a major transformation and been turned into a gastropub. The former upstairs living quarters were now a smart restaurant, and the main bar had been filled with solid timber furniture and leather sofas and chairs. The restaurant menu also applied to the main bar, but the tap room had been left more or less as it had been since the late fifties.

Roscoe ordered a bottle of Miller and carried it across to a table that looked out through a set of glass doors onto the small patio at the side of the building. From there he could see the foot traffic from South End Green and the parking spots right outside. He hoped that he could pick out Marnie Stone before she stepped through the front door. He took a drink of beer and looked around the room. There was a bald man in a dark suit at the bar sipping from a tumbler of scotch, and at the foot of the stairs a waitress was chalking up the night's menu on a large blackboard which she rested across her knees. She had blonde hair bundled up on top of her head, and slim, tanned legs that stretched from a short black skirt to leather sandals. On her ankle, a small tattoo of a snake in red and blue made him think of the scar on his own ankle. Her hands were covered in chalk dust and there was a thick streak of blue chalk like a tribal mark across the centre of her forehead. Roscoe could just about make out the word "Specials" across the top of the board.

"Frank Roscoe?"

Roscoe blinked and turned to see an attractive woman in her late thirties standing before him. She had thick brown hair cut short, matching brown irises that burned with a quick intelligence, a broad nose sprinkled with a light touch of freckles, and a wide, generous mouth. She wore a loose suit that hid her figure and told him that she liked to keep on the business side of a situation. She offered him a luminous smile that created brackets in her cheeks, and Roscoe felt heat rise in his face as he remembered the phone call from earlier.

"Marnie Stone," said Roscoe, starting to climb from his seat. "You want something to drink?"

Marnie held up her hands, palms out. "That's all right, I'll go to the bar," she said. "You want another beer?"

"No, I'm fine at the moment, thanks," said Roscoe, resting the palm of his hand on the top of the bottle for a second.

Marnie headed for the bar, and returned two minutes later with a glass of red wine in her hand and took a chair opposite Roscoe. She took a quick sip and then looked around the room. "This place has changed," she said, and then turned in her seat and pointed in the direction of the front of the building. "Didn't there used to be a sign up on the wall outside?"

In April 1955, Ruth Ellis had shot and killed her lover, David Blakely, on the street outside the pub. She had then stood and put another three bullets into his chest as she waited for the police to arrive. She had been the last woman to be hanged in Britain. Her story had been made into the film *Dance with a Stranger*, Miranda Richardson starring as Ellis, and for some time there had been a small plaque on the front of the building pointing out how the bullet holes in the tiles had been made.

"That's right," said Roscoe, smiling. "It went up about the same time as the landlord took a chisel to the tiles and put in the bullet holes. That must've been in about 1975 or so."

Marnie let out a short laugh. "You mean they're not the actual bullet holes?"

Roscoe smiled again, shook his head. "No, they're fakes."

"And you know that for a fact, do you?" Marnie took a sip of her drink.

"I'd just started at William Ellis at the time," said Roscoe, referring to the high school on the far side of Parliament Hill. "Some of the older boys . . . it was a fifth formers hangout, I think. They used to drink in here all the time, the older brothers of friends and the like. It was just a dark little pub back then, it had fallen a long way from the glamorous place it used to be back in the fifties. There used to be all these framed photos on the walls of film stars who drank in here. Richard Burton and Elizabeth Taylor, people like that. A new landlord put up the sign and made the bullet holes to try and turn the place around, bring back the good times."

"So there were never any real bullet holes in the tiles?"

Roscoe shook his head, no.

"That's a great story," said Marnie. "Far better than the bullet holes being for real. What're you, some kind of local historian?"

Roscoe smiled and took a sip of beer. He could see the shimmer of humour in Marnie's face, the lines, and pink roses had bloomed in her cheeks. "I've lived around here all my life," he said. "I reckon that if you live in one place long enough then it eventually lets you into its secrets."

"That's a good theory," said Marnie. "I can see why you became a police officer."

"Well, that's one of the reasons, I suppose," said Roscoe.

"You mean there's more than one reason?"

"Some other time, perhaps," said Roscoe, firm and final.

"Yeah, all right," said Marnie, struggling to hide her disappointment. "Anyway, do you still have any information in that head of yours about Lee Rooker?"

"You'll've heard of a man called Bar Code," said Roscoe.

"Known to his mother as Malcolm Percoda," replied Marnie, nodding. "One of the top drug men in Camden Town."

"Lee Rooker runs the doors for him at some of the clubs around Camden Town, controlling which dealers are let in and stuff like that."

"And that's all that he does? Bar Code doesn't have him doing anything else? Like any of the really bad stuff?"

"Well, there's honest gossip out there that he's killed before. Street dealers who skimmed the product, stuff like that. . . . You're not still looking at Rooker for this, are you?"

Marnie told him about the reward.

"That's a bad situation to be in," said Roscoe. "Having to react to public pressure like that. But I think Fletch was right the first time around. Rooker's a company man, in for the duration, and I can't see him making a move like this on his own. If he did do it, then it would have to've been on Bar Code's say so, and if that's the case then his alibi'll be rock solid."

"Even if he was just following his own dick?" said Marnie. "This looks like it all came down after a fight over a girl."

Roscoe grinned, took a pull on his beer. "You might have a point there. What's the girl have to say about it all?"

"So far we haven't been able to find her."

Roscoe looked off across the patio for a moment, then shook his head. "Ballard was just one of a large number of runners on the estate, dispensable. You're sure there's nothing else?"

"Kid might as well've fallen down a black hole for all the interest we've got on this one," said Marnie, shaking her head.

★　★　★　★　★

Barney pulled on his jacket and slipped out of the flat, left his mother stuck in front of *Changing Rooms*. "Ten," she called out after him. "I want you in by ten, okay, Barney?"

He took the stairs to the ground floor, immune to the kaleidoscope of sounds that bounced out at him from behind locked doors: people singing and fighting, solid beats and old time guitar music, the full spectrum of childhood emotions from cries to squeals of laughter. The front door had been propped open and a couple of kids stood waiting for the lift. Bloodshot faces and curled fists clutched tight to their chests to keep from rattling. The taller of the two was bundled up inside several layers of clothing as if he felt the cold a season ahead of other people. Barney recognised him as one of the new faces around the estate, had seen him crashed out on one of the benches in the playground, slumped in the shade of the community centre.

Barney kept his head down and hurried out the door. He took a sharp right and then checked across his shoulder to the far side of the estate. There were a lot of people hanging around the phone booths: little ones no more than ten or eleven out to make an impression, a reputation, and older ones still climbing the ladder and who moved with a resentful sluggishness. Barney knew that the dealers used a number of flats on the estate to store their drugs, either through intimidation of the tenants or by driving them out of their homes altogether. One of the kids in his class, Ethan Jones, his grandfather had been forced to come live with Ethan and his mother after the old man had returned home from the bookies one afternoon to find a couple of men with guns in his front room. The men had made it plain that he had no choice about the situation. The dealers had covered the rent and slipped him another hundred a week to keep it neat.

He headed up to Camden Lock and turned north on Chalk Farm Road. Past the Roundhouse and over the bridge into Primrose Hill. Ten minutes from his front door, junkies in the lift and dealers on the phone booths, and he strolled through one of the richest parts of London. He passed nice restaurants and designer clothing stores, then cut around the back and came upon a solid fortress of red brick, the Primrose Hill Estate. He pushed open the gate to the fenced-in sports court and stepped inside. Floodlights bathed the court in a thick sulphur sheen, and he took a seat on the tarmac beside the goal, leaning back into the fence to catch his breath. In front of the goal at the far end of the pitch, a group of kids kicked a football around, practising free kicks and corners. Perspiration bubbled on their foreheads and stained their clothes in darker shades.

He watched them until one of the footballers, a black kid in a Ben Sherman T-shirt and a blue bandana tied around his head, noticed him and raised a hand in his direction, grinning.

Barney returned the wave and pushed himself to his feet. He stuffed his hands inside the back pockets of his jeans, waiting for his friend to trot the length of the pitch.

"Look at the stranger over here, man," said the black kid. "Back in the world."

Barney felt a fat smile split his face.

"I haven't seen you in an age, man. Where you been hiding?"

Lincoln Fuller had started at Auden Place kindergarten on the same morning that Sarah Price had first dropped off her younger son at the school. Two three-year-olds scared of their own shadows, and the pair of them had been firm friends ever since. They had attended Primrose Hill infant and junior school together, but at the age of eleven their paths had split. Lincoln had gone on to Haverstock School, the school nearest to his home on the Primrose Hill Estate, while Barney had been accepted at William Ellis on Highgate Road in Kentish Town. The pair had remained friends despite the separation, but the depth of the friendship had lessened over time and distance, their characters altered by the different elements that surrounded them. It had been some months since the old friends had last seen each other.

"Here and there," shrugged Barney, his face lit up like a Halloween pumpkin under the lights.

"Here and there, here and there," echoed Lincoln in a singsong voice. "So what brings you over here tonight and not there?"

"You know I like to slum it now and then, keep it real," said Barney, still with that big grin on his face, all thoughts of the argument with his mother now banished from his head.

"You know that's a lie right there," said Lincoln. "Over in the Castle, I hear the bodies're piling up like a nuclear bomb gon' hit the damn place. That's keepin' it real. But whatever the state of the divide, man, it's good to see you," he added, and then took out a pack of Kools from his jeans, shook one loose. He offered the pack to Barney, but the offer was declined. He pulled out a Zippo from the same pocket and fired up the cigarette.

"You too, Link."

"Let's roll," said Lincoln, cool smoke on his breath, turning and walking out of the court.

"Where are we going?" asked Barney, having to run a little to catch up with his friend and fall into step beside him.

In the near distance he could hear the rattle of a train, the main line from London to Manchester or Liverpool.

13

Sarah Price had an old Richard and Linda Thompson tape, *I Want To See The Bright Lights Tonight,* in the cassette deck. She had been into Richard and Linda, and John Martyn, Cat Stevens, Nick Drake, people like that, at school way back in the late seventies, but she had not listened to their stuff in over twenty years. But in the last three years or so, she had found herself returning to their music once more, picking up secondhand tapes at the Lock and in the market. She reckoned that it must be the aural equivalent of comfort food, going back to the womb. And after all that had happened in the last couple of years, no one could deny her that.

She held the phone in close to her neck, puffing on a Silk Cut. The cigarette tasted stale, no great surprise there since the pack had been open for more than three months. She told herself she had packed it in for good this time, but she still dipped into the pack in the back of the kitchen drawer once in a while. She could hear the neighbours arguing through the wall, something to do with a car. Fat parents and their kids did nothing but argue, their sole means of communication.

Four rings in, the phone was picked up at the other end. "Yeah, hello there," said a male voice.

"Hi," she said. "It's Sarah."

"Hi, Sarah, how are you? I was just about to call you, see if we're still on for tonight."

"Oh. That's what I was calling about."

"That sounds ominous. Everything okay?"

"Yeah, sure, everything's fine," said Sarah, and took a pull on the Silk Cut. "It's just Barney, you know, he's just. . . . I tried to talk to him earlier tonight, but he just got all upset."

The line went silent. The neighbours' argument turned into muffled thumps, crashes against the wall.

"Ralph?"

"I'm still here. So what are you telling me, Sarah?"

"Ralph, can I ask you something?"

"Yeah, sure. Go ahead."

"Do you like Barney?" said Sarah at last, her voice sounding breathless. "I mean really like him, and not just because he's my son."

"He's a good kid. Yeah, why?"

"I don't know. . . . He's having such a hard time at the moment, I don't know if me and you is such a good idea. Right now, I mean. He needs me all to himself . . ."

"You know I'm really fond of you, Sarah. You *and* Barney."

"I know, I know, it's just . . ."

"We can take this at any speed you like, Sarah. Do you want to take a break, is that it? Cool off for a time?"

Sarah took another pull on her cigarette, crushed it in the saucer on the coffee table in front of her. "I don't know, Ralph. I'm in such a muddle about him. He's a teenager, he could be fine tomorrow. I don't know . . . I don't know what to do about him."

"Do you still want me to come over? We could talk about it tonight, work it out together. Is Barney there at the moment?"

"No, he's out right now."

Deep breaths echoed each other on the line, and then Sarah heard a leaden sigh.

"Let's meet up later in the weekend instead," said Ralph. "The three of us could go out to lunch somewhere."

"That'd be nice," said Sarah. "Thanks. Thanks, Ralph. You're a good man. Call me on Sunday morning, all right?"

Dillon pulled the Honda Civic into the small car park at the front of the Denton Estate. He cut the engine and looked around, checking out the walkways and the stairwells. It had just turned nine o'clock and darkness had started to fall. The estate was on his patch and it spooked him to come around after hours, out of uniform. Not that he was afraid as in being weak or scared, but he was afraid that someone might recognise him. He had been doing this particular run for Bar Code for three months now, but this was just the second time since he had been back in uniform. And like he had been told on numerous occasions before, if he took the coin then he had no damn choice in the matter. He took a baseball cap from the side pocket of the door, pulled it down low over his forehead. He climbed out of the car and locked it, took another quick look around. Just a couple of old dears holding plastic baskets stuffed full of faded and threadbare clothes on the trail back home from the launderette. He shook his head and glanced up at the front of the building, took in the warped frames and the weeds that poked out of the mortar.

He took the stairs to the second floor and rapped on a scarred blue door at the end of the walkway. He held his face up to the peephole in the door until he heard the shuffle of footsteps on the other side, and then stepped back.

He heard heavy bolts slide back, and then the door opened on a pale kid called Boo dressed in a dark blue top and mismatched tracksuit pants. His feet were bare and blotched red. His face held splashes of acne like some kind of monster make-up and a thin tuft of moustache decorated his upper lip. He took one look at Dillon and then turned and headed back down the hall.

Dillon closed the door behind him, slid home the bolts again and then trailed Boo into the front room.

Boo had taken a seat in a threadbare armchair set up close to a large TV. Some cable music channel had a video of a pair of black girls in minuscule red bikinis up on the screen, and Dillon noticed that Boo had stuffed his hand down inside his tracksuit pants. Dillon had no idea who the girls were, but he had heard the tune once or twice.

On the far side of the room another kid that Dillon knew to be called Squire was sitting at a wooden table in just a pair of white briefs. He had a set of scales and a large pile of white powder laid out on a plastic sheet on the table in front of him. He was filling small plastic wraps with measured amounts of the powder, and then placing them in a carrier bag at his feet. Some of the product stuck to his skin like icing sugar. His biceps popped and stretched as he worked. Dillon nodded to him and Squire nodded back with his chin, carried on with his task.

"How's business?" said Dillon. "You making a roll?"

"Business is business," said Squire, shrugging. "Ain't no how about it, man, business just is. The product and the market, getting it together." He lifted a thin reefer from a plate on the table. He took a hit and held the smoke deep in his chest, put the reefer back on the plate. Yellow burn marks stained the rim of the plate like some narcotic flower pattern, the centre of the plate a pile of crumbled ash, poisoned pollen. The room stank of marijuana but all the windows were shut tight.

"You've got a good point there, Squire," said Dillon. He remained standing in the doorframe, reluctant to step further into the room.

Squire stopped what he was doing for a moment and looked across at the policeman, a trace of contempt in the petrified set of his mouth. He understood the point of having a copper on the crew, but he also knew that it came with unquantifiable risks. And where was all this supposed inside information that Bar Code was filling his pockets for? Far as he knew, the man had been on suspension for the last few months. He pointed to a bulked-out plain white plastic carrier bag on the floor behind the door.

Dillon turned his head and saw the bag. He took a step to the side and stooped to pick it up.

Boo started to make little grunting noises, his hand pumping hard inside his pants.

"For fuck's sake," said Dillon, standing upright and switching the bag in his hands. "Does he have to do that?"

"Yo, Boo," said Squire. "Go in the fucking bathroom or something, put it out of sight."

The kid continued to stare at the screen and pump his hand.

"Yo, Boo," said Squire again, louder this time, and then, getting no response, picked up a lighter and tossed it at the kid's head. The lighter hit him on the side of the face, landed in his lap. His hand snapped out of his pants and his head jerked around as if he had just been woken out of a rollercoaster dream.

Dillon shook his head in disgust and took a step back into the hall. "Later, Squire," he said, and turned and headed back up the hall. He slid back the bolts and let himself out of the flat.

14

Barney and Lincoln were spread-eagled in the grass near the top of Primrose Hill. Pale moonlight lit their faces, revealing the brittle skin of adolescence. In the distance, the roar of the caged animals in Regent's Park Zoo could be heard. Lincoln popped smoke rings in the air from his Kool. Some late-night stroller's Labrador sniffed at their feet and walked on.

"You've still got a stepdad, haven't you?" said Barney.

"Used to have me one until about three months back," said Lincoln. "Mum's working hard on getting me another one right now. Why, your mum looking to get one for you, too?"

"Looks like it," said Barney. "Man named Ralph."

"Ralph, huh? Women that age, seems like they always need to keep a man around the house. How long since the old man split?"

"Over three years now," said Barney.

"Man, you'd've thought that hole down there would've healed up by now," said Lincoln. "Left some kind of hairy scar. Ralph's goin' to have to work hard to get it workin' again, man."

The pair laughed hard at that image, making that freefall leap of the imagination from innocent child to man of the world.

Lincoln took a last pull on his cigarette and tossed it into the grass past his feet.

"Do you get on with him?" said Barney. "Your stepfather."

"Which one?"

Barney shrugged his shoulders in the grass. "Whichever."

"Ain't no difference," said Lincoln. "Both of 'em just wanted me out of the way. First one used to clip me around the ear and send me up to my room, shit like that. This fresh one, he just hands me cash all the time, a fiver here, a tenner there. How about yours, what's he like? Is he a hitter or a cashpoint?"

"He runs this health food store up in town, and brings us all this organic fruit and vegetables all the time. They've got no colour and no taste, and they're always covered in dirt and shit like they've just been pulled straight out of the ground."

"Don't sound like no cashpoint to me," said Lincoln. "Sounds like you got yourself a hitter right there."

Dillon steered the car into the kerb behind a black Cherokee Jeep and cut the engine. He sat for a moment looking across the street at a small Italian restaurant, the Trevi Fountain. Stuck on the end of a short parade of shops, the restaurant was situated beside a video rental store that looked like it had just closed up for the night. A single light burned at the back of the store and Dillon could see someone moving around there. He looked up the street and then checked the mirror, noticing once more that the foot traffic on this stretch of road was slack. He could see the reason Bar Code had chosen this particular place to run his laundering operation: a neighbourhood restaurant that catered to local families on the weekend, the married couples from those same families during the week for quiet romantic meals without the kids, chances were few strangers ever stepped through its doors. It was from this point that funds went out to a number of other cash businesses in the area: a cab firm, other restaurants, a couple of bent solicitors, and a number of clubs around North and West London. He had no idea how much cash came through here each week, each month, but he knew for certain that if someone had plans, if someone had the stones to come at Bar Code, then this was the place to start.

Dillon reached under the seat and pulled out a bottle of scotch. He took a long drink and then stuffed the bottle back under the seat. He felt the scotch burn into the folds of his stomach, and remembered that he had not eaten since lunchtime. He pulled the bottle out from under the seat again and took another hit to blank the pain, and then wiped the perspiration from his face with the flat of his hand.

He thought about all the knowledge he had on Bar Code, and how it meant nothing. How in truth it meant less than nothing. The more he tried to get up close to Bar Code, the more he seemed to back himself into the kind of corner from which there was no escape. Take the Francis shipment, for instance. Dillon had acted on instinct when the chance came up to put that right, but he had fucked up big time and ended up killing that kid instead. A bad mistake he thought he had made up for when one of his snitches had tipped him to Francis's whereabouts two weeks later, but he had still just been able to recover the cash, the product being long gone. Dillon knew he had been close to the flame on that one, both with Bar Code and the top floor brass, but when one of Bar Code's men had been pushed from the roof of a building on the Castle Estate, it had been Dillon who had come up with the idea of putting up a reward and using the locals to spook out the killer for them. He was sure that this was the one to put him back on track.

He watched a man in a baseball cap and denim jacket come out of the video store, pull down and lock up the metal shutters, and then walk off in the direction of Tufnell Park tube station.

Tufnell Park tube station on the corner of Brecknock Road, the road on which Dillon had killed Karl Burns. He blinked and Karl's face appeared in front of him in a blur of blood and metal, and he felt a cold finger touch the base of his spine.

He grimaced and shook the image from his mind, slapping

the side of his fist on the dash to release the tension. He climbed out of the car and walked round to the boot, popped the lock. Leaning in, he lifted out the four carrier bags he had collected on his rounds and put them all into a leather holdall. Taking the holdall from the boot, he locked the car and then crossed the road and entered the restaurant.

15

Near the Finchley Road end of Eton Avenue, Lincoln stopped short in front of a thirties mansion block covered in scaffolding. Barney, his head down in blind and dumb pursuit—they had been walking in silence for about five minutes now, Lincoln having told his friend to be patient and that all would be revealed in good time—bumped into the back of him, stumbling and bouncing back a pace. He lifted his head in surprise and took a quick look around, nailing himself on the map. "Watch your step," said Lincoln, and pushed out at him in jest, then turned and raised his hand in the direction of the mansion block.

Barney grunted and looked at his friend for a moment, noticing the glint in his pupils, and then he turned and looked at the mansion block. He took in the long steel poles, the knotted clamps, the green plastic mesh that masked the faded red brickwork like a bad skin graft. He had no idea what he was supposed to be looking at.

Lincoln continued to point, a loose smile on his lips.

His hands in his pockets, Barney raised his shoulders in question. "What am I supposed to be looking at?"

"I hope you remember how to climb," said Lincoln, and then all of a sudden he took a step forward and jumped over the fence that bordered the garden of the mansion block.

His friend watched him in confused silence.

Lincoln ran across a short lawn, planted his feet in the centre of a dried flower bed, and then took hold of one of the scaffolding poles. He glanced up the length of the pole, slid his hands up as far as he could reach, and then jumped and wrapped his knees around the pole. Scrambling, he pulled himself onwards and upwards, working until he had his arms laid out flat on the first platform. He inched his hands along the platform, searching for secure holds with the tips of his fingers, his legs kicking out behind him, fighting until he was able to swing his legs around and roll across the splintered planks.

Up on the platform he crouched low and gestured for his friend to join him, mouthing words of encouragement.

Barney felt his heart step up a beat, an unfamiliar hot chill at the back of his neck. On instinct he checked both ends of the street, and then put a hand on the fence and jumped over into the garden. He ran across to the same pole that Lincoln had climbed, but he wasn't as athletic and Lincoln had to catch his arm and haul him up the final couple of feet and onto the platform. Secure on base camp, the two friends stood and grinned at each other like a pair of idiots.

"So what do we do now?" whispered Barney, his voice hoarse and high at the same time.

"There's scaffolding all over the place at the moment," said Lincoln, his arm swooping and taking in the full scope of all he could see. "Like the whole fucking street is about to fall down or something. And you can see the signs, it's all supposed to be alarmed, bells and whistles and shit like that, but most of the time it's all just spin, a load of old bollocks. You just need to know what to look out for. This place, I've been here a couple of times before. It's a piece of piss, man."

"You've been here before?"

"You wouldn't believe the stuff people leave out in the open," said Lincoln, turning and stepping along the platform.

From across the street his movements behind the green mesh

curtain must have looked like a grotesque shadow puppet show.

Barney glanced out at the street, caught in the darkness and emptiness of a silent city, he felt safe and tracked Lincoln along the platform. On the far side of the platform, a ladder ascended to another level. The pair climbed the ladder, and then without a word Lincoln dropped to his knees and started to crawl along the second platform. From what Barney could see, this platform was on the same level as the windows of the first floor flats. He decided to wait for Lincoln from where he was at the top of the ladder. The bottom of the windows were about two feet above the platform, and as he passed each window, Lincoln lifted his head to check if there were lights on inside. Rooms with lights on he passed untouched, and rooms in darkness he tried the windows. He reached the far end without luck then turned around, shook his head, and started back for the first ladder.

The second platform was the same, no luck.

On the third platform Lincoln found a window unlocked and started to push it open. He managed to raise the sash about eight inches and then signalled for his friend to join him.

Hot with anticipation, Barney started to shuffle along the platform on his hands and knees. But when he was just a couple of feet short of Lincoln, he heard someone shout out from below.

"Who's that up there? What's going on up there?"

Shocked and surprised, Barney shuddered to a halt in the middle of the platform. His pupils split wide open, he looked towards Lincoln for some guidance, and saw his friend pulling his head out of the open window. Leaving his hands still resting on the sill, Lincoln turned and stared back at him in panic. The voice came back at them again, louder and angrier this time. Barney crawled to the edge of the platform and tried to look down through the scaffolding and the green mesh to see who was there.

"Come down off that scaffolding this minute," he heard.

When he looked up again, he saw that Lincoln had scuttled to the far end of the platform, dropped to his stomach, lowered his feet over the side, and was inching himself down onto the platform below. In seconds his head and then his hands had disappeared, the sounds of his escape nothing but an echo.

Barney felt the panic of abandonment harden his limbs. He stood like a statue for what seemed like hours, then, hearing no further calls from below, started down the ladders with as much stealth as he could muster. On the last platform he stretched out and peered over the side and saw a man with a shock of dark hair in the centre of the lawn, his outline lit up from a bright porch lamp that had just come on. Broad as a tractor, he looked like he had no real need of the golf club he held in his thick hands.

Unsure of what to do, he rolled onto his back and tried to think. Perhaps Tiger Woods had seen and heard just the one person on the scaffolding. Barney decided to sit tight and wait him out. He rested on the platform for a couple more minutes, but soon grew impatient and started to crawl to the far end. Poking his head out through the mesh, he saw no one around on the lawn, and so turned around and eased his legs out into the air. He inched himself backwards, then took a deep breath and rolled his chest off the platform and dropped to the ground. He bounced off his feet and fell onto his side on the lawn. Then, just as he started to pick himself up, Tiger Woods came roaring at him from out of the darkness.

He scrambled to his feet and made a dash for the fence, but just as he put his hand on the top of the fence, he felt the golf club strike him on the shoulder, and he cried out in pain. The club hit him again on the back of the thigh and he cried out once more. Stumbling, he crashed into the fence, but his momentum was such that it carried him forward, and he fell across the top of the fence and landed in a tumble of limbs on the path. He felt skin being torn from his palms, the tips of his fingers.

"Little piece of shit," shouted Tiger Woods. Seconds later he reached the fence, and on seeing his target spread-eagled and bleeding on the path, raised the golf club and swung it hard through the air. But this time Barney managed to roll out of its path and into the gutter before it could make contact.

Picking himself up, Barney started to run as fast as he could, tears breaking in the back of his throat.

16

"Can I give you a lift anywhere?" asked Marnie outside the Magdala. Night had fallen and turned the bottom of the clouds a darker shade of streetlight amber. She glanced across at the chipped holes in the wall, smiling to herself as she remembered the tale Roscoe had told her, waiting for a response.

"That'd be great," said Roscoe. "Which way are you going?"

"Crouch End," said Marnie, looking off in the direction of South End Green where she had parked her car. She held her keys tight in her hand, in no clear rush to head on home but unsure of the motives behind that feeling. She felt a strange kind of attraction to Roscoe, something she couldn't quite put her finger on. The handsome tilt of his mouth and the brittle light that coloured his pupils, sure, but something more, too. The quiet strength he had shown when he had talked about his failure to track down his assailant, perhaps, and his intention to continue until he was successful. There had been no macho heroics to his words, just the quiet show of determination that she found lacking in her colleagues at the station in her regular hours.

"Tufnell Park," said Roscoe. "Is that on your route?"

"No problem," said Marnie, giving him a warm smile.

As the smile hit him full in the face, Roscoe felt a thrill shoot up his spine. It had been some time since he had been attracted to someone like this, and it had come as a complete surprise to him. He tried to figure out what had happened, what had provoked this heat, and came up clean. His heart and loins out there on their own, working to a hidden agenda. He opened his mouth to speak, but Marnie had turned her back to him and started for the opposite kerb. Smiling to himself, he followed her to the car. He waited for her to unlock the doors, then climbed into the passenger seat and felt a shot of lightheadedness as he dropped his foot onto the scrap of carpet and debris in the footwell.

Marnie fired up the engine, glanced over her shoulder and pulled out from the kerb.

She drove in silence for a short time, taking a left into Constantine Road and heading for Dartmouth Park.

Roscoe settled back into his seat and saw more scenes of past violence. The spot outside a pub where a man had been knifed to death for *not* looking at another man's girlfriend, the other man having splashed out a fortune on a black leather minidress in order to show off his girlfriend, far too much for her to be ignored. The scratches of blue paint on the end wall of a brick terrace where a woman had crushed the legs of her unfaithful husband with the front of his new car.

Red and black, blood and leather: the livery of the dead.

Marnie drove in silence, glad that Roscoe didn't feel the need to talk to her all the time. She hated people who loved the sound of their own voices, peacocking their egos.

On the red light at the junction of Highgate Road, she pushed in the CD that rested in the slot, and seconds later the title track of The Kinks' *Village Green Preservation Society* album came on.

Roscoe pursed his lips and nodded his approval, settled back in his seat to listen to the music.

He pointed to the deck as the track faded out. "I bumped into Ray Davies round here once," he said.

"Yeah?"

"One Sunday lunchtime a couple of years ago. It was a hot day, it had been really hot all week, but he still had on these shoes that were all covered in mud, and I remember thinking, how come he's got mud all over his shoes?"

Marnie held out for a couple of beats, and then, grinning, glanced across the seat at him. "And?"

"And what?" replied Roscoe, half laughing.

"What do you mean, and what?" said Marnie, half laughing herself now. "How come he was wearing muddy shoes, that's what."

"Are you like this all the time?" asked Roscoe. "Always looking out for an ending, some kind of closure? You're police, Marnie, you should know that not all stories have an ending."

"You don't know, do you?" said Marnie, glancing across at him again. "You didn't ask him, did you?"

Roscoe kept silent, the grin on his face lit up red from the taillights of the car in front.

Barney dragged himself up Chalk Farm Road, his lungs burning from having run the mile from the flats on Eton Avenue. He was limping a little, and his leg hurt from where Tiger Woods had made contact with the golf club. His head was spinning and his thoughts sparked and missed connections, making little sense. Light rain crackled on his forehead, and he could taste underground air in his mouth, dead and metallic. Blood pounded at his temples and rippled his vision, tinkering with his balance. Neon drips of colour leaked from the lights on the Stables Market entrance arch before him, and the big chair above the pine shop across the street looked as if it were floating in the air.

He had first run to the Primrose Hill Estate, but there had been no sign of Lincoln in the sports cage, and when he had pressed his doorbell, there had been no one at home either.

Emotions stormed through his head, out of control, a white noise hurricane: one minute he wanted to climb to the top of Primrose Hill and rage at the world, and the next he wanted to run on home as fast as he could and hide under the bed.

He crossed the street and walked down Hartland Road, picking up the pace as he approached the railway arch.

"Yo, Barnabus, what's the fuckin' rush?" came at him from out of the darkness to his right.

"You missed your supper or something?" said a second voice.

Glancing into the darkness, Barney could make out the shapes of two people standing under a basketball backboard, the glow of a cigarette or a joint. The hoop had been pulled down from the backboard some time back and never replaced.

"It past your bedtime, Barnabus?"

"Your mama still read you a bedtime story?"

"You heard the one about the big bad drug dealers who came around and gobbled up little Barnabus?"

"You have a drink of milk before bed, Barnabus, or are you still sucking on your mama's titties?"

"Yo, Barnabus, tell your mama to come and suck on this."

"And tell her she better have a big appetite."

Gurgling laughter filled the darkness, echoing from the roof of the arch.

The shapes stepped out of the darkness and took human form, and Barney recognised two of the runners for the drug dealers who operated on the Castle Estate.

He put his head down and started to run as fast as he could, faster than he had run from Tiger Woods, faster than he had ever run before. He ran straight out into the road without a glance at the traffic, hit the kerb and kept on running through the estate without so much as a look back, his limbs on fire.

The sudden rush of blood to his head brought some kind of cohesion to his thoughts:

His brother had died from drugs.

He hated what that had done to his mother.

In turn he hated what his mother had done to him.

He hated his mother.

He hated his dead brother.

"It's Frank."

"Hello, Frank," replied Rhiannon, her voice little more than a whisper.

"How are you doing? You don't sound too good."

"Oh, you know how it is, Frank," said Rhiannon. "Some days are better than others. What's the time, just after eleven? Almost tomorrow. Maybe tomorrow will be better."

"Yeah. Maybe tomorrow."

"So you went to see Cahill, then?"

"Yeah, this afternoon, right after I left the Echo Barn," said Roscoe. "He was at home, the address you gave me."

"And what did he have to say for himself?"

"Well, I think you're right about him being leaned on," said Roscoe. "He's scared of something, that's for sure." He picked up a glass of beer from the coffee table, took a sip, then put the glass back on the table. "He knows something happened that night, but he's not telling us what. I'm not even sure he knows what himself. One thing he did tell me was that Dillon appeared to be looking for someone in the crowd right after the crash." Roscoe decided to leave out the part about him not being interested in the child that he had just run down and killed.

"You think he was trying to run someone down in the crowd?"

"Well, I don't know about that, Rhee," said Roscoe, dampening her hopes. "It's too soon for me to tell, I need to look into it more, talk to some other people. But it looks like you were right about it not being a straightforward accident."

Roscoe heard tears, then a liquid crackle on the line.

"You okay, Rhee? You want me to come over?"

"No, that's all right, I'll be fine in a minute," said Rhiannon, sniffing back the tears.

"You sure?"

"I'll be fine, Frank."

"You need to keep strong," said Roscoe.

"Frank, can I ask you something?"

"Sure," he said, and waited for her to speak.

"I feel terrible about it, but I can't stop feeling that I want another baby," said Rhiannon.

Roscoe felt something lurch inside his chest, as if she had just asked him to father the child.

"I know it'll never happen, but all the same . . ."

There had been a time when the pair of them might have become more than just good friends, close friends, but Rhiannon had already fallen head over heels in love with Charlie by then, so that particular song was destined to remain unheard.

Roscoe bit his tongue and kept silent, feeling the heat rise in his face.

"But then I think that if I have another baby it might diminish what Karl meant to me," continued Rhiannon. "As if I thought that he was replaceable or something."

"I don't think it would mean that," said Roscoe. "You had a lot of love for Karl, a great love, and it will always be there. You'll always love Karl just the same as if he was still with us. Another child . . . I don't know, maybe if you and Charlie can work it out. Where is he, anyway? How come he's not there with you?"

"That's all in the past now," said Rhiannon. "You know that, Frank. We had our time and now it's gone."

Roscoe drank his beer, then held the chill glass against his cheek. "How could he let you go like that?" he said, true sorrow in his words. "How could he let Karl go like that?"

"It's not all his fault," said Rhiannon. "I had a major part in the drama too, remember?"

"Yeah, I remember," said Roscoe, although he had not seen much of them throughout their troubles.

"Anyway, call me tomorrow if you hear any more," said Rhiannon, and then the line went dead.

17

Friday, 22 October

Marnie Stone lived alone in a small studio flat on the top floor of a converted Victorian house just off Stroud Green Road in Crouch End. When she had first moved in she had decorated the place in a Santa Fe colour scheme in an attempt to create the illusion of space, but when she had hauled in all her furniture and her stacks of books, videos, and CDs, most of the desert colours had been obscured and the place had ended up looking just as cluttered as if she had painted it black. The one remaining item of the intended scheme that could still be seen was a framed print of one of Georgia O'Keeffe's skull paintings. A friend had once asked her why she had not chosen one of O'Keeffe's more sensual flower paintings, and Marnie had replied that, on the contrary, she found the skull paintings far more sensual. There was something about the animal being stripped back to the bone and opened up to the elements that had once been its habitat that appealed to her sense of belonging. The print now rested on a pile of faded paperbacks behind the dining table.

Marnie had lived alone all her adult life. The result, she knew, of having to share a bedroom, and even her clothes, sometimes, throughout her childhood with three younger brothers and never having any space, however small, to call her own. Her mother had died from breast cancer when she was fourteen. So, as the only female left in the house, and with her father working nights as a security guard out at Heathrow, she had ceased to be a sister and instead become a surrogate mother to her brothers, particularly the youngest, Ben. He was just eight when his mother had been taken from him, and despite his father's and Marnie's best efforts, the trauma had fired him into one kind of trouble after another. It had been a full-time job looking after him, reassuring teachers and calming irate neighbours, let alone taking care of the other two, running the home, and still finding the time to do her own schoolwork. It had been one of the reasons she had decided to join the police force, after gaining no small measure of insight into how some people could fall through the cracks despite the best intentions of their loved ones. That, and the fact that she felt more comfortable in the presence of men. Despite the PR puff, back in 1988 there was still no institution more male-dominated than the police.

Marnie walked across to the window that faced the street, raised the wooden blind and looked out at the fresh morning. She squinted as a beam of autumn sun cut across the rooftops opposite, and felt the beam warm her face as she glanced up and down the street. It was a few minutes after seven and the place was deserted, just one man heading for the bus stop at the end of the street. She noticed that the trees looked darker than usual, and that the leaves had started to shift colours and break loose from their branches, falling to the earth and drifting into small piles at the side of the road. Autumn heading down the pike, her favourite season. She loved everything about it: the change in the landscape, the light, the smell, and most of all, the melancholic mood it engendered in her. She opened the window a fraction and felt a puff of chill air on the back of her hand.

She remained at the window for a couple of minutes, then took a deep breath and turned back into the room. She grabbed the copy of the *Camden New Journal,* the local free newspaper, she had picked up from outside Tufnell Park tube station the night before after dropping off Frank Roscoe, and dropped herself into the armchair in front of the window. She sipped her coffee and flipped through the paper until she came to the Ballard reward story at the top of page seven:

£10,000 reward offered by family in hunt for youth's killer

Marnie shook her head at the headline, the implied criticism at the lack of progress by the police, and then skimmed the rest of the piece: the usual deadpan stuff about how the parents wanted to find out what had happened to their child, their need for closure, more stuff about what a decent and loving son Ballard had been—it never ceased to baffle Marnie how little parents knew about their offspring—and then her heart sank as she noticed that her name had been offered as the contact point for the public. She cursed Belmont under her breath and decided to keep out of the office for the rest of the morning and let Spencer deal with the inevitable calls.

She opened her wardrobe and stood for a moment looking in at the racks of clothes, deciding what to wear. She noticed that her robe had fallen open, her naked left breast reflected in the mirror, and an image of Frank Roscoe popped into her head. His appearance came as no surprise, because she had felt the burn of attraction the moment she met him, the surprise being that he had not appeared earlier in her dreams. She grinned back at herself in the mirror and hoped that she bumped into him again soon. She slipped the robe from her shoulders and let it fall to the floor. She took a moment to skim her contours, and then selected a black blouse and a pale blue suit, crimson underwear. She dressed, ran her fingers through her hair, and then picked up the phone and called Spencer at the station.

"All right, Spence," she said. "Tell me about all the calls

we've had on Ballard so far."

"There's just been a couple so far," he replied, flicking through his notebook. "The first one: this kid claims to have been on Castle Road at the same time that Ballard hit the ground. He said he heard a scream and when he looked over he saw someone land on the path in front of the building. Then a minute or so later a man who he's seen around the estate before coming out of the building and running off towards Kentish Town Road."

"Did he tell you why he happened to be near the estate at that particular time?" asked Marnie.

"He said he'd just been for a drink with some friends at the Man in the Moon up on Chalk Farm Road, and he was on his way home. He lives on Hammond Street with his parents. Neil Ford, nineteen. I think he said he was a student. And as far as we can tell, he's clean. There's nothing on him in the computer."

"That's it, that's all?"

Marnie heard a page being turned, then Spencer sighing.

"No, that's not all," he said. "He also said that the day before yesterday, he saw the man who he claims ran away from the scene out near the phone booths on Kentish Town Road. It's the first time that he's seen him since the night Ballard died."

Marnie pushed a loose strand of hair back behind her ear. "So it was a drug squabble."

"Lifted straight from the template," said Spencer. "Someone ripped him off and now he wants to get his own back. He was very keen to come in and pick someone out of a line-up for us."

"Jesus," said Marnie, smiling a humourless smile. "Is this the only time we can get people to talk to us, when they want us to do their dirty work for them? Okay, I'll go and talk to him."

"Okay," replied Spencer, ruffling through his notebook once more. "The second call just came in from a couple of pensioners who live on the estate. Sisters, I think. Anyway, they share a flat in the building that overlooks the spot where Ballard fell."

"Sounds good so far," said Marnie.

"One of them, Connie Parker—that's the pair's mouthpiece, Connie Parker—she told me that earlier that same afternoon a group of lads started to push them around outside the community centre when they were on their way home from Safeway's. One of them tried to distract her while another one tried to snatch her purse, stuff like that. She managed to hold on to it, but she said that it shook them both up a little. She didn't report it because it's not the first time that it's happened, and as no one had been able to help them the first time around, she didn't see the point in reporting it this time."

"So why is she telling us now?" asked Marnie.

"Well, she saw the piece in the *Journal* yesterday and thought that we might need her help."

"I don't understand," said Marnie, frowning. "What's all this got to do with Paul Ballard?"

"Well, from what she could remember, it was Paul Ballard who tried to steal her purse."

"Ballard tried to steal her purse?" repeated Marnie, surprised. "Is she sure about that?"

"At nine fifteen on the night Paul Ballard died, she said that she went into the kitchen to make a cup of tea, and when she looked out of the window she saw a man spread out on the ground right in front of the building opposite. He had on the same clothes as the man who tried to steal her purse, and from that distance and in that light she thinks that it was the same man."

"Does her description match the one we have on file for Ballard when he was found?"

"Right down to the trainers," said Spencer.

"Sounds promising," agreed Marnie. "Maybe we should take

a closer look at the kids who flop around the community centre."

"And that's not all," said Spencer. "She also told me that right after she saw the man on the ground, someone else came out of the building and ran over to him. They were only there a couple of seconds, though, because as soon as a third person turned up, that sounds like it was Henderson, the man who called 999, they ran straight back inside again. She didn't recognise them, but she said that there was something about them that looked familiar. She said they were wearing a dark hooded top and tracksuit bottoms with stripes down the sides."

"A man or a woman?"

"She couldn't tell," said Spencer.

"So what do you think? A drug deal gone bad?"

"Could be," said Spencer. "But then why run back into the building, why not just get the fuck out of there?"

"Maybe they left something up on the roof," said Marnie, thoughtfully. "Something personal." And then another thought struck her. "Or maybe because they live in the building."

"Do you think we should canvas the place again?"

"Let me talk to this Connie Parker first," said Marnie. "See if I can get a clearer picture of what she saw. She couldn't offer us any more than the hooded top and tracksuit?"

"No, that's the lot," said Spencer.

"Okay, give me the address. I'll call round on my way in."

18

Roscoe woke tired and disoriented. Once again he had not slept well; a thick, persistent pain in his foot, as if a nail was jammed down in beside his Achilles tendon, had kept him awake most of the night. He had taken a handful of paracetamol before he retired, and then another handful some time before dawn, but his foot still hammered in tune with the disturbed pulse of his heart. In the few minutes of fitful sleep that he had managed to accumulate, his dream theatre had screened the film of the moment when he had been shot, over and over again. The face of the shooter morphing from one person to another, people he had arrested, people he had worked with, even his own father and brother appearing at one point, never settling on one face for more than a split second at a time. The dream had not disturbed him because it had been the same dream he had been having ever since the shooting, but his frustration at its regular screening had started to bleed into his waking hours.

The image of his father appeared in his head once more, and his thoughts turned to the old man.

Jack Roscoe had never been a man to let his emotions show. He used nicknames not as terms of affection, but as a means of keeping people at arm's length, as if by admitting that he knew someone's given name he would also be admitting to a dependence on them. Roscoe did not think that he had ever heard his father call either him or his brother by their real names. Or his mother, come to that. Like most of his generation, born and steeled under the hammer of the Luftwaffe, Jack Roscoe had been a closed man, prone to letting off steam in bouts of pugnacious temper. And he was not prejudiced about who he chose to fight: his wife, sons, neighbours, colleagues, and even his bosses at the bus depot where he worked as a mechanic for over four decades had all been subject to his anger. Now that he had retired, he was as lonely as only someone whose enemies have all died could be. Most afternoons he would sit alone, in his kitchen or in the local pub, and run old arguments through his mind, reframing ideas, choosing the right words, getting it right this time. Getting angrier and angrier because there was no one left to listen to him. Roscoe knew this and felt no sorrow, because his father had worked all his life to come to this point and it was a torment he deserved. But Roscoe also knew that he himself was suffering from a different strain of the same condition. It was as if something had been handed down in the blood. Since the shooting he had found himself running the incident through his mind again and again, dreams bleeding into waking thoughts, attempting to figure out who had shot him and the reasons behind it. Spending too much time at the Echo Barn hoping to spark some kind of memories among the other regular customers. The fact that he appeared to be turning into his father bothered him almost as much as the fact that he did not know who had shot him. He did not want to end up like his father, bitter and resentful towards an unseen hand, but he was afraid that he lacked the skills to change. So despite his own great personal sadness, he was filled with bittersweet relief when Rhiannon came along and handed him something to help take his mind off it.

He climbed out of bed, headed into the bathroom, and stepped straight into the shower.

He lathered himself with soap, and as he ran his hands over his torso, he felt the ripples of fat around his midriff. Since the shooting he had put on almost a stone in weight. Dr. Jenkins had advised him to look after his diet while he was laid up, and Roscoe had tried his best to cut out starch and eat as many fresh fruit and vegetables as possible, but it had been far easier for him just to order in takeaway most of the time. But now that he was back on both feet, Roscoe had no doubt that the shape of his body would soon return to normal.

He stepped out of the shower and, grabbing a towel, walked through into the bedroom. He clicked on the stereo and the opening track of Richard Hawley's *Lowedges* came forth. He found the albums of the Yorkshire Roy Orbison perfect for either starting the morning or ending the evening, and one of them had been on the stack beside the stereo in his bedroom since he had first discovered them.

He towelled himself off and then dressed in a faded black sweatshirt and tan chinos, pulled out a pair of old black suede Campers from the back of the wardrobe and slipped them on. The left shoe felt good, fitting loose around his injured foot. The sole had split on both shoes, but Roscoe still found them to be the most comfortable of all his footwear, and that was just what he needed if he planned to walk off those loose folds of flesh around his stomach. He slipped on a blue Harrington jacket and checked his pockets, then went into the bathroom and took another couple of painkillers. He let himself out of the flat, walked down the stairs to the front entrance and stepped out into the street. He glanced up at the dark clouds bunched over Kentish Town, and then set off in the direction of the rain.

As he reached Kentish Town Road, he was reminded once more that it was one of the seediest and best high streets in London. He walked past a curious combination of people: schoolchildren with greased-down Caesar haircuts, teen mothers in nicotine-taut masks, people in their twenties and thirties in high street reproductions of celeb splendour, and a number of crumpled elders who had used the sixties revolution to back up their fall into a dissolute routine of pubs and bookies and afternoon naps that stretched into darkness. The street itself was one of the few high streets in London which had not been homogenised and still retained some kind of local character, despite the fact that its character was like something out of the 1950s. For the most part, the shops on Kentish Town Road had not changed since the war, and the few chain stores represented were small branches of Boots, Woolies, Betterspecs, and a couple of the smaller bookies. Regeneration in the borough had been targeted at the tourist hot spots of Camden Town and Hampstead, and because of this the people of Kentish Town had a stubborn pride and sense of self that residents in the other places lacked.

Roscoe strolled on past an Indian restaurant, a store that sold international phone cards, a carpet store, a kebab shop, and the DIY store which had been a record store for as long as he could remember until a branch of Virgin Records had opened down in Camden Town and pulled all of its trade. Passing a pawnbroker, he glanced inside and saw a woman holding up her wedding band to an indifferent man in spectacles behind the counter: love for sale.

Just before he reached the corner of Holmes Road, the location of the police station, he stopped and pushed open the door of the Mediterranean, a small restaurant he often used when he was working, and stepped inside. Over time he had come to think of Jim Larrieu, the owner, as a good and trusted friend, but he had not been in the restaurant since he had been shot. He had not wanted to put his friend in the uncomfortable position of having to offer tender mercies. Their friendship had been built on gruff companionship, the kind of friendship that could span months of silence, not on open shows of affection, and he knew that he could not have put his friend through it.

He was sure that Jim would have understood.

When the noise of the street followed him in through the door, the man behind the counter looked up to see who had entered and a warm and crinkled smile spread across his face.

Roscoe felt the smile pull at the corners of his own mouth.

"Hello, Frank," said Jim Larrieu.

Like he had never been gone . . .

Roscoe opened his mouth to speak, but as he did so Jim turned on his heel and disappeared into the kitchen. Roscoe shook his head, his smile intact, and looked around for a table. He saw a clear one near the back of the restaurant and headed for that. "Nice to see you too," he said to no one in particular.

He took a seat facing the front and glanced around. Steam coloured the windows and the smells that drifted in from the kitchen were as promising as he remembered. He picked up the menu but he knew that he would order what he always ordered at this time of the morning: poached eggs on toast and coffee.

Just then Sophie, Jim's daughter, came out of the back room. She was seventeen, no, eighteen now, and often tried to hide her smile, but there was no mistaking the beautiful dark looks that she had inherited from her mother, a gift made all the more attractive under her seeming indifference. The curls of her thick black hair rested on her bare shoulders, and her green irises darkened to a rich brown as the dark of night approached. She had a talkback mouth that cracked into a bright smile as she approached the table, and Roscoe suspected that she had broken more than a few hearts in her time without even realising it.

"Have you only just got out of hospital?"

"No, I've been out a few months now," replied Roscoe. "But the foot's still on the mend and so I can't walk too far."

"And what, you're too cheap to get a cab?"

"I know, I know," said Roscoe, a little ashamed. He knew

that she was only teasing him, but he felt about two inches tall.

"Leave him alone, Sophie," called Jim from across the restaurant. "Just take his order and leave him alone."

Roscoe offered her a sheepish smile, and then looked out into the street for a moment and then back at Sophie.

"Some kind of hero you turned out to be," said Sophie, and the heartbreaker smile coloured her face once more. "The battle-scarred cop who needs a fat chef to fight his battles for him." She pointed the sharp end of her pencil at his face. "The usual?"

"Thanks," said Roscoe, breathing a sigh of relief.

He watched her cross the room, her hips ducking around the tables as if she were practising a dance routine, stopping to pick up used plates, and then pulled his mobile out of his pocket. He punched in the number for the station around the corner and asked for DI Brian Dineen. There were a couple of clicks and rings and then a harassed voice said, "Dineen, CID."

"Brian, it's Frank."

"Jesus, Frank, I'd almost forgotten about you," said Dineen, surprised. "You're not due back at work yet, are you?"

"No, not yet," said Roscoe. "I need to learn how to walk again first, and then how to walk and talk at the same time, and then all I have to do is convince the shrink that I'm not still too traumatised from the shooting to make a comeback."

Roscoe heard a deep breath on the other end of the line.

"No, the reason I called is because—"

"You need help looking for the shooter," interjected Dineen.

"No, it's not that. Look, Brian, I don't suppose you could nip around to the Med for ten minutes, could you?"

"What, right now?"

"Yeah, I'm in there now. That's where I'm calling from."

"Frank, I'm up to my balls in paperwork at the moment. I can even feel paper cuts trimming my short and curlies. I'm in court this afternoon, and there's a big pile of other stuff I need to take care of before I can leave tonight. How about I meet you in the Pineapple later? What's it all about, anyway?"

Roscoe took a deep breath. He had known Brian Dineen for almost two decades, trusted him in full. Yet he had no idea how he would react if he told him what he was up to. But if he wanted to help Rhiannon then he needed the information. He had no choice. "It's about the kid who was killed on Brecknock Road in May," he said. "The mother is an old friend of mine."

There was a pause, nothing but the background noise of the CID room on the line. Roscoe thought he recognised a voice, a stray inflection, but he couldn't put a name to it. "Sure," said Dineen at last, hesitant. "About seven all right for you?"

"Thanks," said Roscoe, and shut off his mobile.

Jim approached with two cups of coffee. He set them down on the table and sat himself down opposite Roscoe. "You're still not back at work, then, Frank?"

"No, the foot's still on the mend," replied Roscoe. "Should be about another month or so, something like that."

Jim nodded, said nothing. He knew that if Roscoe wanted to talk to him about what had happened he would do so.

"And I've still got no idea who shot me," said Roscoe.

Jim nodded again, hunched over the table.

Roscoe took a sip of coffee, and then held the cup in his hands before his mouth. "I keep having this dream where the shooter's face never quite comes into focus," he said. "Like when there's a face in the flames of a fire or something . . . We picked up some CCTV footage of his car from about ten minutes before the shooting happened, but it's impossible to make out a face. That's what it's like in the dream. It's so frustrating."

"You think whoever it was might try again?"

Roscoe looked off out of the window and saw a man with a

can of beer in one hand peering in at the counter, his other hand rubbing at his crotch. Sophie came out from behind the counter, a knife in her hand, and the man turned and ran out into traffic.

"I try not to think about that," replied Roscoe.

Sophie came over and put Roscoe's plate in front of him, clattering the knife and fork down beside it, and then turned and headed back without a word. Roscoe pointed after her. "Is she like that with all her customers, or just the ones she likes?"

Jim lifted his shoulders and let out a deep breath, raised his palms in defeat. "Her mother was like that when I first met her and she turned out fine."

"She's a good kid," said Roscoe. "She'll be fine once she comes out from behind that black cloud she likes to hide behind."

Jim nodded his head in silence, then looked at Sophie in the kitchen as she talked to the chef, an older man with dark hair. He wore a black vest and had a snake tattoo on his left shoulder, curled around into his bicep. He spoke to Sophie with a tenderness that her father could see from a distance, a tenderness that appreciated her potential rather than her age.

"You're right," said Jim. "But I can't help but worry about her. Out there in this world that we've made for her."

Roscoe cut into his eggs and toast and forked some into his mouth. "She's a strong person," he said. "She'll survive."

"You remember that protest walk that some of the mothers from around here made about eighteen months ago?" said Jim.

Roscoe nodded. After a nine-month period in which seven local teenagers and men in their early twenties had been murdered on the streets of Kentish Town and Camden Town, a couple of the bereaved mothers, together with the local pressure group MAD, had organised a walk from the Forum club in the north part of Kentish Town down to the Castle Estate in Camden Town. The route had taken in the sites of all the seven murders and, despite an initial forecast of around a hundred, more than a thousand people had trekked the mile-long trail of blood. For a short time it had made a difference, but of late the statistics had started to climb once more.

"I think it must be time for another march," said Jim.

"Are you sure it's got that bad again?" said Roscoe, unsure himself now that he came to think about it. He had not been keeping track of things while he had been laid up.

"Since Christmas there must have been at least another five murders. There was that French tourist on the canal down near the Lock, and that girl who was found dumped in the skip over on Leverton Street. And just this morning I read in the paper about a man who's put up a reward to help find out who murdered his son. You remember, the one who was pushed from a roof down on the Castle Estate? How terrible is that, having to pay someone to admit that they witnessed the murder of your child?"

"I don't think it's as simple as that," said Roscoe. "It's more about the fear of reprisals. I don't think it's because no one's interested or that no one cares. Most trial cases fall down because of witnesses not turning up due to intimidation and threats. And even if the accused is convicted, there's still the family and friends to contend with. Trying to get people to testify is like trying to get blood out of a stone."

"So ten thousand pounds, not much to risk your life."

"Not much at all," said Roscoe, and forked some more eggs into his mouth. "But lives have been snuffed out for far less."

"That's true," said Jim.

"But putting up a reward. . . . I don't know, some parents are so blind to the truth about their children that you have to wonder sometimes if they even know them at all. One of the kids who was a subject of the last march, Jake Robinson, I don't think even his mother would have marched on his behalf if she had known the truth about all the stuff that he had got up to."

"I don't remember reading anything about that," said Jim, squinting across the table.

"We tend to keep that kind of stuff out of the papers," said Roscoe, picking up his coffee and taking a mouthful. He had finished his food and pushed his plate to one side of the table. He pulled a pack of Marlboro Lights out of his pocket and fired one up, dropping the match on to the plate. "There's no point in dragging up all that stuff afterward when it's too late to do much about it. But this kid. . . . We couldn't find one person to make a statement against him, but we knew for a fact that—"

"What did he do, Frank?"

"What didn't he do more like," said Roscoe, and took a pull on the cigarette. "One thing he did do—pack a lot of life and death into his short time on the planet. For a start we had him pegged for over three hundred burglaries, most of them on the same estate where he lived all his life. His friends and neighbours, some of them three or four times in a month. One time he and his friend ran into two Danish students up on the heath, offered to show them around. A couple of hours later, one of them went into the bushes for a pee and Robinson followed her in and raped her. She told the police, but when Robinson denied it and said it was consensual, she withdrew her complaint and flew home to Copenhagen the same night. Another time he beat up an old man in his own home so bad that he made him deaf and blind on his left side. He died three weeks later from a heart attack. We knew that Robinson had killed him but we just couldn't prove it."

"That's terrible," said Jim.

"That's the justice game," replied Roscoe, and pushed back his chair and stood up.

Roscoe pulled out his wallet and left a ten on the table,

promising Jim that he would call in more often now that he was back on his feet. Calling out his farewell to Sophie back in the kitchen, he stepped out into the autumn sun. Pushing his hands into the pockets of his coat, he turned and headed north.

He walked up Kentish Town Road and crossed at the junction with Fortess Road. Stopping outside the North Star pub for a moment, he looked in at the barman lifting down chairs from the tables, and then walked around to the side of the building. Stacked against the wall were about fifteen cellophane-wrapped bunches of flowers and a couple of bunches hand-pulled from nearby gardens. Poked into the top of most of the bunches were small handwritten cards. All the cards and flowers were faded now, some of them crumbled into dust. Two weeks earlier a drug deal in the pub had turned sour and the teenage dealer had been dragged out of the pub, beaten about the head and then stabbed in the heart. He had died before an ambulance could be called. The pub had been packed at the time, but no one would admit to having seen what had happened. Roscoe could not know for sure, but he suspected that the reason no one had come forward was not because of the fear of reprisals, but more because people were glad to see the death of a member of a gang that had terrorised the area for months. Above the flowers someone had stuck a photo of the dealer, Robbie Laverick, his grinning face beaming out from a greenhouse of marijuana plants.

Roscoe had no doubt that if asked, Laverick's mother would not hesitate to take part in a march to help make the streets of Kentish Town safe from the kind of people who had killed her son.

19

O'Brien had been a PC since forever. On the force for almost two decades, the idea of promotion had not crossed his mind for almost eighteen of those years. Sure, there had been a time when his enthusiasm and ambition had been high, but it had not been long before the truth of his abilities had surfaced and he had been forever nailed to the bottom rung. And just as he had accepted his own stagnation, he bore no resentment to other fresher faces on the force that clambered over him. He had less than fourteen months until his pension, and just as he had blinkered himself to the furious ambitions of his colleagues, he also had no interest in the dirt on their hands. And he suspected that Sean Dillon had the dirtiest hands he had ever seen.

Dillon and O'Brien were on their way to the Denton Estate to pick up a man called Stuart Pember, a suspect in the burglary of an optician on Kentish Town Road two weeks earlier. The previous day, Pember had been seen attempting to unload a case full of Armani frames to a stallholder at the indoor market in the old Electric Ballroom in Camden Town. Witnesses reported an argument over the price of the frames, and there was some hint that the frames had been stolen to order. But when a couple of adjacent stallholders tried to intervene, Pember kicked the stallholder in the shins and then slammed him across the face with the case and stormed out of the building. The stallholder had suffered some bruising and had needed four stitches in a cut to his temple. Pember had done time for a number of offences ranging from possession of cocaine to GBH.

O'Brien steered the patrol car up to a short brick terrace on the edge of the Rochester Estate, just off Camden Road. Behind the east side of the terrace, a chain link fence bordered the car park of a small electrical goods warehouse. At the far end of the street, the solid concrete end of a brace of Victorian houses blocked the traffic and the sun. Graffiti littered the concrete in black and red letters, a cartoon street scene depicting a game of basketball and a number of names that O'Brien could not make out. He pulled the car to the kerb and killed the engine. He looked out of the window at the line of houses on the near side and squinted at the numbers on the peeled-paint doors.

"Over there," said Dillon, pointing out the other side. "The one with the brown door." He looked over his shoulder at the end of the terrace and noticed the entrance to an alley which led around to the back of the houses on that side. "How d'you want to play this?" he asked. "Do you want to take the back?"

O'Brien looked over at the entrance to the alley, then turned back to Dillon. He took hold of the door handle. "Give me two minutes," he said, and pressed down on the handle.

"Take your time," said Dillon, nonchalantly. "Pember's in a dead end out here, there's no escape for him."

O'Brien raised his chin in response, then slipped out of the car and crossed the street. Dillon watched him disappear behind the side of the terrace, and then took another look at the house. Similar in appearance to the other houses on the estate, its sole unique feature was a polished brass knocker on the faded door, like a fresh autumn raindrop fallen to the hardened earth.

Checking his watch, Dillon looked up and down the street as he waited. Then as he reached for the handle, he noticed someone in the room above the front door, a flash of pale flesh.

In the upstairs room, a woman in her late twenties stood and admired herself in a mirror hidden from his view. She had a blue towel wrapped around her head, and her hands rested on her hips as she turned from side to side. She had medium breasts that looked quite firm, and he could see a small black tattoo, or a birthmark or a scar, high on her upper arm. Beads of water shone like diamonds on her skin. Dillon watched as she raised her hands and cupped her breasts one at a time, probing the flesh for alien lumps, and felt blood pool in his loins. He shook his head and then opened the door and shuffled out of the car. He crossed the street pressing at his crotch, making himself comfortable before he rapped on the door with the back of his hand.

Moments later the door opened and he came face to face with an old man dressed in a pair of crumpled trousers and a pale green T-shirt. He had a roll-up in his mouth and some ash had broken loose and crashed onto the front of his trousers. He blinked at Dillon and held onto the door frame for support.

Dillon looked past him into the house. "I'm looking for Stuart Pember," he said. "You must be his father?"

The man hesitated but then nodded in response, unsure. He risked a quick look back into the house, but as the man turned back to face him, Dillon noticed that something had sparked fear in his pupils. The man picked up on this and took a step back and tightened his grip on the door. "He's not home right now . . ."

Dillon reached out and pushed the door back into the wall. "Then you won't mind if I come in and take a look," he said, and lifted the old man's hand from the edge of the door and let it fall. He stepped up and slid past the old man into the house.

"Who's that at the door?" came a female voice from upstairs, querulous and pinched.

"You can't just come in here . . ." started the old man.

Dillon pinned him to the wall with a hard stare, and then

turned his full attention to the woman at the top of the stairs. She still had the towel wrapped around her head, but she had now put on a pale blue cotton dress that stuck to her damp frame like a second skin. He could see her raised dark nipples and the silhouetted outline of the inside of her thighs through the thin material. She looked scared, and he sensed an appetite for defeat in the stance she had adopted, loose and low and curled in upon itself.

"Where's Stuart?" said Dillon.

"He's not here at the moment," said the woman. "I don't know where he is. He stops at his friend's place sometimes."

"You're sure he's not upstairs?" said Dillon, taking a step closer to the stairs.

"No," said the woman, and her body twisted and turned under the burn of his stare.

"Don't piss me about," said Dillon, and put his foot on the bottom step, his hand on the rail.

Just then he heard the clatter of feet on the kitchen roof at the back of the house. His head jerked in the direction of the noise for a second, and then jerked back again. He saw a flash of blind panic pass across the woman's face, and so he ran through into the kitchen. There was a key in the lock, but by the time he had unlocked and torn open the door, Pember had run across the garden and started to scramble up the wooden back fence.

Dillon shook his head and smiled to himself. He leaned into the doorframe and folded his arms across his chest, watching Pember and waiting for him to fall into the arms of O'Brien.

Seconds later, Pember disappeared over the top of the fence, and then Dillon heard the scuffle of limbs and voices.

"Whoa, what the fuck's going on back there?" Dillon said after a moment, grinning, and took a step out into the garden.

He heard more scuffles, the sound of flesh on flesh, flesh on tarmac, and flesh on timber, and then O'Brien calling out. More scuffles, harder this time, and then the sound of rapid footsteps that faded into the other sounds of the morning. Dillon took another step out into the garden but then pulled up. He turned and stepped back into the house, a chill smile on his face. "Stupid old fucker," he muttered under his breath.

Back in the hall the woman had come down the stairs and now stood beside the old man in front of the door. She had pulled on an old cardigan and the rise and fall of her breasts had been buried in its folds. She had also removed the towel from her head and her damp auburn hair tumbled onto her shoulders.

Dillon tossed them a contemptuous glance, and then headed up the stairs. He pushed open each door until he came to the main bedroom and stepped inside. The curtains had been pulled back and a keen autumn sun laid a sepia sheen across the furniture. Bundles of clothes were spread across the floor, and on the far side of the room, beneath the window, a sports hold-all rested on its side. It looked like Pember had tried and failed to grab it in his rush to leave the house. Dillon stepped around the clothes and picked up the holdall, tipping out its contents onto the bed: spectacle frames, a hammer, some electrical tape, more tools, and a couple of small sachets of what looked like cocaine. Dillon opened one of the sachets, licked the tip of his finger and dipped it into the powder, lifted it to his lips and took another lick.

"Mmmm, not bad," he muttered, and dropped one of the sachets into his pocket.

He poked his head into each of the other rooms again, taking a couple of minutes to check out the bathroom to see if Pember had tried to hide more stuff in the cistern or flush it down the toilet. One of the bedrooms had been painted in blue and white, and newspaper pictures of Chelsea footballers formed a mosaic on all four walls.

Back downstairs, he found the old man and the woman seated on the sofa in the front room. "Are you going to tell me now that you didn't know that Stuart was up there?"

The old man started to speak, but Dillon help up a hand to silence him.

"You think this'll make it easier for Stuart? You think that we'll get tired of chasing him around and leave him alone?"

The woman pressed her hands together between her knees, kept her eyes away from him. The old man reached out and put his hand on top of her wrists.

"Is this your father?" said Dillon.

"I'm Stuart's father," he said. "David Pember."

"You live here as well, Mr. Pember?"

"No, I—"

"Well, in that case," said Dillon, cutting him off. "You won't mind if I talk to Miss . . ."

"Corcoran," said the woman, prompted. "Marie Corcoran."

"Miss Corcoran," said Dillon, then turned to the old man. "You mind if I talk to Miss Corcoran alone for a moment?"

The old man looked at Marie with tearful concern in his eyes, and she repaid him with a small squeeze of his hand.

Dillon waited until the old man had left the room, then he closed the door and took a seat beside Marie on the sofa. He looked at the freckles on her knees, and ideas ran back and forth across his mind. He raised his head and looked around the room, took in its atmosphere of hostile shabbiness.

"What do you do, Marie?" said Dillon. "Do you have a job?"

Marie kept her eyes on the carpet. "I have to look after George," she said. "My son. He's with my mother right now."

Dillon nodded as if processing this new information.

Marie started to bite at her nails, then reached out and took the pack of Silk Cut from the coffee table in front of her. Her hands shook and Dillon had to strike a match for her.

Dillon took out the sachet of cocaine from his pocket. "Do you know what this is, Marie? I found it upstairs."

Marie continued to stare at the carpet, smoke drifting through her fingers.

"Marie?"

She jumped a little in her seat, as if she had forgotten that he was still there, and then turned to look at the plastic wrapper in his hand. She nodded once, and Dillon made sure that she saw him looking at her breasts, the heat in his eyes.

"Then it looks like Stuart's in deep shit," he said. "I don't know . . . three, four years. . . . Think you can handle another jolt like that? How about George, is he going to miss his dad?"

Marie shook her head and smoke spilled out of her mouth.

Dillon fell silent for a moment, then turned to face her. He let his knees brush against her leg, push her dress up her thigh a little. He held his legs there, felt no resistance.

"Marie, I'm going to ask you something now, something that could affect your whole future. Not just yours, but Stuart's and George's as well. Do you understand what I'm saying?"

She turned to look at him, life draining from her eyes, and nodded.

"You do want to keep Stuart out of jail, don't you?" he said, making sure that she saw him put the cocaine in his pocket.

She nodded again, rubbing at the tears on her cheeks.

"If we don't manage to pick up Stuart today, then I'm going to have to come back here again tonight," said Dillon, and then took a deep breath. "And if he's not here, then maybe you could help me . . . help me find a way to make sure that he stays on the outside, where you need him." He paused for a second, hesitant, and then said: "Do we understand each other here, Marie?"

Dillon felt the idea shake her to the frame, and hold her still for a moment, but then she closed her eyes and nodded.

The front door rattled and moments later O'Brien stepped into the room, holding a handkerchief to his bloodied nose.

20

Neil Ford lived with his mother in a basement flat on Hammond Road, a short hop from the north end of Kentish Town Road. Marnie left her car on a meter outside the house and strolled up the cracked path, pressed the bottom bell.

"Who's there?" came the slow response, female.

"It's DS Marnie Stone from Kentish Town CID. I'm looking for Neil Ford."

"What's it about? Is he in some kind of trouble?"

"You need to ask him about that," replied Marnie. "Is he there? I need to speak to him."

"No, he's not here at the moment."

"This is where he lives, though?" said Marnie. "This is the address he gave to one of my colleagues."

"Yeah, he does live here," said the disembodied voice. "It's just that he's at work at the moment. He got himself a job at that electrical store on Camden Road, near the station."

"Thanks," said Marnie, then turned and walked back to her car.

Ten minutes later Marnie pushed another bunch of coins into another meter at the bottom of Camden Road, under the bridge, and then headed into the electronics store. She spotted Ford at once—he was the one who looked out of place. The other two salesmen looked as if they needed the job to eat and make the rent, but from his appearance it was clear that Ford was just here to take the cash and feed it into his thin frame in whatever form he could find. His thick black hair was plastered to his scalp like boiled spinach, and broken spots of acne were clustered near his mouth.

He stood in front of a rack of DVD players, looking at the buttons as if they contained the deepest secrets of life. There were no customers in the place and the other two salesmen chatted behind the counter. Marnie walked across the sales floor and stopped beside Ford. He took a moment to realise she was there, but when he did a blankness remained in his face, and Marnie understood at once that this had been a wasted trip.

"You must be Neil Ford," said Marnie, and flashed her badge in front of his face. "Detective Sergeant Stone, Kentish Town CID. You wanted to talk to me about Paul Ballard."

Ford looked across at the counter, waited for one of the others to notice him, and then said, "I'm just going out back for a smoke. Five minutes, all right?"

The other salesman, a tall black kid with features like a duck, lifted his chin in response, and then Ford headed for a door marked Private at the back of the store. Marnie trailed him into the storeroom, then through another door out to the narrow street at the rear of the building. On one side of the entrance timber pallets were stacked in various piles, and on the other side cellophane angels burst out of a rusted skip. Ford sat on one of the pallets, took out a pack of Old Holborn from his pocket, and started to roll a cigarette.

Marnie waited for him to light the cigarette and then said, "Okay, Neil. You want to tell me what you saw?"

Ford took a couple of puffs on the cigarette. "I don't know," he said. "It was around half past nine, I suppose. I was on my way home from the Man in the Moon. You know, on Chalk Farm Road?"

"I know the place," said Marnie.

"I'd been in there with a mate of mine who lives up on the Gilbey Estate."

Marnie nodded.

"When I left I cut around the back, past the community centre, and then up onto Castle Road. When I passed the estate I remember thinking that it was too quiet, like there was no one around, nothing. But then I heard this horrible scream . . ."

He took a deep pull on his cigarette, his cheeks hollowing as he did so, and then continued, a catch in his throat as he spoke. "And when I looked across I saw . . . I don't know, it looked like there was someone laid out on the ground or something. All messed up, like. And then someone else came out of the flats and ran off towards the other side of the estate."

Marnie pursed her lips. "Where was this man on the ground, which side of the front door was he on?"

"I don't know," said Ford, squinting at Marnie for a fraction of a second.

"Did you manage to get a look at them?"

"He was tall, skinny, and he had one of those soul patches," he said, rubbing at the skin just below his lower lip.

"That's a good description," said Marnie.

"Yeah, well, I got a good look after I heard the scream," said Ford.

Marnie looked across the street for a moment. She watched a magpie pick a piece of silver foil out of a crack in a brick wall, then turned back to Ford. "You ever been to church, Neil?"

The kid shot her another quick glance, confusion creasing his forehead.

"You ever read the Bible?"

Ford ignored her, blew across the top of his cigarette to keep the coal burning.

"You ever read the Bible, Neil?"

"I don't know," he muttered, blue smoke curling out of his

mouth, wrapping around his throat. "At school."

"You remember the Ten Commandments?"

Rocks of ash fell from his cigarette, and Ford rubbed it into the ground under the toe of his trainer.

"Thou shalt not commit murder, all that," said Marnie.

"I suppose so," said Ford, and nodded his head. "Yeah."

"How many of them can you remember? Three, four?"

"I don't know. . . ."

"Come on," said Marnie, her voice hard and low. "How many of the Ten Commandments can you remember?"

"What's this all about?" Ford looked up at Marnie, the side of his face all marked and twisted. "I thought I was supposed to be helping you find a murderer or something."

"Thou shalt not bear false witness," said Marnie, ignoring him. "What do you think that one means, Neil?"

The kid looked at the ground, took a deep pull on his cigarette. He poked his toe further into the gravel.

"You were nowhere near the Castle Estate that night, were you, Neil? Did you get burned on a drug deal, is that what happened, Neil? And now you're looking to use me to get back at the piece of shit that ripped you off?"

"No, it's not like that," Ford protested, but his heart wasn't in it.

All of a sudden Marnie snapped out her hand and slapped the cigarette out of his mouth, scratching his cheek with her nails.

Ford jerked back on his seat, and stared up at her with a combination of fear and surprise on his face.

"Don't make it any worse than it already is," said Marnie, taking a step closer. She folded her hands into hard fists and rested them on her hips, leaned in close to him. "Or do you want me to arrest you for wasting police time, obstruction—"

Ford shook his head, no. He opened his mouth to speak but

Marnie held up the flat of her hand.

"Save it," she said, and shook her head. "Just don't come to me when some crackhead kicks down the front door and beats Mrs. Ford around the head with a baseball bat."

From where she sat on the sofa, Sarah could see into the boys' bedroom. She could see the posters on the wall, Charlie's Angels and the Strokes, and the piles of comics, DVDs, and clothes on the floor. She still liked to think of it as the boys' bedroom despite the fact that Luke, her eldest, had been dead for over two years now. He had been just fifteen when he had been found dead with a needle in his arm.

Luke and his friend Chris Kirchen had returned to the Kirchen home one night after seeing another of their friends perform with his band at the Bull & Gate in Kentish Town. The two had been drunk but had smoked a little puff and drunk some more beer before Chris had gone up to bed and left Luke adrift on the sofa. His father had found Luke the following morning when he got up to go to work. Luke had often slept on the sofa, and Bob Kirchen was used to seeing him among the morning-after debris, but nothing could have prepared him for the sight that greeted him that morning. Luke had turned the colour of a fresh bruise, his limbs looked almost broken, arranged in the attitude of an abstract statue, and black puke stained the front of his T-shirt. He looked like he had been dead for a lifetime, Bob Kirchen later told the police.

Scared and still in shock, at first Chris had told the police that he had no idea that Luke had been using heroin. But later that afternoon, full of remorse, he had confessed that the pair had discussed scoring some that lunchtime, and that Luke had bought some from one of the dealers on the Castle Estate before heading up to meet Chris at the Bull & Gate. Luke had told Chris about the score, but Chris had said that he had wanted to wait until the time was right before he tried it. "I guess Luke thought that the time was right," Chris Kirchen told the police.

Sarah's second child, thirteen at the time, had looked up to Luke as a mentor as well as a brother and had taken this blow to the heart hard. First his father had deserted him, and now his beloved brother had also left him for another place.

Sarah had tried her best after her husband left home, but then when Luke died, she came to see herself as the one left behind. Since she could not understand what had happened herself, how could she offer comfort to the tortured and confused child who blamed her for it all? In time she had come to believe that her own past held the code, that her own liberal attitude towards drugs had encouraged Luke to his death. And all she could now offer her sole surviving child was protection.

She picked up her coffee mug and carried it through into the kitchen. She rinsed it under the cold tap and placed it on the draining board, and then stood for a moment looking out across the estate. In the block to her left, she could see a man in a pair of red shorts drinking from a can of beer, and in the flat beneath him an old woman tried to get up from her sofa, but each time she took hold of the arm and pulled, her hands collapsed and she fell back on the seat once more. Sarah watched her make another couple of failed attempts and then shifted her attention further round the square. In the block opposite, she saw a man in a white vest shaving the tops of his ears, and then in another window an old woman was pointing in her direction. Seconds later, the net curtain shifted to the side and the face of the woman detective who had interviewed her after that drug dealer had been found dead at the base of the building was staring right back at her. She felt a cold fist tighten around her heart, and she had to grab the edge of the sink to keep from collapsing.

Marnie looked out across the Castle Estate to where Connie

Parker's knotted hand pointed. "You mean near the black bin liner?" she said.

Scraps of litter were spread across the path and the grass, drifted up against the iron railings that surrounded the building from which Paul Ballard had been pushed to his death. Ten feet from the front door of the building, a black bin liner had been jammed in between a couple of the railings, about two feet above the ground. Marnie wanted to check that Connie Parker knew the precise spot where Paul Ballard had landed, that she was not just another loon out for a bit of attention, but she also wanted to check that the old woman still had enough of her sight left to make her statement credible. She used the bin liner as a target.

"No, it was further from the door than that," said Connie Parker, shaking her head. "Near that. . . . Near where that newspaper's wrapped around the railings. You see that?"

"Yes, I can see that," said Marnie, nodding, satisfied that there was nothing wrong with the old woman's sight, and that her recollections were truthful. She had picked the correct spot. "And that's where you think he landed, where you saw the body?"

Connie turned from the window and nodded once more. Her shoulders were shaking a little and she clutched a frail hand to her chest, resting the other on the side of the kitchen counter. "At first I just thought that he was drunk," she started, and then trailed off. Marnie had noticed that it was a peculiar habit of hers, ending her sentences on a fade as if she had forgotten what she was going to say, or maybe she thought that she had said it already and was afraid to repeat herself.

"And this was the same man who tried to steal your purse?"

"Yes, that's right."

"You're sure about that?"

"Of course I'm sure, dear," said Connie, and touched Marnie

on the arm in emphasis.

"Just checking," said Marnie, smiling. She glanced at the hand settled on her arm, the lightness of its touch, the pale blue veins like string holding the brittle collection of bones together. "And this happened earlier the same afternoon?"

Connie nodded again. "Outside the community centre."

"What time was that?"

"It must have been about three o'clock, I suppose."

"Do you know who else was with him?"

"Well, I'm afraid I don't know their names, dear," said Connie, shaking her head. "But I do know there were two of them. Apart from the one who was killed later, I mean . . ."

"Did you recognise either of them?"

Connie thought for a moment, her forehead lined in concentration. "Yes, I think so," she said at last. "I think I might have seen one of them around the estate before."

"You mean around the Castle Estate?"

"Yes, I think so . . ."

"How about if I get a car to take us around, see if we can pick him out?"

"That sounds like a good idea," said Connie Parker, a touch of congratulation in her voice.

"Err . . . thanks," said Marnie, hesitant, feeling a blush rise in her cheeks. She had never been told that she had had a good idea before. "I'll try and sort something out when I get back to the station." She leaned back on the kitchen counter, and folded her arms. "Okay, now what about the other one? The one who came out of the building straight afterwards?"

Connie started to shake her head. "I don't know . . ."

"Black, white . . . tall, short . . . male, female?"

Connie continued to shake her head. "No, I can't remember," she said again. "All I can remember is the tracksuit."

"Could it have been one of the other kids from earlier?"

Connie shook her head, no, certain. "Whoever it was seemed to be much older, less quick on their feet . . ."

Marnie glanced over towards the shops, saw a line of closed shutters splattered in graffiti, racks of dried out fruit.

"Okay, thanks," said Marnie.

21

The Linton Tree sat on the corner of Brecknock Road and Linton Street, two hundred metres from Tufnell Park tube station. On the other side of the junction from the pub stood Callahan House, one of the numerous blocks of council flats that peppered the area and made up the Linton Estate. It had been in front of Callahan House five months earlier that Rhiannon Burns had seen her son killed under the wheels of a police car.

After leaving the Mediterranean, Roscoe cut through the backstreets of Kentish Town and come out on Brecknock Road opposite the Linton. On the kerb he paused for a moment in thought. He glanced in the direction of the tube station, then crossed the street and pushed open the door of the pub.

He had been in the Linton before, after dark, and he was surprised that in the light of the afternoon it looked shabbier than he would have imagined. But then he thought that most pubs looked shabbier in the light. Solid blocks of autumn sun fell from the front windows and turned the dark furniture a shade of orange, and spotlit wisps of smoke danced across the tables like dreams leaving the heads of the clientele. There were large mirrors on the other three walls, but neither the sun nor the mirrors did much to raise the level of gloominess.

Roscoe stepped up to the bar and nodded to the barman, a squat man in his forties dressed in a black T-shirt and jeans. Self-inflicted juvenile tattoos littered his arms like graffiti.

"Is the landlord about?" asked Roscoe, letting the barman

see a flash of his ID.

The barman blinked and looked towards the front door for a moment, as if to map out his escape route. "In the back having his lunch," he said, jerking a thumb over his shoulder.

"You want to fetch him for me?"

The man shot Roscoe a dark look, held his ground for a fraction, and then turned and headed into the back.

A couple of minutes later another, older, man appeared. He had dark red hair and dark red skin that had dried out from the constant batter of alcohol and nicotine. He held a balled napkin in his hand, and traces of saliva flecked his lips and his chin.

"Sorry, did I interrupt your lunch?" said Roscoe.

"Just finished," said the man, his eyes closed, shaking his head. He raised his hand and poked at some food stuck in his back teeth with a thick nicotine-stained finger.

"You're the landlord here?"

"I think you'll find that's my name over the door," said the man, pointing at the entrance. "Donald Fergus Moon."

"Detective Inspector Roscoe, Kentish Town CID," said Roscoe. "You mind if I ask you a few questions, Mr. Moon?"

"Sure," said Moon. "What can I do for you?"

"Do you remember the accident that happened outside here about five months ago?"

"The kid who was run over," said Moon, narrowing his eyes. "That was no accident."

"So you did see what happened," said Roscoe.

"No, but I heard enough about it," said Moon, pushing back his shoulders.

"You heard enough about it," repeated Roscoe, deadpan. "That's strange, because we never heard much about it."

"People talk," said Moon. "I work behind a bar, I hear things."

"You want to tell me what people were talking about?"

Moon blinked and looked off across the pub. He seemed to

focus on something through the doors for a moment, and Roscoe could see a conflict of emotions in his pupils.

"What's all this about?" said Moon at last. "Are you still looking for someone to take the blame?"

Roscoe should have known that it would come to this: the belief that the police were just out to look after their own. He thought about telling Moon the truth, that he was not part of the official investigation, that he was here on behalf of the child's mother. But then from what Moon had just said, it sounded like he had not heard about the result from the inquest, the verdict in Dillon's favour, and he decided to go with his instincts.

"The inquest is in a couple of weeks, and there are still a number of discrepancies between what the policemen involved are telling us and what forensics and the mother are telling us," he said. "So what I need to do is find someone prepared to talk to me, someone who was out there that night, and ask them what happened. I don't need a formal statement at the moment, just an impartial view so I can start to pick out the truth from all the stuff that I can get together."

"What happened was he was going far too fast," said Moon, anger and sadness in his voice. If he had heard about the verdict, then it had been pushed out of his mind in his desire to pin the forked tail on Dillon. "Couple of local hotheads arguing in the street, for Christ's sake. What was the fucking rush?"

Roscoe shook his head and offered Moon a sad smile, indulged him in his moment of righteous indignation. He let Moon blow off a bit more steam, his nostrils flaring, and then said, "I don't suppose you remember who was out there that night?"

Moon hesitated for a long second, and then nodded to two women sitting at a table in the far corner of the room. "The one on the left, the brunette," he said. "She was out there when it happened. I remember she came in afterwards and tried to get a free drink out of me, said she was in shock."

"You give it to her?"

"That's me, the good doctor," said Moon, half-laughing.

"Let me take care of that now," said Roscoe. "What's she drinking?"

"That night she wanted a brandy."

"Give me two brandies, and I'll have a ginger ale."

Moon filled the order and Roscoe handed over fifteen pounds, told the landlord to take one for himself.

He carried the drinks over to the table where the brunette and her friend, a woman with blonde hair, bloodless lips, and parchment skin sat and chatted. He introduced himself and offered the women the drinks, took a seat opposite the brunette.

"You remember the child who was knocked down and killed outside here at the start of the summer?"

The two women looked at each other for a moment, and then the brunette looked at Roscoe and nodded.

Roscoe turned to her friend. "You weren't here that night?"

"No, I was over at my cousin's flat in Cricklewood, she'd just had twins, two girls, but I heard about what happened."

"All right, thanks," said Roscoe, smiling. "But do you mind if I talk to your friend here alone for a minute?"

The blonde shot Roscoe a look of bruised surprise, and then slipped out from behind the table and stepped up to the bar.

"I'm sorry, the landlord didn't tell me—"

"Nicole Rains," said the brunette.

"Thanks for talking to me, Nicole."

"Thanks for the drink," she said, and took a sip.

"That's okay," said Roscoe. "Right, Nicole, do you think you can remember what happened that night?"

"I'm not making a statement," said Nicole, folding her arms across her chest and pushing herself back into the seat.

"I don't need a statement," said Roscoe. "I just need to get the chain of events clear in my mind. Like I told Donald—"

"Donnie," Nicole corrected him.

"Donnie," echoed Roscoe, a brow raised in question.

"He likes to be called Donnie," said Nicole.

"He likes to be called Donnie," repeated Roscoe, glancing over at the landlord.

Nicole gave him a crooked smile. "He still lives with his mother," she said.

Roscoe raised his brows and shook his head, once. "All right, well, like I told Donnie," he said, smiling like he was in on the joke, "I'm just here to get people to talk, to get people to tell me what they saw the night that Karl was killed."

"Karl. That was his name?"

"That's right," said Roscoe. "Karl Burns."

"Oh," said Nicole. "I never knew that."

"Anyway," said Roscoe. "Like I said, I'm not interested in a formal record. I just want to hear as much as I can from as many people as I can, and then try and pull it all together."

"I don't have to make a statement?"

Roscoe shook his head, no.

Nicole thought about this for a moment, looking around the room, a flutter of apprehension high in her chest. No one seemed to be all that bothered about her or who she was talking to, there was just the occasional sidelong glance in their direction. Even her friend the blonde had found someone else to talk to.

"Well, I was standing right outside the door, talking to a friend of mine, Jean Blake," she said at last. "And before you ask, no, she didn't see anything. I was standing with my back to the wall, looking towards the tube station. Jake and Pam came out of the pub fighting, and carried on fighting until they reached in front of Callahan House. I saw Jake hit Pam a couple of times, and then when the siren started . . . I don't know . . . I didn't see the boy . . . Karl, I didn't see him before that . . . I wasn't watching all that much, it gets pretty boring seeing them fighting all the time like that. But when I heard the siren get up close, I looked over and saw Pam hit Jake with a good one, and that's when he fell and knocked the boy out into the road. . . . Knocked him right into the path of the police car . . ."

"So it was an accident," said Roscoe, feeling something hard stick in his throat.

Nicole picked up her drink and took a sip, nodded.

"And you're sure about that?"

"I think so."

"Okay," said Roscoe. "And what about before the accident?"

"I don't understand. What d'you mean, before the accident?"

"Before the accident," repeated Roscoe. "Did you see anything before the accident? Anything unusual, anything at all?"

"I don't know. How d'you mean, unusual?"

"I don't know," said Roscoe, shrugging. "Was there anyone standing in the road watching the fight, for instance? Did you see anyone run away when the siren started to get closer?"

Nicole shook her head, no.

"How about on the other side of the crowd?"

"I couldn't see over there," said Nicole, and shook her head again. "There were people all around, in front of me."

"Did you see the police car before it hit Karl?"

"No, but I remember that I saw Colin Carpenter over there. He and his son were over on the far side of the crowd."

"Colin Carpenter?" The name had not been in the file.

"We were in the same class at junior school."

"Do you know where he lives, this Colin Carpenter?"

"On the estate somewhere. Donnie'll know the place."

"What about his son?"

"I think he's away at university somewhere. Up north, I think."

"Okay, Nicole, thanks for your help," said Roscoe, and left her to her drink.

He collected Colin Carpenter's address from the landlord, and then stepped out of the pub and into the afternoon sun. He crossed the road and walked over to the point in front of Callahan House where the accident had taken place.

He noticed that a bunch of withered flowers wrapped in cellophane were still tied to the railings in front of the building. Sometimes it seemed like there were more bunches of flowers on the streets of the capital than there were in the cemeteries, as if a resigned London had decided to celebrate its own version of the Mexican Day of the Dead every day of the year.

Roscoe stood for a moment looking at the dried flowers, wondering if the next MAD march would come this way.

22

DC Rob Spencer handed a slip of paper to the uniform seated at the desk beside him, a bald and tired man in his late thirties named Cutler, and asked him to add the name written on the slip to the list of names to be checked out. It was the fifth name he had considered promising since he had last spoken to Stone and told her about the calls from Neil Ford and Connie Parker. Five names out of around fifteen calls, not a bad strike rate so far. But then Spencer told himself that the weekend, when most people would pick up the paper, was still to come. Cutler took the slip of paper and put it on the pile at the side of his desk.

Spencer leaned back and tried to roll the stiffness out of his shoulders. It seemed like he had been at his desk for hours, listening to desperate and outlandish stories of altruism that masked greed and revenge, until his mind felt as numb as his bones. He pushed back his chair and climbed to his feet, told Cutler he needed some coffee, and headed for the door.

Three steps from his desk and the phone started up again. Spencer ignored it and kept on walking.

A couple more steps and he heard Cutler call out his name.

Spencer turned on his heel and shot the PC an irritated look. "Jesus Christ," he said. "Can't you deal with it, Cutler?"

"It's Ballard," said Cutler, deflecting the stare. "Said he wants to talk to either you or Stone."

Spencer shook his head, attempting to shake the frustration out of his mind, then walked back to his desk. He snatched the phone from Cutler's outstretched hand and sat on the edge of the desk. "Mr. Ballard? It's DC Spencer. What can I do for you?"

"You wanted me to let you know about the man who put up the reward," Ballard reminded him.

"That's right," said Spencer.

"Well, I just spoke to him," said Ballard. "And he told me that he doesn't see the point in talking to the police himself. All he's doing is putting up the cash for the reward. Past that, it's got nothing to do with him, he says. It was my son that was killed, so it's me that you should be talking to."

"I can understand that," said Spencer, although it was not something he had come across before.

"But he did agree to let me tell you his name so that you can check his credentials."

"That's very public spirited of him," said Spencer, but he could not keep the sarcasm out of his voice. He had spoken to enough nuts that morning to curdle his natural empathies.

"Is there a problem with that?" said Ballard.

"Sorry," said Spencer. "It's just that the phones here've been jumping off the hook all morning. The reward, you know. . . ."

"Oh," said Ballard on a tuft of soft breath, and then there was a brief pause. "Have you heard anything yet?"

"There's been one or two possible leads," said Spencer, careful not to raise his hopes. "But like we said before, putting up a reward tends to scramble all the legitimate information that comes in. And with our limited resources being stretched . . ."

Ballard remained silent. Spencer could hear his breath on the line.

"Do you want to tell me his name now, Mr. Ballard?"

"Of course," said Ballard. "He's James Wilkinson and he lives on Lordship Lane in Forest Hill, down there near the Horniman Museum. His eldest son, Simon, was mugged outside the station about two years ago. Some kids after his mobile phone. He tried to fight back but one of the kids stabbed him in the head with a penknife. He died later that night in hospital."

"And the kids that did this've never been caught?"

"That's what he told me," said Ballard.

"All right, thanks, Mr. Ballard," said Spencer. "I'm sure that'll come in useful."

Ballard asked Spencer to keep him up to date then hung up.

Spencer handed the phone back to Cutler, and then wrote the new information in his notebook. He dropped the notebook back in his pocket, and then headed out of the office to the canteen.

Sarah had smoked the last of her dried-out cigarettes the night before, but the one she had going from a fresh pack she had bought that morning still tasted stale. The inside of her mouth felt scorched, and she kept having to cough to loosen the tickle at the back of her throat. She held the cigarette in the same hand as the phone as she listened to a ringing on the other end of the line. Blue smoke threaded around her arm like the ghost of a tattoo. Moments later she heard someone pick up at the other end, and then came the sound of a familiar voice.

"Lucille, it's Sarah," she said, and then realised that it was the answering machine. "For fuck's sake," she snapped under her breath, crushing the phone in her hand. She took another pull on the cigarette, waited for the message to end, and then said: "Lucille, it's Sarah. Call me, please, quick, I've just seen that woman, that policewoman from before, asking questions on the estate."

Marnie was just climbing back into her car when her mobile started to ring. She pulled it out of her pocket and pressed the OK button. "Yeah, Stone."

"It's Spencer, Boss."

"What's up, Spencer? More wild geese been set loose on the streets of Primrose Hill?"

"That's not too far from the truth," sighed Spencer, tired. "No, what I'm calling about . . . Ballard just rang and told me the name of the man who put up the reward."

"That's good," said Marnie.

"A man named Wilkinson," said Spencer. "James Wilkinson."

"Doesn't ring a bell," said Marnie, turning and leaning against the car. In the distance she could see all the cranes that poked into the air around the Lock, as if Camden Town were a work-in-progress. "Do we know who he is?"

"Not in this part of the world," said Spencer. "He lives down in Forest Hill somewhere, south of the river."

"So what's his connection with Ballard?"

"Sympathy, by the sounds of it," said Spencer. "Some kids attacked and killed his teenage son a couple of years ago. Started out going after his phone and ended up putting him in the ground. From what Ballard told me, the kids've never been caught. I think Wilkinson must've heard about Paul Ballard being killed and felt some kind of kinship with his parents, the father."

"So now he wants to go after the kids who killed his son by proxy?"

"That's about the truth of it," said Spencer.

"It wouldn't be the first time," said Marnie, smiling to herself and shaking her head. "Have you spoken to him yet?"

"Ballard said he wouldn't talk to us."

"But he would give us his name?"

"That's right," said Spencer.

"What about his son?" said Marnie. "Do the details of the murder check out?"

"I was just about to get on to it," said Spencer.

"Okay, let me know how it turns out," said Marnie.

"Sure," said Spencer. Then: "There's one other thing."

"Yeah, what's that?"

"Dineen wants to talk to you."

"What's that about?"

"I don't know, he didn't say," said Spencer. "Something about Kilburn, I think. He's in court this afternoon, but he said that you can catch him in his office around five-thirty."

"Okay, thanks," said Marnie again, and then clicked off the phone and dropped it in her pocket.

23

Kentish Town City Farm sat on a five acre plot of land at the point where two sets of railway tracks crossed. To the north of the farm behind the main buildings, a grass embankment ran down to a chain link fence that prevented a couple of goats from wandering onto the track that ran east-west, and to the east of the buildings, the land disappeared into the brick support arches of the line that ran north-south and also bridged the first set of tracks. On the farm, the rattle of trains filled the air like a mechanical backbeat to the rise and fall of animal noises.

Besides the goats, the farm also boasted ducks, chickens, geese, cows, pigs, and a number of horses. Throughout the seasons, the farm supplemented its meagre council grant with horse riding lessons to both neighbourhood kids and adults alike. There was also a garden full of apples, pears, figs, pumpkins, sweet corn, and giant sunflowers that visitors were encouraged to sample and take home.

Towards the back of the farm there was a small picnic area where school parties could eat their packed lunches.

Marnie sat at one of the benches in the picnic area, across from Shona Kilpatrick. Behind the smell from the goat pen, on the rockiest part of the embankment, she could detect the delicate fragrance of basil and dill in the organic garden, and in the near distance she could see a group of schoolchildren gathered around a couple of chickens, clucking back at them in some kind of strange communication.

"I suppose you're going to rat on me," said Shona, sulking.

Marnie had called at the Kilpatrick home and been told that she could find Shona on the farm. Her mother had said that Shona had become enamoured of the place after a school trip there some eighteen months earlier, and had soon started hanging around the place after school and at weekends. One of the volunteers had befriended her after a time, and when she had asked Shona if she would like to help out, Shona had jumped at the chance to get up close with the animals. Finding a kind of calm there that she could not find in her life outside of the farm, she was soon spending more and more time there until she was jumping school two or three afternoons a week. The farm manager and the volunteers had tried to get her to return to school, banning her from the farm during school hours, and Shona had tried her best to stick to her desk, but despite all their best efforts she had run back to the farm time and time again until it had become easier all round to just let her follow her heart.

"For bunking off school? No, that's another bunch of cops altogether," said Marnie, smiling. "No, like I said, now that the Ballards have put up a reward, we need to go back over all the original statements and see that it all still holds together."

"You don't think I was telling the truth?"

"It's not that, Shona," said Marnie. "It's just that after all this time—"

"I'm not scared of Lee Rooker," said Shona, tilting her chin up in the air and flaring her nostrils.

"He has got a formidable street reputation," said Marnie.

"He's nothing but a thug," said Shona, scowling. "That's how we started hanging around with him in the first place—he bullied Jenna into going out for a drink with him until she felt that she couldn't say no. Just to see if he could, I think, because

I don't think he liked her all that much. We were in the Subterranean getting drinks one night, and he was standing at the bar beside us. He chatted to Jenna for a couple of minutes or so, seemed to be getting on with her fine, and then all of a sudden he turned his back on her and walked off. But when he saw that someone else was interested in her, he came bouncing back like he'd left his dick on the bar or something."

"And that someone else was Paul Ballard," said Marnie, nodding to herself.

"Paul Ballard?"

"I thought Rooker and Ballard got into a fight over Jenna."

"That wasn't Ballard," said Shona, her own face reflecting the confusion. "No, he was another bloke Jenna met later on. I don't remember this guy's name, but what happened was . . . Rooker arranged to meet her in the club one night, the Subterranean, but he forgot to tell her that he'd be working the door. So of course Jenna gets bored and starts talking to someone else, this other bloke. Rooker spotted them and that's when he started to throw his weight around."

"Oh, right," said Marnie, nodding, struggling to put this fresh information into the timeline. "So where's Jenna now, then? I tried speaking to her father . . ."

"There's another thug right there," snorted Shona. She looked off towards the group of children in front of the chicken shack, and Marnie caught a glimpse of the innocence that Shona still held beneath her hard shell, the girl beneath the anger.

"Do you know where she is, Shona? It might be important."

"Last I heard. . . . I got a postcard from Cornwall about two weeks ago," said Shona. She shook her head and two thick curtains of hair fell across her face. "I had no idea she was there, she didn't tell me she was going. She just disappeared, and then one morning this postcard dropped through the door."

"So if the fight between Ballard and Rooker wasn't about Jenna, what was it about?"

"I'm not going to court," said Shona, curling one curtain of hair back behind her ear, leaving the other one free.

"You won't have to go to court," Marnie assured her. "This is just between the two of us, background information."

Shona thought about this for a moment, spiralling emotions contradicting each other. At last she spoke. "You know that Ballard was working the booths on the Castle Estate."

"He was selling drugs," said Marnie. "Yes, we know that."

"Well, I heard he was getting a lot of grief from some of the people on the estate."

"Some of the other dealers," said Marnie, thinking about the bloodshed that had come from other territorial pissings.

"It was nothing to do with the other dealers," said Shona, shaking her head, her hair falling in front of her face again. "I think this was just some woman on the estate. One woman . . . I don't know, I don't know who she was, but he couldn't handle it. He didn't know what to do about it, how to get her off his back, and so he went to Rooker and asked him to help. But Rooker just laughed in his face, told him that if he couldn't deal with it then he should get off the estate and get back on the tit."

"So Ballard knew Rooker beforehand," said Marnie, running the changes through her head.

"Both of them were working for Bar Code, so I guess—"

"Do you know Bar Code, Shona?"

"I don't know him, but I know who he is," she replied. "I think everyone in Camden must know someone who works for him."

Marnie nodded. "So what did Ballard do after Rooker told him to deal with the problem himself?"

Shona flattened her lips and shook her head. "I don't know," she said. "Next thing I heard, he was dead."

★　★　★　★　★

Roscoe stopped for a cup of coffee in a small Italian restaurant near Tufnell Park station, and then headed for the Linton Estate.

Reaching Callahan House, he pushed open the front door and started to climb to the third floor. As he climbed he felt his breath shortening, and the extra pounds he had put on since the shooting start to pull him back. And his foot had started to ache, too, the pain tightening around his calf like a tourniquet.

He rested for a moment on the landing in front of the Carpenter place, breathing hard, and then pressed the bell.

The door opened on a man in his late forties. He had a cropped scalp and wore a tracksuit and trainers. He squinted at the warrant card Roscoe held up for him to inspect.

"Frank Roscoe, Kentish Town CID."

Carpenter lifted his chin in response.

"You mind if I come in for a moment, Mr. Carpenter?" said Roscoe, glancing along the corridor.

"What's it about?" asked Carpenter. One hand rested on the edge of the door and the other high on the frame, creating a barrier that separated him from the stranger on his doorstep.

"The accident out front back in May," said Roscoe.

Carpenter stared at him for a moment with flat eyes, then some kind of sadness crossed his face and he dropped his hands to his sides and let his natural defences fall. He stepped back and motioned for Roscoe to follow him into the flat.

"It was a terrible business," said Carpenter, shaking his head. "I know his grandmother, have ever since we moved in here about ten years ago, a lovely woman. She's got bad arthritis now and doesn't get out much. Karl and his mother used to live here for a while after she spilt up with her husband, but I guess they wanted their own space. I used to hear him jumping around in her front room, but now all I can hear is her crying."

"She lives upstairs," said Roscoe, pointing at the ceiling.

"That's right," said Carpenter. "The flat right above me."

Roscoe tried to picture the old woman, but the face remained out of focus. He thought that perhaps he should go up and see her, but in all the time that he had known Rhiannon, he doubted that he had met her mother more than three or four times.

He followed Carpenter to the kitchen.

Carpenter crossed the floor, rested his hands on the edge of the sink, and looked out the window at the debris on the back of another building on the estate: the kids' bikes stacked on short balconies, the pale plants in broken pots, and the clothes that snapped in the air. He stood firm and silent and appeared to be listening for something familiar. The sound of a child's bouncing footsteps on the ceiling, perhaps.

"I understand you have a son yourself," said Roscoe.

Carpenter turned his head to the side a fraction and nodded. "Jonathan," he said, and then corrected himself: "Jon."

"And he's away at university at the moment."

"Huddersfield," said Carpenter, and Roscoe thought he detected a touch of pride in his voice. Jon must have been the first of this particular branch of Carpenters to go to college.

"Does he like it up there?"

"Well, he's always going on about how the beer's a lot cheaper than down here," said Carpenter, shrugging. "But I don't think he plans to stop on after he finishes his studies."

"He spent the summer here in London," said Roscoe.

"Yeah, with his mother for the most part," said Carpenter, and then he turned around and folded his arms across his chest, resting his backside against the sink. "She lives up in Golders Green with her second husband. He's a secondhand car dealer, got a couple of places near the bus terminus. He gave Jon a job cleaning cars for the summer, or valeting them as he put it, and so he ended up stopping at their place most of the time."

"But he was here on the night of the accident?"

"That's right. He was going to Greece later that night, and I offered to give him a lift to the airport. I think we must have left here about ten or so."

Less than an hour after the accident, thought Roscoe. "What about the police?" he said.

"What about them?"

"I don't remember seeing a statement."

"Jon had a plane to catch," said Carpenter, knotting his arms tighter. "Besides, there were enough people out there that night who saw what happened without me having to stick around."

Roscoe offered him a rueful smile. "Seems that's just what most other people thought as well."

Carpenter looked at Roscoe for a second as if he did not understand, and then turned back to the sink. He lifted the kettle from the counter, shook it, then clicked it on. He took a seat at the kitchen table, clasped his hands together, resting them on the scratched Formica in front of him. One of his thumbnails had been torn off some time ago making the tip of the thumb look like a solid piece of air was being pressed into the flesh, and he kept running the other thumb across the pale scar.

Roscoe pulled out a chair and took the seat opposite him.

"You want to tell me what happened?" said Roscoe. "You want to tell me what you saw?"

Carpenter blinked at the apparent abruptness of the question, as if he had been asleep, and then took a deep breath and started to speak. "Well, when the fight started—"

"I know all about the fight," said Roscoe. "Tell me about the police car, tell me about the accident."

Carpenter looked at him again, surprise and something more in his face.

"It's all right, no one's handed me a brush and a bucket of whitewash," said Roscoe, anticipating the clear question in his face. He had also decided against telling Carpenter his own connection to Karl in case it pushed him in the other direction.

Carpenter flattened his lips and nodded. "I think I first heard the siren when the car was still back near the station," he said, hesitant at first. "But I had no idea that it was coming to break up the fight. I mean, Jake and Pam are forever at each others' throats, and the police've never been called to them before. So I heard the siren coming, but when I looked over and saw the car, it didn't look like it was in that much of a rush. There were a couple of cars in front of it, and when one of them pulled over to let it past, it didn't seem to be that bothered.

"Close to the fight there were a couple of men standing in the road watching, and when the police car saw them it seemed to speed up all of a sudden and the men had to jump out of its path. . . . The car swerved a bit. . . . That must have been right before the boy was knocked into the road. . . . The driver can't have been able to see him because of the men standing in the road."

Roscoe kept silent for a short time, processing the information and attempting to picture the scene in his head.

Carpenter kept nodding his head, telling Roscoe that he had got it right, his mind had kept the memories intact. Just then the kettle clicked off and he glanced across at Roscoe, but Roscoe motioned for him to remain seated.

"The police car," said Roscoe. "You said that it seemed to speed up as it approached the scene. Tell me about that."

"Well, when I first—"

"It had its siren on," said Roscoe, almost to himself.

"That's right," said Carpenter.

"Tell me when it started to speed up."

Carpenter blinked, taking a second to catch up on the questions. "When it saw the men standing in the road."

"The two men standing in the road watching the fight."

Carpenter nodded.

"And both of them had to jump out of its path . . ."

"Run for the kerb," said Carpenter, nodding once more.

"And Karl," said Roscoe. "You think the driver couldn't've seen him because of these two?"

"Yeah, I think so," said Carpenter.

"Right," said Roscoe. He looked out of the window for a second, fine tuning the images in his head. "You know either of the two men who were standing in the road?"

Carpenter started to shake his head, but then changed his mind. "I think one of them must've been a minicab driver."

"You think one of them was a minicab driver?"

"Right after the accident I saw the car drive off. . . . One of the men was sitting in the back and the other one, the driver, had what looked like a radio in his hand. I remember the car had a sticker on the side that I recognised."

"You recognised a sticker on the side of the car? You mean like a logo? You remember which firm it belonged to?"

"I don't use cabs all that much," said Carpenter, shaking his head. "But I remember that the logo was black and red."

"Black and red," said Roscoe, almost under his breath. There were a number of cab firms in the area, and he could think of at least four that had a black and red logo. He pressed Carpenter further, tried to help him recall more about the logo, but he could remember no more about either the logo or the car.

"What about the man in the back?" said Roscoe.

"What about him?" said Carpenter.

"You didn't recognise him at all?" said Roscoe.

"No, I don't think so," said Carpenter, shaking his head.

"Where was the cab parked when all this was happening?"

"In front of one of the parking meters, about a couple of feet or so from the kerb," said Carpenter. "I think there were about another two or three spaces in front of it."

Parking meters ran the length of the street from the tube station to the area near the crossing in front of Callahan House. Roscoe reckoned that the cab had been parked no more than ten metres from the scene of the accident.

"You remember which house the fare came out of?"

Carpenter shook his head, no.

"You remember seeing the fare walking towards the cab?"

Carpenter shook his head again.

Roscoe thanked him for his time and then handed him a card with his mobile number scratched on the back, the station number crossed out, and told him to call him if he remembered more.

24

Walking past the front of Shake Records, Barney turned his head and glanced inside, but he could see no sign of Mel. Just that pinhead Archie, putting in time on his tortured life. He hunched his shoulders and hurried on through the street market.

He had first met Mel when his father had left home and hooked up with Mel's mother, and Barney had taken an instant dislike to her. Her mother had just stolen his father, for fuck's sake, and in his book that made her just as much of a creeping thief as her mother. But in the last couple of months, since things had started to turn bad at home, he had begun to see more and more of her, got to know her a little better, and he found that she had been just as hateful and bitter about him as he had been about her. She had been on the same roller coaster ride of loss and rejection after her own parents had split, been through that slot of hatred for all things Price, but now much to the relief of the old timers, he and Mel were more like brother and sister.

He checked the traffic and crossed the High Street, heading up towards the canal and then turning onto Hartland Road. Mercurial touches of Mel flitted across his senses as he walked, distracting him from the other people around him on the street.

As he approached the community centre at the foot of Hartland Road, across from the Castle Estate, he saw a group of kids pushing around a basketball on the forecourt, pitching it at a rusted iron hoop attached to the front of the building.

Graffiti coated all four sides of the brick and timber structure, and some colours had also been stretched across parts of the tiled roof. Barney seemed to remember his mother telling him something about it being designed and decorated like that to stop people from slapping it with their own signatures. It looked like it too; most of the pics and tags looked fake and out of time.

He recognised some of the kids from around the estate and knew that at least a couple of them did shifts on the phone booths on the far side of the estate on Kentish Town Road. One of them, a small black kid nicknamed Polo, had been there the night Barney's mother screamed at them after she caught them attempting to sell wraps of heroin to Barney and some other kids on their way home from school. She had stood in the centre of the pavement and screamed until her face had turned crimson, blood throbbing in her temples, her tongue flicking out streams of anger that had been buried inside her since Luke had died. The dealers and runners had looked on and smirked, hitching up onto the stairs and walls around for a better look. Later, his ego sunk in teenage embarrassment, Barney had tried to tell her that it was no big deal—it happened all the time—but her ears had still been filled with blood and she had not heard him. But the damage had been done, and now each time he came across Polo and his friends he had no choice but to accept their jibes.

He tucked his chin onto his chest and quickened his step, hurried across the stretch of pavement.

"Yo Barnabus, what's with the sprinting?"

"You in a rush to get home and get high or somethin'?"

"Check out the walk, fellas, like he just peed his pants."

"Oh man, I can hear it slopping around in his shoes."

"You sure that ain't the shit running down his legs?"

"Linford Christie on his ass."

"Chickenshit more like."

"You need something to bring on that night chill."

"Those Pampers, man, those nappies're not *designed* to hold the amount of shit that comes out of a kid as big as *that*."

"Cluck, cluck . . ."

"You sure mama up there don't need no gear, man?"

"P'aps he got one of them *bags* to collect his shit."

Laughter and curses chased him down the street.

He heard the scuffle of footsteps behind him, and then the basketball bounced off the back of his legs and caused him to stumble. His face burned with embarrassment and he wanted to run, but he forced his feet to maintain his pace. The ball bounced up close once more, and then one of the kids was beside him. Not Polo, but another black kid who he recognised from the class behind him in school. The kid kept pace beside him, and he could smell the smoke on his clothes, the chocolate on his breath.

"You like to get high, Barnabus?" asked the kid, holding up a foil wrap in front of his face and turning it in his fingers.

Barney bunched his shoulders and hurried across the pavement, stepping out into the street.

"First one's free," said the kid, grinning, and a cloud of poisonous laughter erupted from his friends. Encouraged, the kid took a couple of quick steps up ahead of Barney, and then turned and stuffed the wrap into Barney's jacket pocket.

Barney pushed his hand into his pocket and tried to pull out the wrap, but the kid grabbed hold of his arm below the elbow and held it tight, pulling him close as he walked beside him.

"Let me go, let me go," squealed Barney, and tried to pull himself free, but the kid just held him tight, grinning from behind stoned pupils. The pair continued to wrestle across the street as cars scooted past them on either side, hot air and fumes in their faces, and solid blocks of noise pressing on their eardrums. On reaching the far side, the kid appeared to get bored and let go of his prisoner before heading back to his friends.

Barney hurried on towards the estate, his breathing ragged and loose. He looked around him as he walked, and seeing no one up close, pulled the foil wrap out of his pocket. He held it tight in his hand, and then took a quick look back at the kid who had put it in his pocket, but both him and his friends seemed to have lost all interest in this particular game. He looked down at the wrap again for a second, and then started to open it, intending to dump its contents on the ground, but when he unfolded the wrap all it contained was a smudge of chocolate.

He crunched it up into a ball and hurled it on the ground.

Hot tears spiked his cheeks, and he wanted to get out of there as fast as he could. Rubbing at the tears, he started to run, feeling a rush of blood fill his head like the taunting chant of a thousand tormentors. He thought of his mother and the humiliation she had caused him in the name of his long gone brother, and rage and hatred filled his heart. If she felt so much about him, he told himself, couldn't she tell that he had nothing in common with Luke, nothing at all, and that he had no inclination to head in the same dark and truncated direction?

He reached the front door of his building and let himself in, the reek of stale beer, urine, and glue hitting him in the throat like a punch. He crossed to the stairs, crushing a plastic Coke bottle and a couple of KFC cartons underfoot, and then climbed as a combination of dance beats hit him at each floor.

Letting himself into the flat, he headed straight to his room. He heard his mother in the kitchen, the chop of a knife on the board as she prepared supper, and behind that he could hear the signature tune to the ITN news on the TV in the front room.

He shucked off his jacket and hung it on the back of the chair beside the bed, then crossed to the window and dropped the blinds on the scene of his humiliation. He pushed off his trainers, and rolled onto the bed. Lifting the headphones from the mini-stereo, he slotted them over his ears and then punched the start button on the latest Chili Peppers CD.

Seconds later the door opened and his mother pushed her head into his space. She motioned for him to turn off the stereo, but he pretended to not understand, and so she came into the room, crossed to the stereo and pressed the button herself.

Barney spun his feet around and sat up, his legs on the opposite side of the bed from his mother. "What was that for?"

Sarah said nothing, just stood firm and stared back at him, her face as cold and dark as he had ever seen it. There was a knot of muscle in the centre of her forehead. "Never mind about that," she said. "I want to know what happened out there just now."

"I don't know what you're talking about," replied Barney.

"In front of the community centre," said Sarah.

Barney felt his heart drop in his chest, and his blood run cold. He had a flash nightmare of his mother running out into the street and confronting the basketball kids, more humiliation.

"It was nothing," he said.

"Tell me what happened," said Sarah once more. "I was standing at the sink looking out of the window . . ."

"It was nothing, it doesn't matter," said Barney. "You know what they're like, those kids. After . . . you know . . ."

"The one who spoke to you," said Sarah, stepping further into the room and crossing to where he had dumped his jacket.

"It was just jibes and stuff," said Barney, shucking his shoulders and sticking out his bottom lip like a petulant child.

"And that's all," said Sarah, looking around. She hesitated

CRESTWOOD PUBLIC LIBRARY DISTRICT

for a moment, and then picked up his jacket from the chair. "He didn't just give you something?"

"What d'you mean?"

"He didn't try and sell you anything?"

"What're you talking about?"

"You didn't buy anything from him just now?"

"No," said Barney, his frustration caught in his throat.

"You're sure about that?"

"Of course I'm sure," snapped Barney.

Sarah started to poke her hand into his jacket pockets, one at a time. She pulled out a fistful of coins, some old tube tickets, a leaking pen, and then pushed them back in again.

"Hey, what's happening," said Barney. He stood and made a half-hearted attempt to take the jacket from her hands, but she lifted it out of his reach and he fell back on the bed.

Sarah continued to search his pockets.

"I don't know what you think you'll find," sneered Barney.

Her search completed, Sarah tossed the jacket on the bed. "Tell me what happened out there just now," she said.

Barney looked into her face, the furious darkness of her pupils. "I don't know what you're talking about," he said.

"Don't lie to me, Barney," said Sarah. "I just saw him put something in your pocket."

"It was just a chocolate wrapper," he protested.

"Don't make me ask again," said Sarah, folding her arms.

"Mum, he was just messing about . . ."

"Show it to me, then," said Sarah, and stuck out her hand.

"I threw it on the ground."

"You did what?"

"It was just a piece of foil, some rubbish . . ."

Sarah stared at her son. She wanted to believe him, she *did* believe him, but something pushed her on. She could not back down. It was that kind of weakness that had killed Luke.

"Go and fetch it," she said, pointing in the direction of the front door and the estate. "Go and fetch it for me."

"I don't believe this is happening."

"Just go and fetch it for me."

"It was just a piece of foil, Mum," pleaded Barney. "Stuff like that happens all the time, it's no big deal."

"Go on, humour me."

"Oh for fuck's sake," snapped Barney. "I've had enough of this shit. You're mad, fucking mad . . . Just because Luke thought that it was fucking cool to stick a needle in his arm."

Barney snatched up his jacket and stormed out of the flat, the door slamming and rattling behind him.

25

Back home, tired and with his foot aching after walking around most of the afternoon, Roscoe took a nap. Later, with his foot still thrumming with pain, he popped a couple of paracetamol and made himself a mug of strong coffee. He dug out the Yellow Pages from the back of a cupboard, stuck a Bill Nelson CD, *The Alchemical Adventures of Sailor Bill,* on the stereo and carried the phone over to the coffee table.

He shucked off his shoes and rested his damaged foot up on a cushion on the table.

From the two hundred or so minicab firms listed in the Yellow Pages, he managed to pick out the four that he knew had red and black logos and copied their numbers into his notebook. Then he added the numbers of another three firms that had their main offices within half a mile of the scene of the accident.

Drinking his coffee, he pulled the phone across the table and dialled the first number.

"Abacus Cabs," came a singsong female voice.

"This is Detective Inspector Frank Roscoe from Kentish Town CID," said Roscoe, his tone strong and confident despite the white lie. "We're looking to trace someone last seen getting into a minicab, and I wondered if you might be able to help us."

"You think it was one of our cabs?"

"I don't know," admitted Roscoe. "All we have is a witness

statement that puts our man in a minicab."

"Well, I'll see if I can help," said the dispatcher, after a brief pause. "You want to tell me the details?"

Roscoe told her the date. "It was a Saturday night, sometime between nine and ten. . . . Going from somewhere on Brecknock Road in Tufnell Park to we don't know where."

He heard the dispatcher repeating the information to herself, as if to remember it as she wrote it down. Then he heard the sound of another phone ringing in the background, and the dispatcher asking the caller to hold for a second.

"Look, Inspector, I'm sorry, but I'll have to get back to you on this," she said as she came back on the line. "I'm on my own here at the moment, and it's just starting to hot up. We must get at least three hundred calls on a Saturday night."

"That's fine," replied Roscoe, and then recited his home phone number and asked her to call him in her own good time.

He made a note in his notebook, then took another sip of coffee and dialled the second number. But this one told him that their records were kept for just a month and then discarded.

Roscoe fell silent, remembering the numbing sensation of frustration that sat at the heart of police work. Then he shook the idea loose, thanked the dispatcher, and hung up. His thoughts on his future in the force would keep for another time.

Fifteen minutes later he had two firms that no longer held the required records, two that held computerised records and told him right off that no one had called a cab to Brecknock Road on the night in question, and three that kept paper records and promised to call him back as soon as possible.

He returned the phone to the table, and then rubbed his hands across his face until he could feel the tiredness start to fade. He stood for a moment listening to the music, then walked across to the front window and stared out at the cars lining the street, the setting sun highlighting the fresh colours of autumn.

★　★　★　★　★

The basement flat looked to be in darkness as he approached from the tube station, and Barney felt a little stupid that he had not bothered to call ahead, but there was no way that he was going home again if it turned out that his father was out for the night, even if it meant him sleeping rough. But as he neared the flat, he saw a band of orange leaking from beneath the curtains in the front room, and he felt a rising sense of relief as he descended the stairs and pressed the bell.

Moments later Mel opened the door and he followed her into the front room. Apart from a light in the hall and the light from the TV, scattershot oranges and blues, the room was in darkness.

"Are you on your own tonight?" Barney broke the silence.

Mel folded herself into an armchair. "I think Mum and John were meeting up in town to see a film or something," she said. Dressed in a loose white T-shirt and a pair of khaki shorts, her tanned feet were pale where the straps of her sandals fit. She picked up the remote and muted the TV, cutting short some nobody's moment of fame.

Barney dumped his jacket on the floor and dropped back onto the sofa. He caught sight of the bruise on the side of Mel's face, large in the light of the TV, and let out a fast shock of air.

"Jesus Christ, what happened?"

Mel lifted a roll-up from a plate on the coffee table and sparked a Bic to its ash, pulled the cigarette back to life. The bruise shifted its shape in the light from the flame.

"Tell me what happened," he said again.

"It's nothing," said Mel, and flapped a dismissive hand in front of her face. "I got mugged, that's all, it's no big deal. . . . I lost the mobile, but I can get another one tomorrow."

"What about the bruise? Did you put up a fight?"

"I was using the phone when he snatched it," said Mel. "I

think he must've caught me with his watch or something."

"It looks like it must've hurt."

"It was more of a shock than anything," said Mel. "You know what it's like in Camden Town, stuff like this happens all the time."

"Yeah, I suppose so," said Barney. "You could've at least told Archie, though. When I went into the record store yesterday, he sounded like he wanted to stick one on me or something, give me the other half of the matching set."

"He's such a jerk," said Mel. "I don't know why I bother, with what he pays me. Besides, what's his problem anyway, no one ever goes in the fucking place, except the drunks from Arlington House, and then only when it's fucking raining." She took a deep pull on the cigarette and then crushed it out on the plate beside her, curling up her feet beneath her. "What're you doing round here, anyway?"

"Oh, you know, the same old shit at home. Luke this, Luke that, Luke blah blah blah."

"Your mum," said Mel, nodding. It had been the same complaint for as long as she had known him.

"She talks to me as if I'm still a child, like I'll be dead in the morning if she doesn't keep an eye on me."

"Her problem is that she still thinks that she can save Luke," said Mel with an air of wisdom beyond her years. "It's as if she's forgotten that he's dead. She needs to take a look out of the window and see that the world's moved on."

"But that's all that she ever does," said Barney, sighing. "Looks out of the window, keeping an eye on all the dealers out there. Hey, maybe she could tell us who pushed that one off the roof last month. You know his folks've put up a reward to find out who it was? Ten thousand quid, I heard."

"Ten grand? Jesus, that'd come in useful," said Mel.

"Enough to get me out of her grasp forever. . . ."

"I'd never have to feel Archie's eyes on my tits again. . . ."

Barney shook his head and looked across at her, grinning.

"You wouldn't make me write a begging letter," said Mel.

"Oh, I don't know," he said, warming to the idea. "If word got around that I'd given you some of the money, who knows what kind of other people it'd bring out of the woodwork. All the friends I never knew I had, the cousins I'd never met before."

"Maybe even Luke'd come back from the dead and demand his slice of the cake," said Mel, laughing.

"Hey, don't laugh," said Barney, his smile oscillating between laughter and frustration. "At least it'd get my mum off my back." He pointed at the pack of tobacco on the coffee table.

"Sure, help yourself," said Mel, and reached across and slid the pack across the table. Her T-shirt stretched tight across her chest, her nipples dark and hard against the white cotton, and Barney felt the air lock in his throat.

It had started to happen more and more of late, this rush of attraction for her, and it left him not a little confused. He knew that there was no law to prevent them from getting it on, but it still filled him with an unassailable sense of guilt, and the thought of telling Mel about his feelings terrified him.

He took some tobacco from the pack and started to roll a cigarette, tried to push these thoughts out of his head.

"Hey, Barney, before you roll that cigarette, I think you'd better stick some of this in it," said Mel, tossing a plastic bag of marijuana into his lap.

Barney took one look at the bag and jumped back in his seat, grinning, his hands snapping up in the air, palms out, as if he had been burned.

"Don't worry," laughed Mel. "I'm not going to tell your mum or anything."

26

Roscoe reached the Pineapple just short of seven. The place was filling up fast, with customers standing either alone at the bar or in little satellite groups. Roscoe bought a bottle of Miller Lite and managed to find a spare table in a back corner of the bar. He pulled out a seat and sat down. His foot felt like an anchor tied to his leg, and so he lifted it and rested it on the crossbar of the seat opposite, took off the pressure. He poured the beer into a glass, took a long drink and looked around.

The Pineapple had catered to a local crowd from as far back as Roscoe could remember, a crowd that stretched from a number of TV faces to the man who ran the flower stall at Kentish Town station. Hidden from the main stretch, it had retained its local flavor despite a number of outside threats. The latest had been from a firm that had wanted to turn the upper floors into smart flats, the bar into a gastropub. The lease had been about to run out on the pub, and the freeholder had wanted to capitalise on its success, but the faces had put their muscle to some use for once and turned the press onto their cause, forcing the freeholder to back down and offer the landlord a fresh lease.

Fifteen minutes later, Roscoe had finished his drink and was wondering what had happened to Dineen. He was just about to head up to the bar for a refill when, across the crowd, he saw Dineen walk through the door. And right behind him, Marnie Stone.

Roscoe felt his heart lift and his breath catch in his throat, but then he remembered the reason he had asked Dineen along in the first place—to get the dirt on Dillon, the man who had run down Karl Burns, and his head clouded with irritation. Dineen should have come alone. He had been a trusted friend for a long time, so no doubt he had his reasons for bringing Marnie along, but he could have at least warned him about it. He thought about skipping out of the back door, but then Dineen spotted him and sketched a hand in the air. Marnie made no sign of having seen him; she just tracked Dineen across the room, her head held low.

Roscoe gritted his teeth and, deciding to ride it out, climbed to his feet.

"Looking good," said Dineen, stepping up close and sticking out his hand.

Marnie pulled up beside him, her hands on her hips. She was wearing a pale blue suit and a black blouse.

"Thanks for coming, Brian," said Roscoe, and shook the other man's hand.

"No problem," said Dineen, and turned a palm towards Marnie. "Frank, this is Marnie Stone, our new DS."

"Marnie," said Roscoe, and offered her a questioning smile. She reflected the smile, and Roscoe thought he detected a touch of embarrassment there, and warmth, as if she was just as surprised as he was to find themselves meeting again like this. He acknowledged the smile and felt his tension ease back a little.

"I was just telling Marnie about the shooting," said Dineen. "Your foot. How long ago was that now?"

"Seven months, three weeks, two days, nine hours, and ten minutes," deadpanned Roscoe. He paused, and then shook his head. "No, I don't know," he said, smiling. "About seven months, I suppose. That sounds about right. Seven months. It seems longer."

"And we're still no nearer to catching the shooter?"

"And you're still no nearer to catching the shooter," returned Roscoe at once, shaking his head.

"That must be hard to deal with, the not knowing," said Marnie, a complicit smile on her lips, and in that smile and in the echo of their conversation from the night before, Roscoe felt a secret world being created, one that included just him and Marnie, and it filled him with an adolescent thrill.

"Well, I'm still waiting on a good night's sleep," said Roscoe, grinning. "But at least it's given me a little insight into how the public must feel when we don't close a case, I suppose." He pointed to his foot. "You mind if I sit down? I've been walking around all day and my foot's hurting like mad."

"No, sure, whatever," said Dineen. "Now, what can I get you both to drink?"

"I'll get these," said Marnie. "What're you both having?"

"Miller Lite, thanks," said Roscoe.

"I'll have a Scotch," said Dineen.

Marnie nodded, then turned and headed for the bar. Roscoe watched her go, the smooth rise and fall of her hips as she stepped around a pile of sports bags on the floor beside a group of red faced men in football shirts and jeans. One of the men took his face out of his beer for a moment and tracked the same motion right up to the bar, then dipped back into his glass.

Dineen pulled out a chair and sat down, scooting himself up to the table.

"So who's the new girlfriend?" said Roscoe, hard and low.

"You mean Marnie? Don't be ridiculous. You know Carol. You think I would ever risk lifting up her stone to see what's underneath? Jesus Christ, life's too short as it is, thanks. No, like I said, Marnie's the new DS. She came on rotation a couple of months back."

"So what's she doing here tonight?" asked Roscoe. "I thought we were going to have a quiet word."

Dineen looked at him from the side, shook his head. "I thought you wanted to know about Sean Dillon."

"Yeah, so?" said Roscoe.

"Yeah, so he's been at KT for about six months now," said Dineen, leaning across the table. "But before that he was over at Kilburn, and Marnie also came to us from Kilburn. Four months after Dillon, but at least she was there around about the same time that he was. I spoke to her earlier because I thought she might know something about him. His street rep, I don't know, something . . ."

Roscoe nodded, appeased, and gestured for him to continue.

Dineen glanced over towards the bar, saw Marnie heading towards them with the drinks. "Anyway, I'll let her tell you."

Roscoe leaned back in his chair, fell silent.

Marnie put the drinks on the table, lifted a glass of red wine to her lips and drank. The wine left a little moustache on her upper lip, and she licked it cat clean. "Cheers," she said, and then took a seat beside Dineen.

"Cheers," said Dineen.

Roscoe poured some beer into his glass, raised it in front of his face in a salute and then took a long drink.

"You wanted to know about Sean Dillon," repeated Dineen.

Roscoe glanced at Marnie, glimpsed the seed of a conspiratorial smile on her lips. "That's right," he said.

"So what's it all about? What's the sudden interest?"

Roscoe shifted in his chair, feeling uncomfortable under the spotlight. He did not want to make a fool of himself in front of Marnie. "The kid who was killed in the accident on Brecknock Road—Karl Burns—his mother's an old friend of mine. She's asked me to take a look into what happened that night."

Dineen kept silent, his features blank.

"She told me that Ian Cahill, the sole witness, withdrew his statement at the last minute," said Roscoe, soft and careful. "And so she asked me to go round and have a word with him, find out what happened. Well, I've spoken to him now, I went round there yesterday afternoon, and he didn't tell me all that much, but I did get the impression that someone had leaned on him." He blinked and broke the spell, took a drink. "She also told me that she thought that Dillon had speeded up as he approached the scene, as if he was aiming for someone in the crowd."

Marnie shook her head and twisted in her seat.

"And you think it was Dillon who warned him off?" said Dineen.

"Who else could it have been? If not Dillon, then someone on his behalf . . ."

"That's quite an accusation," said Dineen, and lifted his glass from the table and took a sip.

"I also talked to someone else who saw what happened—"

"I thought there was just the one witness," said Dineen.

"One that came forward," said Roscoe. "But after I spoke to Cahill, I went around to the Linton Tree and managed to dig up someone else who saw what happened that night. It wasn't too difficult, a couple of brandies, that's all it took. Whatever, the point is I found someone, someone who saw what happened but left the scene before the police started asking questions. The reason being he had to take his son out to the airport, Gatwick."

Dineen looked off across the bar, scratched at the stubble on his chin with a fingernail. "This new witness. He also said that the car was aiming at someone in the crowd?"

"That's what he told me," said Roscoe, picking up the bottle and glass from the table. He poured beer into the glass with studied concentration, then looked over at Marnie and found her watching him, the flicker of quiet intelligence in her pupils, and he felt blood flood his skin.

"So what do we have on Dillon, then?" he managed to get out.

"Nothing concrete," replied Dineen. "But since he's been at KT he's had more than his fair share of street talk."

"How do you mean?" said Roscoe.

"John Francis," said Marnie, looking at Dineen.

"John Francis," echoed Dineen, nodding in agreement.

"I think I heard something about that," said Roscoe.

"Five months ago a man named John Francis was found beaten to a pulp outside a pub in Highgate. From the wounds it looked like it was a baseball bat or something similar. The Boogaloo, up there on the hill near the tube station. You know it?"

"I think I've been there," said Roscoe.

"Francis was a small time crook from Kent, on the coast down there near Folkestone somewhere, Dover. A known associate of two men who were picked up recently trying to smuggle a RIB—that's a Rigid Inflatable Boat to us landlubbers, Frank—trying to smuggle a RIB full of cannabis resin into the country. Apparently, with all the increased security at airports now, ever since September the eleventh, villains are turning to more traditional methods of smuggling drugs. I hear that they're even using the same caves on the coast near Ramsgate that the old pirates used back in the eighteenth century. And it looks as if it's working, too. The Coast Guard reckon there's at least one drop a night on that stretch of coast, and they're so overworked it's like a joke. Anyway, from what this pair told the Coast Guard, all three of them used to work for a firm in London. Up here in Camden Town, so that means Bar Code. Everything was going along just fine, everyone making a load of money, until a few months ago when Francis got greedy. It all started one night when they were out at sea and the Coast

Guard started chasing them. So of course they did what they always did in the circumstances, they tossed their load over the side and wrote it off to bad luck. Anyway, a couple of weeks later, it's just Francis and one of these other guys out at sea, and Francis decides he wants to tell his paymasters that he's been chased by the Coast Guard again. Only this time, he wants to take the stash up to London to sell it himself. He tells the other guy on the boat he'll cut him in for half, but when he gets up to London he just disappears. So of course the other man grasses him out to the chief, and within the hour there's a bounty out for the recovery of the drugs."

"So where does Dillon come into all this?"

"This is where it gets interesting," said Dineen, and took a sip of his scotch. "It was Dillon who found him."

"He was the one who found Francis?" said Roscoe.

"That's right," said Dineen, nodding. "In his statement he said he was just driving past when he saw this fight going on in the street by the side of the pub, and so he stopped to break it up. He said he had no choice but to go through the lights, turn around, and park up first, and so by the time he got back to the pub the attacker had run off and Francis was unconscious."

"And when did all this happen?" said Roscoe.

"Sometime around the end of May, I think," said Dineen.

"A couple of weeks after Karl was killed," said Roscoe, and then took a drink from the glass and glanced around the bar.

"So what happened at the Boogaloo?" said Marnie.

"Well, from what I know of the place, and I drive past there most nights, it gets dark down that side of the pub where the attack took place, and so it'd be difficult if not impossible to make out something going on there from just driving past," said Dineen.

"You think he was there when it happened?" asked Roscoe.

"There were no other witnesses, no one else came out of the

pub and saw what was going on?" asked Marnie.

Dineen shook his head, took another drink.

"He was there when it happened," said Roscoe.

"It looks like that," said Dineen, trying not to go where Roscoe was leading him, despite the evidence.

"And Dillon beat him up," said Roscoe, persistent.

"Well, there were no other witnesses, and it was Dillon who called it in, but I guess that could just mean that someone else did come out of the pub and see him beating up Francis but never came forward. But Dillon wasn't to know that, and so perhaps he thought he had no choice but to call it in."

"What about forensics?" said Marnie.

"Dillon said that he had to roll Francis onto his back to check if he was still alive, so I suppose that would account for the blood on his clothes."

"Clever," said Marnie.

"Where was Francis living at the time?" asked Roscoe, thinking about the cabbie and his fare on Brecknock Road.

"According to his father he was still living in Dover," said Dineen. "But he also said that Francis'd been staying with some friends up in London for a while, a couple of months or so."

"Have you any idea where that might have been?" said Roscoe.

Dineen shook his head, no.

"So the thinking is that he was still up here because he couldn't shift the drugs," said Roscoe.

"I don't know," replied Dineen.

"Dillon might have taken the drugs from Francis," said Roscoe. "Found out where he was and set up a fake meeting."

"I don't know," said Dineen again.

"But it seems certain that Dillon is in Bar Code's pocket," said Roscoe, his tone becoming more aggressive.

"We don't know that for certain," said Dineen, running a

hand across the top of his head. "But there is one other thing that you should know before I go. Right after the accident on Brecknock Road, Mike Hooper—he was the other PC in the car with Dineen, a good copper . . ."

"I know Hooper, a good man," said Roscoe.

"A good copper and a good man," said Dineen. "But right after the accident he walked out of the job. Just took off his uniform, stepped out of the door, and kept right on walking."

"That's not too difficult to understand," said Roscoe. "After going through something like that."

"But Hooper had the job running through him like a stick of rock. From when he was a kid, all he ever wanted to be was a copper. You talk to his wife or his friends—and all his friends were on the force, believe me, he had no time for anything else. It was in his blood. I can't see him just walking out like that . . . Something rotten happened that night," said Dineen, and drained the last of his scotch and put the glass on the table.

"Mike Hooper," said Roscoe. "Do we know where is he now?"

"Last I heard he was patroling the O2 centre, the mall down on Finchley Road, chasing truants and bag ladies out into the rain," said Dineen. "Still, I guess he at least still gets to wear a uniform."

Roscoe looked over at Marnie, hiked his shoulders and turned his palms out in a gesture of disbelief.

"Well, he has got a point," said Marnie, raising a brow.

"Right, that's it for me," said Dineen, pushing back his chair and standing up. "I have to pick up Jeanette from her school concert rehearsals." He turned to Marnie. "You'll let Frank know all about Dillon's time over in Kilburn, right?"

"Sure, no problem," said Marnie.

"Great, thanks," said Dineen. "And Frank . . ."

Roscoe climbed to his feet, and shook his friend's hand.

"Call me," said Dineen. "We'll have a real drink. You can let me know what I've got to look forward to when I retire."

"I don't think you need my help on that score," said Roscoe, laughing. "The word is you retired some time ago, you just haven't got around to leaving the building yet."

Dineen echoed the laugh and clapped him on the shoulder, and then headed off across the room. Roscoe watched him raise a hand to the landlord, and then he was out of the door.

Roscoe turned to Marnie, a little uncomfortable now that Dineen had gone. Since the shooting he had not been able to feel at ease with people he did not know well. That, and the fact that he fancied the pants off her. He sensed that there was some kind of reciprocation, too, but it had been a long time since he had been in that kind of situation and he was out of practise. He put his hands in his pockets to keep them from flapping around. "I'll get another round in and then we can talk about Dillon," he said.

"Just come and sit down for a minute," replied Marnie, and head motioned to his seat. "There's not that much more to tell, but we might as well get it out of the way. There's no point in letting that little shit ruin the whole evening. It won't take long. You can get the drinks in afterwards."

"All right," agreed Roscoe, a little cautiously, and lowered himself into his seat.

Marnie leaned across the table, pushing a loose strand of hair back behind her ear.

Roscoe eased back in his seat, laced his fingers together.

"Sean Dillon is a disgrace to the job," said Marnie. "He shouldn't be allowed to wear the uniform. He just uses it like a stick to beat people, cajole them into doing what he wants."

"You know this for a fact?"

"I've heard the stories, and there're a lot of stories . . ."

"So there's some truth in the rumour that Brian was telling us about?"

"The only reason it's still a rumour is that he hasn't been caught yet," said Marnie, contempt wrapped around her words.

Roscoe smiled at her, feeling his heart rise in his chest. He had wanted to believe Rhiannon on this one, but his instincts told him otherwise, his head holding out over his heart. But now it felt that she had been right all along, and it made him want to wrap it all up and let Rhiannon get on with her life.

"The night that Karl was killed," he said. "Is it possible that Dillon saw someone in the crowd and tried to kill them with his car, and Karl just happened to fall in his path?"

"You spoke to the witnesses . . ." Marnie let the sentence drift.

Roscoe looked off across the bar for a moment, ran it all through his filters, cop and friend and human being, and came up with the same response: "I think that's exactly what happened," he said.

27

Dillon sat in his car watching the front of the house that Stuart Pember shared with Marie Corcoran and their son George. He had been there half an hour, since the end of his shift, smoking cigarettes and sipping from a bottle of scotch, waiting for Marie to take the kid up to bed. There was no sign of Pember, and Dillon knew he would not be back tonight. Some people in leather coats passed in front of the house, and slices of laughter and talk shimmered on the brisk night air. Dillon watched them pass and then tossed the butt of a Silk Cut onto the street and took another pull of scotch to cool his throat. Marie had the curtains open, and he could see her sitting on the sofa with the kid beside her, their faces rapt and flecked in blue TV lights.

Dillon kept on watching, patient as a hawk.

Soon after nine Marie unfolded her arms and pushed herself up from the sofa, her limbs leaden and stubborn. She stretched and said something to the kid, echoing her words with loud hand gestures, and the kid climbed to his feet, and then the two of them left the room. Dillon took a final pull on the bottle, and then capped it and stuffed it under the seat.

Seconds later the landing light went on, and then another light at the back of the house.

Dillon pulled out the bottle back out from under the seat, took another final hit as he waited some more.

Ten minutes later, the second light went off again, and Marie reappeared in the front room. She pulled the curtains, and Dillon caught a glimpse of her midriff and remembered the heat of her thigh earlier that afternoon. It had been some time since he had rattled the bones of a roll, as he liked to call the wives and girlfriends of suspects, and he was looking forward to getting back in the saddle. Just the thought of it made him hard, and he slipped his hand inside his jeans to readjust himself.

He climbed out of the car, locked it, and then headed across the street and rang the bell.

When Marie opened the door, Dillon saw the pain and injustice of the current situation etched on her face, and he knew that he had her in the palm of his hand.

"Hello again, Marie," he said, and the curl of a cruel smile spread across his face.

"He's not here," said Marie, a shake of fear in her throat. "He's not been back here since this afternoon."

"What about the phone, has he tried to call?"

"Mmmm, no," said Marie, shaking her head, keeping it low.

"You tell him I'd be coming back again tonight?" said Dillon, hard and fast, stamping on her brittle lie.

Dull and beaten, Marie looked up into his face. Crimson shame gripped her throat, and she looked close to tears. "In the morning, he wanted me to fetch him . . . He made me promise . . ."

"Where is he at the moment, Marie? In the neighbourhood?"

Marie blinked, holding back the tears. "He's over at a friend's place in Kilburn. In the morning, he wanted me to . . ."

"Whoa," said Dillon, raising the flat of his hand. "Too much information. You want me to have someone pick him up?"

She shook her head, just the once, as if she no longer had the strength to protest further, and then stared at her feet.

"Well then, keep that information locked up," said Dillon.

Marie muttered something inaudible, and her shoulders slumped a little further as if another string had been cut.

The rumble of traffic and the crackle of the TV in the background were the sole sounds on the air.

"Now," said Dillon after a time, "are you going to let me in so that we can talk about how to keep Stuart out of jail?"

A shrunken Marie stepped aside and let him into the house.

Charlie Burns eased away from the lights at the Albany Street junction and headed down Parkway towards Camden Town.

At the bottom of the street he hung a left and turned into Arlington Road. He passed the Mecca bingo hall, and then on his right he saw a group of men gathered around a battered white transit van parked at the end of Inverness Street. A hand painted sign on the side of the van read Free Hot Meals. Most of the men had the stiff limbs and blank stares of alcoholics and came from Arlington House, the huge red brick building at the end of the street. Built to provide accommodation for single working men at the turn of the 1900s, the hostel had long since fallen into a state of disrepair, but it still housed around four hundred men. For the most part Irish, the men had come to London in the sixties and seventies looking for casual work on building sites to support their families back home. Most of the men who made the trip had returned home after a time, but the ones that had remained, the stubborn and the proud, the lost and the damaged, had come to regard the hostel as their home.

With a feral hunger, the men forked food into their mouths from foil containers. In the background, a man with a face so pockmarked it looked like his skin was melting held the container in his hands and stared at its contents as if he had just been told that it was this particular food that was responsible for sustaining a life that had long since ceased to be bearable. Charlie knew just how he felt; such was the direction his own life had been of late. It had been bad enough separating from Rhiannon, her taking Karl out of Brighton and all but out of his life, but ever since Karl's death he felt as if he had been sent to a place from which he could never return. A place without light, without the gradations of sense and emotion that told him that he was still alive, a place without hope, a place without a future.

He pulled up at the end of Arlington Street, across from the new Ice Wharf development, a hotel and designer flats. Through the iron gates he could see Camden Lock market on the far side of the canal, and on the near side to the right, the old lock-keeper's cottage that had now become just another Starbucks.

He shook his head and turned into Jamestown Road.

Camden Town was changing, being developed out of all recognition. Two decades back, when Charlie and his friends had first started mapping out their territories, it had been a ramshackle grid of pubs, workingmen's cafes, secondhand book-shops, independent cinemas, record stores—he remembered seeing Elvis Costello walk out of Rock On in Kentish Town Road once, a stack of old soul records tucked up under his arm right before he cut *Get Happy!!* It had been a cheap area, rough and accepting of the marginalised and the disenfranchised. But all that had started to change in the late eighties when the old stables behind the Lock had been redeveloped, and from then on all kinds of other places had fallen like a stack of loaded dominoes.

"George!"

Dillon heard the name like a bark in his ear, and before he knew what was happening, Marie had pulled up her knees, pushed back his shoulders, and rolled out from beneath him.

He landed on the bed on his side in a knot of limbs, and it took him a moment to pull himself together. He took a couple of quick breaths, blinked, and then just about managed to focus in time to see Marie pull down a nightshirt over her naked but-tocks. Behind her, backlit from the landing light, stood little

George with a look on his face as if he had just seen a ghost.

"Jesus Christ," muttered Dillon under his breath, and ran a hand across his face.

Reaching down to pull up the sheet across his naked skin, he rolled onto his front. But he soon felt an ache start to build in the base of his cock, pressed hard against his stomach like that, and so he rolled back onto his side, raising his knees to hide his nakedness, and the poke in the sheet, from the child.

"Mummy, who's that man in your bed?" said George, pointing, before his mother snatched him up and bundled him out of the room, slamming the door behind her without a word or a look back.

Dillon stared at the closed door for a moment, and then fell onto his back. The ceiling was a map of cracks that led nowhere amid patches of inhospitable terrain. He could hear mother and son out on the landing, confusion in the kid and a spiral of fear and sadness rising in Marie, and in that moment he knew that he had taken this one as far as it would go. Not that it had been much to start with. Marie was scared and not looking at it as a route to something else, so it had been more like rubbing himself against a marble statue, cold and rough. He shook the image out of his head and took hold of his cock, conjured up a picture of Uma Thurman, and finished himself off, shooting his load into a bra that he snatched from the chair beside the bed. He wiped himself on the sheet, and then climbed out of bed and pulled on his clothes.

Ten seconds later he was striding back to his car.

28

It was little more than an hour since Dineen had left, and the Pineapple was packed, the air an emulsion of smoke, alcohol, and words torn loose from conversations. A couple in their thirties had taken two of the spare seats at their table, and from the way in which they sat staring into their drinks with tired eyes, Roscoe reckoned that they were parents of young children, lost and alone out on their own for the night.

"Jenna Barnes is long gone now, but I did manage to track down that friend of hers," said Marnie. "Shona Kilpatrick."

"I don't suppose she happened to point the finger at Rooker," said Roscoe, glancing to the side. He could sense the man leaning into their conversation.

"She hasn't got much time for Rooker, she called him a thug, but she did back up what Jenna told us, and that more or less puts him in the clear. But she also knew Paul Ballard quite well, and she told me something interesting."

"What was that?"

"She told me that a couple of weeks before he died, Ballard had moaned to Rooker about a woman on the Castle Estate who'd been giving him a hard time. I don't know what he wanted Rooker to do about it, but Rooker just laughed in his face and told him to deal with it himself."

"That stuff happens all the time," said Roscoe. "And it's always the older women. I don't know, maybe they think that when they get to a certain age the dealers won't fight back."

"There might be something in it," said Marnie.

"Have you spoken to Lucille Hook? You know she helps run the MAD outfit. It doesn't sound like them, direct confrontations are not quite their style, but she knows pretty much everything that goes on on the Castle Estate."

"I know Lucille," said Marnie. "She was the first person I went to after we heard about the reward, but she just told me that she wouldn't be our senses down on the estate."

"That doesn't sound like Lucille," said Roscoe.

"You're right, but . . ." Marnie shrugged, paused, and then continued. "If someone was hassling Ballard, then it's more than likely they were hassling some of the other dealers, too."

"You want to head over there now?" said Roscoe, sensing the other man at the table eavesdropping on their conversation. It was something that always annoyed him.

"What?"

"You want to head over to the estate right now, see what we can dig up?" He glanced at the man beside him, but the other man had turned his attention to a tall blonde at the bar.

"You're not serious," said Marnie, smiling and arching her back in her seat.

"Friday night," said Roscoe. "It must be one of their busiest times, the traders'll be out there in numbers."

"You know someone we can talk to?"

"You mean like an informant?"

"Yeah, like an informant."

"Not on the Castle Estate," said Roscoe, shaking his head. "Other places around. Unless I've been forgotten, of course."

"Somehow I find that hard to believe," said Marnie, smiling. She pushed back her chair and climbed to her feet. "Come on, let's go to work."

Roscoe smiled to himself as he followed her across the pub and out of the door.

Marnie had left her car around the corner from the Pineapple, and as the pair walked through the dark streets, Roscoe noticed a dried bunch of flowers tied to a gatepost on the corner, another marker on the Murder Mile. He remembered the case, a drunken tourist taking the wrong branch of the Northern Line and then stepping out at Kentish Town to ask for help and getting himself robbed and killed instead.

"So what's the rush," said Marnie. "Are you that keen to get back to work?"

"Something like that," admitted Roscoe, surprising himself. It was the first time since the shooting he had felt like that. He looked off across the street for a second, caught a black cat staring back at him from the top of a wall. "But that bloke was starting to get on my nerves, leaning in and flapping his ears around like that . . ."

"What bloke?" said Marnie, laughing a little.

"The bloke on our table, of course. He was starting to invade our space."

"He was starting to invade our space?" smiled Marnie.

Roscoe shot her a guarded look, not sure if she was taking the piss or not. "That's right," he said, cautious.

"So it was our space, was it? Yours and mine."

"You know what I mean," said Roscoe. "You're out for a walk on the heath one morning, and there's no one else around except for some joker and his mad dog about three feet behind."

"You live alone, Frank?"

"Yeah," said Roscoe, laughing now. "But I don't see what that's got to do with it."

Marnie stepped out into the street and walked around to the far side of a dark Saab, unlocked it. Roscoe pulled up beside the passenger side door, rested his hands on the roof of the car.

"Because I have the same complaint," said Marnie, and ducked inside the car.

Roscoe felt another smile tear at the corners of his mouth as he climbed in beside her.

In the darkness, Kentish Town Road looked like an old tattoo, smudges of forgotten colour on a weathered background. Marnie drove in silence, parking at last on the rim of the Castle Estate opposite the phone booths. The pair sat for a few minutes watching the movements of those across the street.

"Did you hear about that rogue website?" asked Marnie, breaking the silence. "Crack in Camden dot com or something. Webcams and photos of people making deals and injecting their toes, stuff like that."

"Webcams and CCTV," said Roscoe. "The new witnesses."

"What's that?"

"I think I read about it in the *Camden New Journal*," said Roscoe. "Someone who lived across the street from a crack house set it up. To shame the police into action."

"The Castle Estate was one of the three or four places featured on the site," said Marnie.

"I guess he just got sick of waiting for someone to do something about it," said Roscoe.

"But it's like we're King Canute," replied Marnie, tracking a Cherokee Jeep making a purchase. "For every one we put away, there's two more stepping off the train at King's Cross."

The inside of the car had started to steam up, small bubbles of heat were trapped on the glass. Marnie opened the window and the immediate smell of petrol hit her like suffocation. She shut it up tight again at once, cranked up the air conditioning.

"There's three basic kinds of soldier on the booths," said Roscoe, pointing across the street.

"I think I remember all that from basic training," smiled Marnie.

"I'm just trying to see if it's still like I remember it," said Roscoe. "It's been a long time. Bear with me, all right?"

"Go ahead," said Marnie. "I'll be the rookie."

"That's the idea," said Roscoe, offering her a smile. "All right, first up, there's the point man, the maitre d' if you like. See that kid there, the one with his left foot up against the wall, the one with the baseball cap down low . . ."

"I can see him," said Marnie. "The one that looks like his head's on a spring or something."

"That's right," said Roscoe, still smiling. "And that'll be him, the one that'll front all the approaches from the punters: the hookers and the junkies, the derelicts and the kids just out for a good time, the cars that pull up at the kerb. He's the one who'll pull in the orders and take the cash . . ."

"Okay," said Marnie, nodding.

"Then behind him, there's the runners . . ."

"The runners . . ."

"When the front man makes a connection, the runners are the ones that'll go and get the stuff from the float and hand it across to the punter further on up the road," said Roscoe.

"Second stringers," said Marnie, nodding again.

"And then behind the runners are the shelf stackers, the ones responsible for making sure the float is kept topped up."

"So where's the main stock kept?"

"Most of the time it'll be kept in one of the flats on the estate," said Roscoe, tilting his head to face her across the seats. "Some poor fucker'll have been intimidated into letting them use their spare room or something. Other times, people'll get bribed or do it just for the kudos or a touch of product."

"So it moves around, it's never in one place for long . . ."

"It's never in the same place for long," agreed Roscoe.

Marnie thought for a moment. "Okay, so that's the background check done. Now, how does that help us with Ballard?"

"The runners are the lowest cards in this particular deck, and the ones that'll be the easiest to turn. But that means stepping up to the gang, and that's for another time. No, I reckon our best bet is to come at them from behind and aim to corner one of the shelf stackers."

"Sounds like a plan," said Marnie, pursing her lips.

"You see that kid there?" said Roscoe, pointing.

"Where?"

"Back there behind the booths, on the right. . . . He's got a cigarette going. . . . You see the ember? You see him? Looks like he's got a small head, but that's because he's got about four sets of clothes on. Like he feels the seasons a month ahead of most other people. . . . It must be winter in his world."

"Yeah, I can see him," said Marnie, a laugh in her throat.

"This shouldn't take too long," said Roscoe, opening the door and putting a foot out on the asphalt. "Park up on Castle Street and come at him from the north. I'll head around to the front of the estate and come at him from the rear."

"This plan is getting better all the time," said Marnie.

"If I make it too complicated, how's he going to know when it's his time to be caught?"

"You might have a point there," said Marnie.

Three minutes later, Roscoe stepped through the wedge of shadow along one of the buildings on the south side of the estate and pulled up beneath a graffiti tag that read *rain man.* Across a stretch of buckled tarmac he could see the kid in the multiple sets of clothing kicking at the ground. He looked bored and, for the moment, out of the immediate action. Roscoe reckoned that if the kid was spooked he would make a run into the nooks and crannies of the estate rather than out towards the booths and risk the abuse of his peers. He knew that Marnie would think so too. Taking a deep breath, he stepped out onto the tarmac and started walking towards the target. Fifteen me-tres out, he spotted Marnie near the building to his left and made a slight shift in his angle of approach, forcing the kid in her direction. Seconds later the traffic out on the street quieted a little, and Roscoe scuffed his heels on the tarmac to signal his approach. The kid snapped his head around and, on seeing Roscoe, coloured him blue on the spot. He spun on his feet and took off for the far north of the estate, but ten metres on he came to a sharp halt as Marnie stepped out of the darkness and pinned him to the wall with a locked arm to his chest. Roscoe grinned and walked over to the pair in his own good time.

Behind his streetwise façade the kid looked scared, and Roscoe let him dangle for a couple of minutes.

"Right, here's the one time deal," said Roscoe at last, motioning for Marnie to return the kid's heels to the ground. "For the moment we're not interested in what's going on out there at the booths, and it'll keep like that just so long as we get to hear what we want to hear. You understand?"

The kid stared at the ground, nodded his head once.

"You have a name?" said Marnie.

"People call me Herbie," said the kid.

"That's a good name," said Roscoe, and then pointed to his chest. "You warm enough, Herbie?"

The kid looked up, a question on his face.

"Doesn't matter," said Roscoe, slapping the question aside. "You been in the game long, Herbie?"

Herbie shrugged and looked off in the direction of the phone booths. "I suppose . . . I don't remember."

"You don't remember? Go on, have a guess. Your skin's still looking clear. A couple of weeks, a month . . ."

"Since about June, I think."

"So about four months, then," said Roscoe.

"Sounds about right," agreed Herbie.

"That's long enough for us," said Roscoe, accepting a nod from Marnie. "You remember a kid called Paul Ballard? Used to hang around the booths."

"The one who fell off the roof?"

Roscoe and Marnie traded glances.

"That's the one," said Marnie. "You remember him?"

"Yeah. I remember him," said Herbie.

"You knew him well?"

"I seen him around. You know how it is."

"You know who was causing him grief?"

Herbie looked confused, that crease in his forehead again.

"Someone was giving him a hard time," said Roscoe. "We think that it was someone from the Castle Estate, one of the residents."

"The residents are on our backs all the time," said Herbie, rolling his shoulders as if to show them how he managed to shrug them off.

"You'll have to be a bit more specific than that," said Marnie.

Herbie thought about it for a moment. "I don't know for sure, but there's this kid who lives in the same building that Ballard fell from. His mum's out here all the time raging at someone or other. I don't think she picks on one person in particular. But it could be that Ballard felt it more than most."

"What did she have to rage about?"

"You want me to be specific again?"

"Be specific again, Herbie," said Roscoe.

"I think she wanted people to stop offering her kid and his friends drugs and shit," said Herbie.

"You ever offer him drugs, Herbie?" said Roscoe.

Herbie shook his head, looked off towards the booths again.

"You want to tell me this kid's name?"

"Name's Barney," said Herbie. "Like the dinosaur."

"You know his other name, too?"

"Price, I think," said Herbie. "Barney Price. Yeah, that sounds right. Barney Price."

"All right, thanks, Herbie," said Roscoe. "You can go now,

but you better stay away from those booths tonight, all right?"

Herbie shot him a look like thunder, then shuffled off in the opposite direction to the booths.

Roscoe watched him go and then turned to Marnie. "Think he's telling us the truth?"

"No reason for him not to," replied Marnie.

"For these kids, lying to the police is their first language," said Roscoe.

"Come on, I'll get the drinks in," said Marnie, laughing.

Roscoe laughed too and fell into step beside her, and the pair walked back towards Castle Street. Seconds later Marnie glanced back just in time to see Herbie disappear around the corner. His shoulders were slumped and she knew that this was because he felt ashamed that in four months he had not learned enough street smarts to spot Roscoe and herself coming up on him like that and then to keep his mouth shut. Kid was no more than fifteen and she wondered what had made him nail his pirate colours to the mast at such a tender age.

The blast and counterblast of stereos and TV sets echoed from open windows on all four sides of the Castle Estate, and Roscoe had the sensation that he was walking through a Roman amphitheatre with the crowd chanting for their blood. But he felt good walking beside Marnie, his heart up from being back in the game, and he chanced a look across at her face to take in her warm profile.

Just then Marnie snapped her hands to her face and fell to her knees in a tumble of limbs. "Ah, fuck," she cried out.

Roscoe froze on the spot, his heart ricochet around in his chest like a pinball.

"Jesus Christ," cried Marnie, blood leaking through her fingers and stringing around her arms. "The fuck was that?"

Roscoe dropped to his back foot and scanned the balconies, all the sounds of the night crushed together in his head. Seeing no motion up high, he jumped across to Marnie and pulled her into the nearest shadow. He checked that she was all right for the moment, then glanced out to check the scene once more. There were still no shifting shapes up on the balconies, or in the hidden corners of the estate, so he turned back to Marnie and lifted her hands free from her face. Streaks of blood lacquered her skin and her hair. The blood seemed to be coming from a wound in her left brow. Roscoe peered at it for a moment, tilting his head and squinting in the darkness. He wiped at the edge of the wound with his thumb. She pulled her head back from him, then let him close in again. "Well, considering the amount of blood, it doesn't look too bad," he said at last, and wiped some more blood clear.

"Jesus, what the fuck happened?" said Marnie, blinking back tears of shock and frustration. Some blood had run into her mouth and she spat it out on the ground.

"Someone must've been throwing stuff at us," said Roscoe.

"I don't see anyone else bleeding around here," she said, blood on her teeth. There was a sparkle of amusement in her pupils, light in the darkness.

"It must've been one of Herbie's crew," said Roscoe.

"You're not going to chase them," said Marnie.

"There's no one out there," said Roscoe, looking around. "They've all disappeared."

"Let's get out of here, then," said Marnie.

29

"Place is still dark," said Barney.

"Weekends, John likes to keep 'em in the pub until chucking out time," said Mel, the words slopping out of her mouth.

It felt strange to hear Mel refer to his father by his first name.

The pair had spent a good couple of hours sitting on a bench overlooking the North Circular, sharing a few joints, staring out at the monotonous rush of traffic that sped past, and talking about the curse of blood relations. The bottles of lemon Hooch that Mel had sprung for at the off-licence had flattened her head out but she still felt high. "It'll be after midnight before we hear from them again, and then it'll be Mum singing one of those songs from the decade that music forgot."

"You mean the seventies," said Barney.

"Fuck no, I'm talking about the eighties," shrieked Mel.

"That's what I meant," said Barney, although he had no idea of the difference between the two. Since Luke had died there had been precious little music around the flat, whatever the decade.

"You still need to be schooled in all that kind of shit," laughed Mel. "If there's one thing that working in Shake has taught me, it's how to spot the real from the fake."

"You mind if I stop over tonight?" said Barney, his thoughts turning to home and the long trip he would have to make.

"It's your place as much as mine," replied Mel.

"Yeah, I suppose it is," said Barney, and felt an unusual sense of warmth flood his heart.

"That's the great thing about being middle class and coming from a broken home," said Mel. "You've always got an escape route when the current domestic situation looks like turning to shit."

"Tell me about it," agreed Barney.

Back at the flat he followed her into the kitchen.

Mel reached into the cupboard beneath the sink and took out two cans of Heineken. "This is where John keeps his beer," she said, handing him one of the cans. Froth bubbled out of her own can as she popped it open, and she pressed her lips to the opening in a burlesque imitation of a kiss.

"Let's go and see what's on TV," she said, licking her lips.

Barney snatched a large bag of tortilla chips from the cupboard and followed her into her bedroom.

Kicking off her boots, Mel stretched out on the bed and propped up her head on a pile of cushions. She hit the remote and the TV came on and flashed blue in the corner, some late night game show where people could win cash for dating the ugliest people in the audience. Barney had seen it before and had no time for the knuckleheaded jokes that had the audience in squeals, but he reckoned that with the alcohol and dope in his bloodstream it might at least raise a smile. He tossed the chips across to Mel and looked around for somewhere to sit. She slapped a hand on the bed and so he tugged off his trainers and climbed up beside her. The bed sagged a little in the middle and she fell towards him. She rested her head on his shoulder and made herself comfortable. She opened the bag of chips and stuffed a handful into her mouth, and then handed the bag back to him.

The pair sat and watched TV for a time, drinking beer and munching tortilla chips. But Barney soon became bored and started to look around the room. He had never been in her bedroom before. The walls were covered in posters and photographs, and stacks of CDs and DVDs were spread around like little rickety staircases. On the wall behind the bedside cabinet there were a couple of postcards of beach huts. One of them was of a long line of pastel huts in the bright summer sunshine, but the other one looked far more interesting, a single hut in darker hues, and he pulled it from the wall for a closer look. The blue and white paint on the hut had started to peel in places, and some of the timber boards were twisted at the ends, but there was something almost serene about the structure, a weathered calmness in the face of the storm curling up out of the sea, that reminded him of an old man sitting in a deck chair as his grandchildren splashed in the surf.

He started to lean back into the cushions, but Mel had rolled into his space and he almost fell on top of her. Sticking out his hand to stop himself from falling, it slid across her bare stomach before catching on the bed. Her skin felt hot and sensual, and the brief contact electrified him and he felt himself getting hard. But Mel seemed not to have noticed in the confusion and so he put a hand on her shoulder and pushed her back onto the other side of the bed.

The rocking motion seemed to rouse her a little, and she blinked and looked up at him with a curious squint.

"Where is this place?" He held up the postcard.

"Place called Deal, down in Kent," said Mel, glancing at the card. "It's been dead since about 1950, but that's cool."

"You've been there," he said, desperate to get rid of his erection. He tried to think of the cold sea curled around his cock and balls, his cock back in its threadbare nest.

Mel glanced across at the postcard again and lifted a shoulder, pursed her lips. "Last summer," she said. "We all went down there for a weekend of rain and fish and chips."

"It looks nice," he rasped.

"It was much better than I thought it would be," said Mel, reaching for the postcard. Her forearm brushed across his lap and she felt the bump in the front of his jeans.

Barney slapped his hands into his lap.

In what seemed to be slow motion, Mel looked up at him with a wicked smile on her lips. "Hello, what's going on down here, then?" she said, shuffling onto her side and resting her chin in the cup of her hand. She rested her other hand on his thigh.

Barney tried to speak but his mouth felt parched, and the words remained stuck to his tongue. He tried to lift his feet from the bed and leave, but his feet had turned to lead.

"I think I think I'd better be going . . ."

Mel ignored him and stroked the inside of his thighs and the material around his groin, his hands still in his lap. Her mouth fell open a fraction and he saw her teeth sparkle in the blue TV glow of the room. Lifting his hands onto his stomach one at a time, she slowly unfastened his jeans, slipped her hand inside his pants, and took hold of his cock. Grinning, there was a mischief in her pupils that he had not seen before, and she started to stroke him in a loose kind of hold.

Seconds later he felt a rumble start deep in his balls, the base of his cock. The rumble built into a crescendo of heat and lust, and then his skin prickled and he shot his load across the back of her hand in a moment that he could not control.

Mel continued to stare into his eyes until he returned the look, and a fat smile broke across his face.

"I bet that feels better," she said, then rolled off the bed and disappeared into the bathroom. He heard a tap running and the flush of the toilet, and then she returned a moment later and handed him a wad of toilet paper. She picked up the can of Heineken from the bedside cabinet and took a long drink, and then a handful of tortilla chip crumbs from the last of the bag.

Feeling a curious state of tired satisfaction descend upon him, Barney wiped himself clean. He had jacked off before, sure, but this was different, and it somehow changed the feelings he had for Mel. He leaned across the bed and kissed her on the cheek, an act that surprised him as much as it did Mel.

30

Roscoe dabbed at the cut on the side of Marnie's forehead with a piece of material torn from an old Uncle Tupelo T-shirt and soaked, in the absence of antiseptic, in scotch. He had also fetched her a tumbler of scotch and ice. She was now on her second. Flecks of blood were scattered among the freckles on her face, the colours like autumn leaves spread across a white sheet that had blown free from a clothes line. He had put a Chuck Prophet CD on the stereo, *No Other Love,* and the title track came from the speakers, Chuck at his most laid-back and seductive.

"It looks like it might leave a little scar," said Roscoe.

"That's all right," said Marnie. She raised a tender hand to her head and touched the bruised skin around the cut, felt the hot touch of blood. "What kind of scar does it look like?"

"You mean there's more than one kind of scar?" said Roscoe.

"The shape, I mean," said Marnie, a little flustered. "I meant what sort of shape will it be."

"You want to know what shape the scar will be?"

"Tell me what you think it'll look like," said Marnie.

On his knees, Roscoe shuffled closer and peered at the cut in the centre of the bruise. He tried to wipe free more of the dried blood without reopening the wound. "It looks like. . . . I don't know what it looks like. . . . A crescent moon, perhaps."

"A crescent moon. Mmmm, that's not too bad, I suppose."

"Not too bad? You mean you'd prefer something else? You

want me to go and fetch the kitchen knife, work on it some more?"

"No, that's all right," said Marnie, laughing. "A crescent moon's quite romantic, don't you think? Sexy."

"You're not one of those people who thinks scars are sexy, are you?"

"The skin remembers what the mind forgets," said Marnie.

Roscoe lifted his glass from the coffee table and took a mouthful of scotch, thought for a moment. "Well, I suppose some of them can be quite sensual . . ."

"Sure, just some of them," agreed Marnie. "Not those from a Caesarian, or a heart operation, or anything like that of course. But the right scar in the right place can be beautiful, romantic. The minor blemish that heightens the true picture."

"I can see the attraction," said Roscoe, leaning back on his heels to admire his handiwork. But almost at once he felt the tension start to build in his damaged tendon, so he shifted his feet around to the side and sat on the floor. "You have a scar worth talking about, or will this one be the first?"

"There's one or two," said Marnie, smiling.

"I've been in a couple of battles in my time, too . . ."

"Let's have a look, then," said Marnie.

Roscoe hesitated for a moment, scanning her face, and then caught the spark of humour in her pupils. Encouraged, he rolled onto his back and pulled off his shoes and socks. Then he raised his left foot in the air, smiling, and rested it in her lap. Marnie leaned forward and ran her fingers across the thick cord of hard skin that snaked around his ankle. Roscoe felt her soft touch seep through his skin and into his blood, heading for his groin. "That's one great scar," admitted Marnie, her fingers tracing the area around the scar, soft and ticklish.

"Your turn," said Roscoe, pulling his foot back onto the carpet.

Without pause, Marnie sat up straight and unbuttoned the top three buttons of her blouse. She turned her head to the side and pushed the blouse off her shoulder, then hooked a finger under the red bra strap and pushed that off her shoulder too. Roscoe saw more freckles on her shoulder, and her skin seemed to radiate a singular heat that he could feel on his face. And then where the collarbone faded into the muscle of her shoulder, he saw a thin blade of rucked white skin about an inch long.

"That doesn't look too bad," said Roscoe.

"I got it falling out of a tree when I was about eight," said Marnie.

Roscoe tilted his head to the side.

"You don't think it looks sexy?"

Roscoe shook his head, no.

"Yeah, you're right," agreed Marnie. "Too rough and tumble, too childish."

She left the blouse undone as she leaned forward, rested her arms on her knees. "Your turn again."

Roscoe took a deep breath and pulled in his stomach, then tugged the hem of his polo shirt free of his chinos and raised it to his chest. He held it under his chin and pointed to a small circular scar a couple of inches to the left of his sternum.

"I got this in a fight outside a pub in Camden Town back in seventy-eight," he said. "The leather jacket I was wearing stopped most of the blade, otherwise I wouldn't be here to-night."

"That's more like it," said Marnie, her pupils darkening.

Roscoe looked at her again, his gaze jumping from her shoulder to her face and back again like a frog in heat.

Marnie caught his look and held it for a moment, the tumble of alcohol and adrenaline in her blood freeing up her true senses, and then she unbuttoned the rest of her blouse. Roscoe felt himself becoming hard, the firm contours of her breasts pulling his concentration into erotic focus. She pulled aside the left side of her blouse and ran the tip of her forefinger around a small jagged scar on her stomach. "I got this from helping a woman get free of her brute of a husband. She was drunk and tried to hit him with her high heel shoe but caught me instead, punctured the skin."

She lifted her head and offered him a dreamlike smile.

Roscoe returned her smile, adrift on his senses.

"So that's it then," said Marnie after a couple of loose beats. "There's nothing more to see, there're no more scars."

There were other scars, but with his mind fogged from heat and desire Roscoe found it difficult to concentrate. He blinked and tried to break contact, blinked once more and that seemed to do the trick. Climbing to his feet, he started to unbuckle his belt, snapping loose the button and sliding his chinos across his hips. He turned at right angles to Marnie and pushed down the top of his shorts. "I don't know if I should tell you about this," he said. "This is from back before I joined the force as well. I think you can tell that I was a bit of a hothead back then."

"Your secret's safe with me," said Marnie, looking at the faint scratches that ran across his hip like lines of cocaine.

"I was pushed out of a moving car on the North Circular—"

"Jesus Christ, what happened?"

"That's for another time," said Roscoe.

"You know," said Marnie, her smile lighting up the room and dimming the lights at the same time. "I think I've got one just like that. Nothing as traumatic as being pushed from a speeding car, but still." She pushed herself out of the chair and climbed to her feet, then unfastened her trousers and let them fall to the floor in one quick motion. She turned to the side a fraction and tilted her left hip up towards him, then, slipping her fingers inside her panties, she slid them down over her buttocks and held them there. Roscoe saw at once the pair of puncture marks on the lower left side, a dog bite he supposed, but his full attention roamed the sweet roll of her hips and thighs, the triangular silhouette beneath her matching panties.

"I think I can see it," said Roscoe, taking a step closer and resting his hand on her hip. He ran it across the scar and then leaned in and kissed her. Marnie put her hands on his biceps and kissed him back. Roscoe hooked his thumbs inside the waistband of her panties and twisted. Marnie felt his hardness on her stomach. She let out a muffled groan and pulled him tighter.

Just then there came a loud knocking at the door.

"What the fuck," said Roscoe, pulling back.

"Come on, let me in," came from behind the door.

The moment gone, Marnie felt naked all of a sudden and folded her arms across her chest.

"It sounds like Charlie," said Roscoe. "You know—Karl's father."

"Open the fucking door, Frank."

"You better let him in," said Marnie, stepping back from him and rubbing her hands up and down her arms, feeling a chill on her skin. "He sounds all steamed up about something."

"It's not *his* head of steam I'm worried about," said Roscoe, grinning. He hesitated for a moment, torn between old bonds and fresh desires, and then came to a decision and pulled up his chinos and belted them tight. He looked at Marnie and touched the scar on her stomach. "And just when I was starting to appreciate a new natural art form too . . ."

"That's the good thing about a scar," said Marnie, smiling. "It'll still be there in the morning. Now go and let him in before he breaks down the door and I have to arrest him."

Roscoe kissed her on the forehead and then watched her gather her things and retreat into the bathroom. He tucked his polo shirt into his chinos and headed for the front door.

The knocking started up once more, and as Roscoe opened the door, he found Charlie Burns on his doorstep with his right fist raised in the air. His mouth was slack, his face pale and slick with perspiration, as if he had just seen a ghost.

"I've just been around to see Rhee," said Charlie, pushing past Roscoe and stalking into the flat. "What's all this about Dillon killing Karl on purpose?"

Roscoe glanced out onto the landing, and then closed the door and trailed Charlie into the front room.

"Is it true what she's been telling me?" said Charlie, picking up a glass of scotch from the coffee table and taking a long drink. "I thought it was supposed to've been an accident."

The Chuck Prophet CD had reached the final track, *Old Friends.*

"Tell me what's going on, Frank."

Roscoe crossed the room and picked up the other glass of scotch from the coffee table. He took a long drink and held the glass in front of his mouth. It took Charlie a moment to pick up on the detail, but then he shook his head and held out the glass in front of him and looked at it as if he had just drunk a magic potion. He opened his mouth to speak, but before he could do so, Marnie stepped out of the bathroom.

"Hello," said Marnie. She had tidied herself up and looked as if the idea of seducing Frank Roscoe had never crossed her mind, but for the crimson rush of blood at her throat.

"This is Marnie," said Roscoe.

Charlie tilted his head to the side and smiled. "One of the Hitchcock blondes," he said, and offered her the glass.

"No thanks," said Marnie. "You keep it. I better be going."

"Thanks," said Roscoe, and kissed her on the cheek.

"Call me tomorrow," said Marnie, and then she was gone.

The two men stood in silence for a short time, and then Charlie repeated his request: "Tell me what's going on, Frank."

31

"John, it's Sarah. I don't suppose the Balloon Kid's out there, is he?" Drunk, sentimental, and full of self-remorse, she used his nickname from when he was a babe in arms, a fat kid with fat limbs that looked like long pink balloons tied together.

"I think I heard him in with Mel earlier on tonight."

"And he's still there?"

"Yeah, I think so."

"You're not sure? You mind checking for me?"

"You two had another fight or something?"

"He's going through a bit of a rough time at the moment . . ."

"He's still a kid, Sarah. You're too hard on him."

"What's that supposed to mean?"

"Oh. You know . . . We talk."

"You talk," echoed Sarah, a snap of offence in her tongue.

"Look, it's late," said John, sighing and shaking his head. He could almost smell the alcohol on her breath down the line. "I don't want to get into this right now."

"You don't know what it's like to be me," said Sarah. "I do the best that I can . . ."

"You've got to stop putting him in nappies, Sarah. Let him grow up and make his own mistakes, make his own path in life."

He took a pull on the stub of a joint in his hand, felt the burn of the smoke on his lips through the cardboard and sucked in air through his clenched teeth to cool them. He crushed the roach in his fingers, and rolled it into a ball.

"You're stoned again," said Sarah, hurt and confusion spiking her blood.

"What's that," said John, licking at the smudges of ash on his fingers and then rubbing his fingers together.

"You've been smoking again," repeated Sarah.

"Sarah, it's no big deal," said John. "You know how it is. You get home from the pub, there's no more drink in the fridge. . . . And since when did you turn from red to blue?"

"This is not about politics, this is about our son."

"It's all about politics," said John.

"For fuck's sake," snapped Sarah, a hard ball of sadness in her throat. "After all that's happened, I would've thought. . . . Jesus, sometimes I think you want him to end up like Luke."

"Don't be so melodramatic. It was just a couple of joints."

"It was seeing us smoke just a couple of joints every night of his life that set Luke off on his downward path."

"It was an accident, Sarah."

"I know it was an accident, I'm not stupid," said Sarah. "But what was he doing taking heroin in the first place? We opened the gate and showed him the path."

"That's ridiculous," said John, anger and frustration thrumming in his throat. "Right from the start Luke had a slow bullet in his head. You know that. Boundaries were for other people. There was nothing that was going to stop him from self-destructing. The number of near death scrapes he had as a kid I'm surprised he lasted as long as he did. There was nothing we could do about it. Let it go, Sarah, for God's sake, let it go."

"But it's the truth," said Sarah, feeling her lashes locking around a hot birth of tears and holding them close, as if allowing them to fall would mean the release of the pain that she needed to feel each second of her life. "I can't let it go."

Charlie sat in mute confusion as Roscoe told him all that he had learned about the accident in which his son had been killed. He told him about the witness who had seen Dillon speed up as he had approached the scene, and the cabbie and his fare standing out in the middle of the road just before the accident happened.

And now Roscoe could see him processing the information as he paced the front room. He had calmed a little since his arrival, but his pupils were still as wide as old pennies.

Distracted, he continued pacing and drinking from a bottle of Miller Lite. At last he pulled up in front of the bookcase. He lifted out one of the books and started to flip through its pages. "I've been looking for this all over," he said.

"Let me see," said Roscoe, homing back in on the talk.

Charlie held up the book for Roscoe to see: George Binette's *The Last Night London Burned,* a slim memoir of the last gig Joe Strummer had performed in London, a benefit at Acton Town Hall for the striking firefighters in the autumn of 2002. "I remember reading about it at the time," he said. "Mick Jones coming out on stage at the end of the encore, surprising Joe and then rocking through a couple of Clash numbers with the Mescaleros."

"Kept the faith right up until the end," said Roscoe. "Ever since the late eighties people'd been offering them millions to reform, but in the end what got them back together on stage was a benefit for a bunch of striking workers and their families."

"Did it for free, too," said Charlie.

"The desk sergeant at Kentish Town, a man called Dobie, he was a rookie PC back when Topper and Paul Simonon were brought into the station after that pigeon shooting incident."

"Jesus, that's going back a long time."

"Spring of seventy-eight," said Roscoe.

"That was around the same time that we used to bunk off school and hang around their rehearsal studio near the Lock."

"Rehearsal rehearsals," Roscoe smiled at the memory.

"That's the place," said Charlie. "Back then we used to see them around the cafés and pubs all the time."

"I heard talk of putting up one of those heritage plaques on 101 Walterton Road over in Maida Vale, the place where it all started," said Roscoe. The Walterton Road squat had been the place where Strummer had got his first band together, The 101ers.

"Better there than in Camden Lock," said Charlie. "I just came past there tonight. It's getting worse each time. The place where the rehearsal studio was is just another bunch of stalls now, selling the same old trash as the rest of the market."

"I guess it must be what the people want," said Roscoe.

Charlie put the book back on the shelf, then turned and faced Roscoe. There were tears spangling his cheeks. "You know, ever since Karl died, I don't feel like it was me back then anymore," he said. "It's like I've inherited someone else's memories or something. I don't recognise myself in them any-more."

"When a man loses a child, he loses so much more than just the child. He loses his self-respect, his pride, and all kinds of other stuff. That's how I feel, like it's all been taken from me. Not just Karl but all of the other stuff, the past and all the memories of what it was like when I was a kid and a teenager."

"It must be difficult," said Roscoe.

"I'm going to get that fucker," said Charlie, grief filling his throat and strangling the words. His tears steamed on his cheeks.

"We still don't know for sure that it wasn't an accident," said Roscoe. "We need to talk to Dillon first, get it straight."

"I don't need to know if it was an accident," said Charlie. "It doesn't matter, all I know is that he killed Karl."

"Think about Rhiannon," said Roscoe. "Think about what she's going through. You don't want to cause her more pain."

"But this is going to help Rhiannon," said Charlie, rubbing at the tear streaks on his cheeks with the back of his hand.

Roscoe climbed from his seat and walked over to Charlie, put his hands on his shoulders. "What about Karl? You think he'd want to see his father like this? He was a good kid, a solid kid, and he cast a long shadow. You're going to be walking in that shadow for a long time. It might be cold and it might be dark, but it belongs to Karl and there's nothing that's going to change that."

"I hadn't seen him for three weeks when he died," said Charlie.

"I'm sure he won't have forgotten about his old man in three weeks," said Roscoe, and offered him a comforting smile.

"No, but it scares the shit out of me that in the future I might forget what he was like," admitted Charlie.

32

Saturday, 23 October

Roscoe stirred in his sleep as the first sounds from the asthmatic motorbike outside his bedroom window split the morning air. Time after time the engine coughed and spluttered as it failed to spark, its rider becoming more and more frenetic with each kick of the pedal. The sounds continued to seep into his head, aggressive and insistent, until at last Roscoe came awake just as the bike shrugged out of its cold morning blanket and sped off in the direction of Tufnell Park. With a tired resignation, he listened as the roar of the bike faded into the distance, then rolled onto his back, blinking at the low autumn sun that sliced in through the blinds.

His thoughts soon turned to the night before, and so he lifted his head from the pillow to listen out for signs of Charlie—some music on the stereo, perhaps, the radio, or even the rattle of him making coffee in the kitchen—but behind the ambient street noise, the flat seemed to be in silence. Perhaps he was still asleep on the sofa. After all, it had been a long night of the soul. Roscoe glanced across at the clock and checked the time: quarter past eight. He decided he could leave it a bit longer, and slumped back on the bed and closed his eyes.

Within seconds he had drifted back into sleep, and his head soon filled with fractured dreams of Marnie. Awake, he might just have been prepared to admit to himself that she was interested in him, and that in turn he found her attractive, but in sleep his subconscious mind told him that she had touched him in a manner that he had not been touched in a long time. There was something about her, a rawness of spirit, perhaps, or the casual belief in the power of her own instincts, that made him feel like he could at last shed the hard shell that had formed around him since the shooting and made him immune to all the simple pleasures that life offered. Now at last he might be able to free himself up to new opportunities.

Roscoe woke again just before nine and headed straight into the bathroom. He took a leak and washed his hands, cleaned his teeth, and rubbed cold water into his face, then walked through into the front room. The blinds were open and bars of mute golden light filled the air. Red lights blinked at him from both the stereo and the ansaphone. The blankets he had lent Charlie the night before were folded and stacked in the middle of the sofa. Roscoe scanned the rest of the room, but there were no strange shoes or items of clothing or other signs to indicate that Charlie was still around. He poked his head into the kitchen, but there was no fresh sign of him there either, just the debris from the night before, mugs and bottles and glasses.

Then he remembered Charlie talking about wanting to make Dillon pay for what he had done, and he felt his skin prickle. He had no doubt that Charlie had meant what he had said, but he had also known Charlie a long time, and in all that time he had never known him to be violent. Sure, he had lost his temper from time to time; it was all a part of growing up and testing your boundaries, marking your territory, but he had never knowingly set out to hurt someone. Then again, he had never lost his son before. Roscoe shook his head and let out a great sigh. He hoped to God that Charlie was not going to be stupid about this.

He walked back into the front room and picked up the phone, punched in the number he had for Rhiannon.

"Hello," came the response, tired and hesitant.

"Hi, Rhee, it's Frank," said Roscoe.

"Hi, Frank, how's it going?" said Rhiannon.

"Not too bad," said Roscoe. "Yourself?"

"Oh, you know," said Rhiannon. "One day at a time."

"Yeah, it must be difficult," said Roscoe, feeling there should be more that he could offer.

"Well, they do tell me that it gets easier with time," said Rhiannon, but there was no real belief in her words.

"I don't suppose it can get much harder," said Roscoe.

"No, but then again I'm still waiting for the shock to wear off," said Rhiannon. "God knows what it'll feel like then, when reality hits. Anyway, have you got some news on Dillon for me?"

"Well, there are a couple of things, but I need to check them out first," said Roscoe. "Maybe tomorrow."

"Tomorrow," agreed Rhiannon. "But you'll let me know if you hear anything in the meantime."

"Yeah, sure," agreed Roscoe.

"So if you're not calling me about Dillon, you must be calling me about Charlie," said Rhiannon, reading his thoughts. "He said he was going to your place."

"You haven't seen him this morning, have you? We were talking until late last night, but when I woke up just now there was no sign of him."

"Sorry, no. I haven't seen him since he left here last night. That must have been about nine, nine fifteen . . ."

"And he hasn't been back this morning?"

"What's going on, Frank? What's happened?"

"I'm sure it's nothing to worry about."

"But he slept over there last night?"

"Yeah, he crashed on the sofa."

"And he's not there now?"

"Like I said, he must've left before I woke up."

"So what happened last night?"

"Nothing, Rhee. We were just talking."

"Talking about what, Frank? Something must've happened, something must've upset him. What were you talking about?"

Roscoe took a deep breath. He looked out the window, gathering his thoughts. In the front garden there were two birds fighting over the last of the breadcrumbs on a saucer that his downstairs neighbours kept filled. He wished he had never called Rhiannon now; he might have known he would just upset her. It was a mistake he would not have made if he had still been working. "Charlie was making noises about going after Dillon," he said, attempting to cushion his words.

After a moment Roscoe heard Rhiannon's breathing become leaden with sorrow and weariness.

"It was just the grief talking," Roscoe assured her.

"Can you find him, Frank?"

"I don't know," said Roscoe. "Maybe he just popped out to get some cigarettes or something, and I'm worrying you about nothing. I shouldn't have called you, Rhee. You've got enough to worry about. But I'll get Charlie to call you just as soon as he gets back, or I'll call you. One of us'll call you, okay?"

"Thanks," whispered Rhiannon, and the line went dead.

Roscoe hung up and walked into the kitchen. He touched the back of his hand to the kettle and felt warmth. It had been at least a couple of hours since it had boiled. Time enough for Roscoe to know that Charlie had not just popped out to pick up some cigarettes.

As the sun angled around the houses on the far side of the street, a pale beam fell across Barney's face and he squinted and came awake. Mel was spooned up close at his back and he could feel her soft sleeping breath on his shoulder. She had fallen into a deep sleep almost as soon as she had turned out the lights, but throughout the night he had not been able to sleep for much more than a couple of minutes at a time. Full of the tastes of alcohol and marijuana and the thrill of her touch, his head had jumped to an adolescent beat and all kinds of romantic blueprints for a shared future together had presented themselves to him on the blank screen of night. In all of them the details had been obscure, but he had no doubt that when the time came the right plan would step up and make itself clear.

From down the hall in the kitchen he heard the radio station that his father liked to listen to on weekend mornings and the hoarse morning-after tones of his father himself as he rustled up some breakfast and talked back to the radio.

He heard the toilet flush, and worried that Dee, Mel's mom, might poke her head into the room to check on Mel, he tried to sink deeper into the bed, but Mel was anchored fast to the mattress and he found himself stranded with his head and shoulders high on the pillow. Instead, he held his breath and hoped that Dee would walk straight past the room, but when he heard her grab hold of the door handle, a spasm of surprise ran through him and he jerked back into Mel, knocking her out of sleep. She let out a little groan and then rolled onto her back, making a strange sound and starting to stretch out her arms. Barney shuffled to the edge of the mattress to offer her a little more space, and just at that moment Dee opened the door and walked into the room.

She took a couple of short steps across the carpet, and when she caught sight of the two heads on the pillow she stopped dead in her tracks. Her mouth fell open and her pupils went wide. She looked around the room, taking in the clothes scattered on the floor, the naked shoulders in the bed. "Don't tell me this is what I think it is," she said at last, her hands reaching out for balance, finding space and falling back again to her sides.

Barney kept dumb and turned his face further into the pillow, pulling the sheet up tight across his bare shoulder.

"What's with all the volume?" said Mel, still adrift on sleep.

"What the hell's been going on?"

Mel shuffled around on the mattress for a short time, then pulled herself up into a sitting position. Her hair looked to have been tied in knots, and her breasts were pink from the heat of sleep. She rubbed at her face and then pulled the sheet up across her chest. "It was late," she said, shaking her head as if that should have been enough.

"I don't want to know what time it was," replied Dee, anger and disbelief rising in her throat. She folded her arms across her chest, feeling almost naked herself in just a long T-shirt. "I just want to know what's been going on here."

Mel kept quiet for a second, looking off across the room to where she had left the empties from the night before. The sight and smell of the dried out bottles and cans ignited her hangover, and she reached up and stretched a thumb and forefinger across her forehead and pinched her skull to help ease the pain.

"I don't understand what the problem is," she said, blinking in the light. "It was getting too late for him to go home, so we thought he might as well stop over. I don't see what all the fuss is about. It's just as much his home as it is mine."

"That's not the point," snapped Dee. "The point is. . . . Jesus, Mel, if you can't see what the problem is, then it's probably worse than what I first thought it was. You're only fifteen, for Christ's sake, you're too young to be. . . . And Barney, Jesus, he's your . . . Christ, Mel, just get dressed and then we can go and talk about this in private, all right?"

"I don't see what there is to talk about," said Mel, her face pinched with teenage knowledge.

Barney lifted his head from the pillow and looked out at his clothes scattered on the floor, like stepping stones from the bed to the door, his route to freedom.

"Just get out of bed and come and talk to me," said Dee, anger turning to frustration.

Mel ignored her and raked a hand through her hair, squinting across the room towards the gap in the curtains.

Dee stared at Mel in disbelief, ran all kinds of memories through her mind and tried to remember when her daughter had stopped being a child. It was a question she had asked herself numerous times before, and each time she had put off answering it for another more distant time. But now that time had come, there could be no more putting it off, and she felt more alone than ever before. She stared at her daughter for a couple of seconds, a lifetime in a couple of breaths, and then turned and called out down the hall. "John, can you come out here a minute, please?"

Seconds later, John appeared in the door, and a look of comic surprise erupted on his face.

Dee tightened her arms across her chest and nodded at the figures in the bed.

John caught the look of seriousness in the stone set of her face, and tried to maintain the mood, but it soon melted as he looked back across the room and saw his son and Mel propped up in bed like a couple of bored porn stars during a break in filming. "Looks like someone had a good night," he said, grinning.

"You don't think we've got a problem here?"

"I don't know what you mean," said John, struggling to contain his amusement.

"So you don't think there's anything wrong with them being in bed together?"

John shrugged and turned out his palms. "They're both

fifteen," he said. "I guess they can do what they like."

"No, they can't do what they like," said Dee, shaking her head. "If they're fifteen then they're still legally children. But that's not the point. The point is that they're our kids, yours and mine. So don't you think there's something wrong with them being in bed together? Something immoral, if not illegal?"

"But they're not our kids," said John. "Not *ours* ours, yours and mine together. Barney's half mine, and Mel's half yours. There's no common parent, no common strand of DNA in their bodies, and so I guess that makes it all right."

"Except that they're both under the age of consent," said Dee.

"Don't tell me you weren't, I don't know, *curious* when you were fifteen? I suppose you're going to tell me you were still a virgin when you got married. If we were in Tennessee or somewhere like that, those two'd be married with a couple of kids by now."

"For Christ's sake, John," said Dee. "Can't you take this a little more seriously, and support me just for once?"

"I always support you when you're right," said John.

"That's not true," said Dee, shaking her head. "You support me when you think I'm right, when you agree with me. That's not the same thing at all. It's like supporting yourself."

John stared into her face for a second, then turned and headed back to the kitchen and his breakfast.

"That's right," said Dee, burning holes in his back. "Just walk away and leave me to clear up your mess. Some parent you turned out to be." She watched him disappear into the kitchen, and then turned to face the bed. "Right, you," she said, snatching up Barney's clothes from the floor and tossing them onto the bed. "I want you dressed and out of here right now."

Barney did not need to be told twice. He bundled up his clothes in his arms and ran into the bathroom. He locked the door and fought himself back into his clothes as fast as he could, all the time listening to Mel and her mother arguing with each other back in the bedroom. Muffled and sounding more like the scraping of raw emotions than an argument, he heard Mel stick up for him, and after hearing his father all but dismiss him earlier, it made his heart swell with love and pride. As he walked out of the flat, not pausing at the kitchen door to look in on his father, he felt that the blueprint he had glimpsed in the long dark night was starting to come into focus.

33

Charlie had been waiting outside the police station in Kentish Town for over two hours when he saw Dillon pull into the car park. He had waited all night for this moment. The back of his thighs ached and his bladder was about fit to burst, but he did not want to miss seeing Dillon while his blood was up. He had no idea what he was going to tell the man, but he felt that he owed it to Karl to put up some kind of protest. He waited for Dillon to lock his car, then climbed out of his own car and trotted across the road. Walking around the barrier, he headed straight towards Dillon as he approached the back entrance to the station. A man in a blue suit and a female PC were smoking there, and the pair watched with blank interest as the scene before them unfolded.

"Hey, Dillon," shouted Charlie, getting closer to his target. "Hold on there a minute, will you, I want to talk to you."

Dillon glanced across at Burns, and a spark of recognition flared in his pupils. Then he glanced across at the station entrance, as if to gauge the distance to freedom, but before he could take another couple of steps Burns had blocked his path.

"I heard about what happened at the inquest," said Charlie. "The thin blue line triumphing once more, pulling out all the stops to protect one of its own."

"Look, Mr. Burns," said Dillon, raising his palms in a gesture of conciliation. "I'm truly sorry about what happened to your son, I really am, but it was just an accident, a tragic accident. I know you must be upset, but there's nothing—"

"How do you know what I'm feeling?" said Charlie. "You don't even know me, so how could you possibly know what I'm feeling?"

Dillon looked over at the smokers for some kind of support, but the couple just stared back at him with colourless faces.

"After an accident like that . . ."

"I think we both know it was no accident," said Charlie.

"If you want to talk to a grief counsellor, or if you think that there might be someone else who might be able to help—"

"I said it was no accident." Charlie's voice grew louder.

Dillon flinched and took a couple of steps to the side, turning his back on his colleagues. "Mr. Burns, please."

"I wonder if the force would still be willing to support you if they knew what really happened."

Dillon shuffled his feet and took another step to the side. He opened his mouth to speak but he struggled to find words.

"You might have intimidated one witness into submission, but there was more than one person outside the pub that night."

"Mr. Burns, please—"

"—and not all of them were too scared to talk to me."

Dillon swallowed and ran a hand across his face.

Burns stepped in close then, and dropped his voice to a harsh whisper. "I know what happened," he said. "I know what happened the night you killed my son. About the face in the crowd, and how you speeded up when you saw who it was."

Dillon tried to hide his surprise, but his pupils flared black and a crimson tide rose in his throat.

"So I want you to think about this. I want you to think about what Karl must have been feeling when he saw your car bearing down on him that night. And then I want you to hold that thought in your head. Because one day soon, Dillon, and make no mistake about this, that feeling is going to be for real."

Mel spotted him as soon as she stepped out of the flat, Barney, sitting up high on someone's garden wall at the far end of the street, kicking his heels. She grinned and stuffed her hands deep in her pockets, and started walking down the street towards him. The traffic on the North Circular hammered the tarmac in the near distance, and the fumes drifted across the area like a poisonous cloud, scratching at the back of her throat and making her want to cough like she had been smoking all night. Poor kid's getting it at both ends, she thought as she got closer. She raised her arm and called out to him, and his face lit up, pulling him out of his trance. He jumped down from his perch and trotted across the street to meet her. Mel glanced back at the flat but there was no one watching them, all the blinds were drawn.

Her mother had gone on at her until she had been able to make her escape into the bathroom. Then the grownups had resumed their own argument, screaming and shouting at each other and making as much noise as possible. For the most part it had sounded just like one of their regular arguments, but there had been short, sharp snaps when the temperature had risen, and Mel had sensed something more to it. Cold stuff that the incident had put to the flame once more.

She met Barney at the end of the street, and he turned and fell into step beside her, sneaking a look back at the house.

"So what's going on back there?" he said.

"You know what they're like," said Mel, shrugging her shoulders. "Both of them are more interested in scoring points off each other than they are about anything to do with us."

"Your mum seemed pretty sparked up about it all," said Barney.

"She'll get over it," said Mel. "It's not like we're planning on getting married or anything."

"Just one of those Jerry Springer moments," said Barney, although he felt his heart sink a little at her comment.

"If she kicks me out of the flat I can always come and stay at your place," said Mel.

"You'll need to get past the dragon on the gate first," said Barney. "Where are you going now, anyway?"

"I thought I'd better go and see Archie," said Mel, a twist of frustration in her voice. "See if I've still got a job."

"I thought you hated that place."

"Yeah, I know, but I still need the money," said Mel. Then, with a sidelong glance illuminated with a bright grin, she took a little sprint forward, turned on her heels to face him, and blocked his path. She smiled and tilted her face up to him for his appraisal. "What's the bruise look like today?"

Barney took a step closer, peered at the discolouration that spread across her cheek. "It's still purple . . ."

"D'you think it'll do? You don't think I need to make it look more elaborate, make the mugging tale seem more realistic?"

"You want me to punch you in the face?" said Barney, laughing.

"Yeah, right," said Mel, echoing his laughter.

"You don't think I would do it?"

"I'd like to see you try," said Mel, her eyes sparkling.

The pair looked at each other for a moment, then Mel jumped forward and planted a well-aimed kiss on his lips, and then turned and ran off laughing in the direction of the tube station.

Barney glanced back at the flat and then chased after her.

The encounter with Burns had spooked Dillon more than he cared to admit, not least because it had happened right in front of a couple of his fellow officers. His first instinct was to fight back, but before he could do that he had a far more important job to do. The reason he was in the station on his weekend off was to bring an end to the Paul Ballard saga.

He spent a couple of hours sorting out old case files in the basement storage room in preparation for them being transferred to computer. Then just before ten, he dusted himself off and fetched a carton of milk from the canteen and carried it up to the third floor, the CID room, where the kettle was.

A couple of detectives were sitting at their desks, working the phones, and in the corner, DS Stone was talking to one of the civilian staff. He knew her a little from Kilburn; she wanted to be one of the lads from what he could remember. To the left of the room, Spencer had the top drawer of a filing cabinet open, a file spread out on top of the open drawer before him. He looked to be deep in concentration, and so when Dillon started across the room towards the kettle, to attract his attention, he bumped his hip into one of the other desks, scraping its legs across the lino with a screech. The ruse worked, Spencer looking across for a second.

"Dobie asked me to bring up some fresh milk," said Dillon, holding up the carton in the air and shaking it.

"Thanks," replied Spencer, distracted.

Dillon picked up the carton that was on the desk beside the kettle. "This one's still half full," he said. "Looks like Dobie forgot he sent up some already."

"Don't worry, it won't go to waste," said Spencer, turning for a second from the file spread out on the filing cabinet drawer. "This place runs on tea and coffee at the weekend."

"You might as well keep this one, then," said Dillon, placing both cartons on the desk, the fresh one to the rear. "There's plenty more downstairs." He took a couple of steps back across the room towards the door, stopped, and turned to face Spencer, a frown creasing his forehead. "Look, Rob, I'm sorry about flaring up in the canteen the other day."

Spencer looked at him, said nothing.

"It's just that sometimes, you know . . ."

Spencer let him squirm for a moment, then dismissed his apologies with a roll of his shoulders. "Forget about it."

Dillon let the relief show on his face, a brief smile.

"How's it going anyway, are you getting anywhere yet?"

"You know what it's like," said Spencer, sighing. He was not one to bear a grudge and, besides, he knew that there was something in what Dillon had said the day before. "You put up that kind of money and all you're going to get are calls from people having trouble with their neighbours, crackheads out for an easy score, and the kind of nutters who want to use the money to paper the inside of their flats with tin foil."

"I know what you mean," said Dillon, laughing. "Like last night, for instance. I got into a bit of a ruck with a couple of kids outside the Underworld club down in Camden Town . . ."

"I know the place," said Spencer, and nodded for Dillon to continue.

"Nothing worth dragging them back to the station for, but one of them got scared enough to offer me up a name for the Ballard case. He didn't mention the reward money, but it still sounded like he was just pulling the name out of a hat."

"It's like a second language to these people."

"You're right there," said Dillon. "This kid last night, the way he was talking, he almost had himself convinced."

"You never know," said Spencer, getting interested. "It's a long shot, but he could be the person we're looking for, the one person who saw what happened. What name did he give you, anyway?"

Dillon looked off across the room for a moment as if the name was written in graffiti on the building across the street. "It sounded like Chris Ellis or something . . ."

"Christopher John Ellison," said Spencer, and then let out a short laugh and shook his head.

"You've heard about this character before?"

"Last night," said Spencer. "Someone called in and said much the same thing. At first it sounded like the same old bullshit, but when we ran his name through the computer it turned out that Ellison is on the run from a couple of robberies on the Regent's Park Estate. Been missing since the end of September."

"You think it could have been him that killed Ballard?"

"I don't know," said Spencer. "It could just be someone who knows Ellison is on the run and wants to take a punt at the reward, but we do still want to talk to him."

"You want me to go and find those kids from last night?"

"That's all right, we can take it from here."

"That might be more difficult than it sounds."

"Why's that?"

"Well, for one thing I forgot to ask for their names," said Dillon. "But I do remember what they both look like, so if you want me to go and take a look around, see if I can find them . . ."

"Doesn't look like we've got much choice," said Spencer, shrugging. "You want me to square it with your guv'nor first?"

"That's all right," said Dillon. "I'm not on the clock this morning, just helping out in the basement, filing and cleaning up and stuff. I'll be glad for a reason to get out of there, tell the truth. But if someone could call me if a real suspect does materialise, so that I'm not out there chasing a ghost . . ."

"Sure, no problem," said Spencer.

"Okay, I'll get right onto it," said Dillon, then headed out of the room. He took one step along the hall, glanced back to check that Spencer was not following him, and then let the grin that had been pulling at his lips for the last couple of minutes break loose across his face. Like a fucking dream, he said to himself. From making the first bogus call about Ellison to talking Spencer into letting him know when a real suspect turned up, his plan had worked like a dream. Now all he had to do was wait for Spencer to call him. It was just a matter of time.

34

Fifteen minutes before ten o'clock, Barney and Mel parted outside Shake Records, Mel kissing him hard on the mouth and making him promise to meet her outside the store at closing time, and then Barney threaded a path through the stalls of the street market. From when he had caught up with Mel at the tube station near her home, she had kept her touch on him: linking arms, holding hands, or just standing close enough for him to feel the heat of her skin on his own. It made him feel like his own private rain cloud had drifted from over his head and left the world looking all bright and new. Even the rotten fruit that rested in the gutters looked like spilled rubies and emeralds. As he reached the High Street, a bus pulled out from the stop outside Superdrug, and he picked up his feet and ran straight across the road. Kept on running until he reached the estate.

He took the stairs two at a time, still full of the energy of promise, and let himself into the flat. He heard his mother in the front room, talking to someone in that strange tongue she had adopted of late, but as he had not eaten since the night before, and his stomach was rumbling loud enough to wake the dead, he headed straight into the kitchen. He made himself a peanut butter sandwich, poured himself a glass of apple juice from the fridge, and then climbed onto the counter to eat.

Two minutes later he had finished the sandwich. He brushed the crumbs from his lap onto the floor, then jumped down from the counter. He drained the last of the apple juice, and put the glass in the sink. He was just about to walk through into the front room, when he realised that his mother was talking to Lucille Hook, the one person above all that he blamed for his current situation. Of course the death of Luke had hit his mother hard—it had hit them all hard—the neighbours too, and its shockwaves would reverberate throughout their hearts and minds for the rest of their lives. But it had been Lucille Hook who had taken that grief and stoked it until it had become something poisonous. She had often spoken about the Castle Estate as being unfit for decent people like Sarah and herself. Going on and on about the drugs and the crime, the graffiti and the stink of piss in the lifts, the police who had all but abandoned the place, Lucille told Sarah if she wanted to protect her second son from the same tragic fate as her first, then she had no choice but to do so herself.

It had been some time since he had last seen Lucille around at the flat, and he wondered what she was doing here now, wondered if she had been coming around while he was at school. Taking a deep breath, he stepped up close to the door to listen.

". . . begin to think what his mother and father must be going through right now," he heard his mother say.

"He was nothing but a drug dealer," replied Lucille, contempt curdling her tongue.

"I know he was a drug dealer, and I know that it was someone just like him who sold Luke the drugs that killed him, but . . . I don't know. . . . You think his parents had to remortgage the house or something to raise the reward?"

"This is not about his parents, Sarah, this is about what's right for us, what's right for all of us in the long run."

"It must be so painful for them."

"And like I said before, Sarah, there's nothing to be gained from going to the police now," continued Lucille in her forceful manner. "But if we let them believe that Ballard's death was part of some turf war between rival drug gangs, then we just might get some decent policing around here for a change."

"But I can't go on like this much longer," said Sarah, her words soaked in tears. "It's tearing me apart."

"And what do you think the police will do if you give yourself up now, after all this time?"

"What do you mean?"

"Well, it's been so long now, they're bound to think that you've got something to hide."

"But it was self-defence," pleaded Sarah.

"But you did follow him up onto the roof, Sarah."

"I know, I know, but he just wouldn't listen to me. I tried talking to him when I saw him down in the lobby, but he just put his hands over his ears and walked away. It made me so angry."

"That's not going to support your claim of self-defence."

"I only wanted him to stay away from Barney."

"You could have said all that to him down in the lobby," Lucille reminded her, frustration tightening her words.

"But I wouldn't have gone so far as to kill him . . ."

"So how come you left it so long to go and see the police? And how come you didn't say anything to them at the time when they were doing their house-to-house enquiries? You told them you didn't know anything. They're going to want to know, Sarah."

And all at once Barney understood what he was hearing—his mother admitting she pushed Paul Ballard from the roof of their building and killed him—and felt his heart drop in his chest. His limbs turned to stone and his face became a cold mask of fear. He reached out his hands and touched the wall for balance.

243

"And what about Barney?" continued Lucille Hook. "What's going to happen to him? You won't be much good to him locked up."

Barney felt his face flush with anger at the sound of his own name coming from Lucille's mouth, and he hated her all the more for using it to attack his mother. He felt the blood come back to his limbs, tingling, and his hands curl into fists at his sides. He wanted to kick open the door and throw her out of the flat, tear her out of their lives forever.

"But he's been brought up to know right from wrong," said Sarah, sobs catching in her throat. "What's he going to think of me if I don't go to the police, if I don't give myself up?"

"If he ever finds out about this, Sarah, then he's going to know that his mother did the right thing."

He could take it no longer; he had to do something. His emotions ricocheted around inside his head, but at the same time a strange calm flattened his thoughts and brought him to a decision. He could see that Lucille was preventing his mother from doing what she felt was the right thing, but he was also now in the unique position of being able to help both his mother and himself at the same time. He hesitated for a second, turning his decision over in his head, and then left the flat in silence.

Roscoe picked up the phone on the second ring. "Rhiannon?"

There was a brief pause and then: "It's Marnie . . ."

"Hi, Marnie," said Roscoe, stepping across to the radio and lowering the volume. "I thought it might be Rhiannon calling back. You know, Karl's mother."

"Why, what's happened?"

"Nothing, I hope. But last night I told Charlie that Karl's death might not've been an accident, that it looks like the driver might've been aiming to hit someone in the crowd."

"Jesus, Frank. What's that going to do to him?"

"I had to tell him what I knew," said Roscoe. "He is the kid's father, after all, as well as one of my oldest friends."

"No point in asking how he reacted," said Marnie.

"He wanted to go straight out and tackle Dillon about it, but I managed to talk him back down. Or at least I thought I had. When I woke up this morning, there was no sign of him. It must be a couple of hours since I called Rhiannon, but she hasn't seen him since he left there last night to come over here."

"You think he might do something stupid?"

"I don't think so, he's not macho like that," said Roscoe.

"Maybe not in the past," said Marnie. "But it's not every day that he's going to find out that someone might've killed his son by accident while they were trying to kill someone else."

"I guess not," said Roscoe, feeling a little chastened. "Anyway, how are you feeling? How's the head this morning?"

"I feel like hell, thanks, and it looks like there's a piece of rotten fruit stuck to my face," laughed Marnie.

"Sounds like it'll leave a bit of a scar," said Roscoe.

"Well, now you put it like that, I suppose there is something to look forward to after all," whispered Marnie, and Roscoe felt his heart step up a beat.

Silence fell on the line with just the sound of their breathing registering across the divide. Roscoe held the phone tight in his hand. After a couple of moments he thought he could hear her breathing get heavier, tense with the unfulfilled promise of the night before. And then the sound of someone in the background on the other side broke the spell, and he found himself clearing his throat to mask his embarrassment.

"And what's been happening on your side of things?" he said, pulling himself back into the here and now.

Marnie took a moment before she spoke, realigning herself. "Last night, you remember Herbie told us about a woman on the Castle Estate, the one who's been having a pop at the dealers on the phone booths for attempting to sell stuff to her son?"

"Kid called Barney Price, right?"

"That's him," replied Marnie. "Well, it turns out his mother . . . she's called Sarah Price, by the way . . . turns out she's got good reason to hound these dealers. She lost her eldest son, Luke, Barney's big brother, to drugs about two years ago."

"How did he die? Was he murdered?"

"Not this one, no. This one went to an overdose."

"And so his mother's just trying to keep Barney from heading in the same direction."

"He's fifteen, the same age his brother was when he died. I guess it must be tough for her right now."

"You think she could have killed Ballard?"

"I don't know, but it was her block that he fell from."

"She followed him up there, they got into an argument . . ."

"It could have happened like that, we don't know, it's too soon to tell. But I better go, Frank, there's a couple of people I need to see here before I head over there and talk to her."

"Let me know how it goes."

"And you can keep me up to speed on Charlie, right?"

"I'll call you later," said Roscoe.

"All right, thanks," said Marnie, and cut the call.

35

Ten minutes after Lucille left the flat, having frightened Sarah into keeping quiet for the time being, Sarah herself stepped out to go for a walk, or perhaps to do some shopping, something, anything, hoping that it would take her mind off things.

She wrapped her coat around her and headed towards Kentish Town Road, the sights and sounds of the estate on the edge of her senses. She kept her head low, but as she approached the phone booths she saw one of the dealers selling a foil wrap to a girl who looked to be no more than thirteen or fourteen. It made Sarah sick to her stomach, but as she knew she could no longer afford to get involved, she quickened her step and pushed on. As she reached the corner of Kentish Town Road, she could not resist a look back, and as she glanced over her shoulder, she saw the dealer staring straight back at her with a look of triumph on his face. She felt her heart skip a beat, and Lucille's words about keeping quiet for the greater good echoed in her mind.

The desk sergeant had lost all of the hair from the top of his head, but when he leaned over his notebook, Barney could still make out a faint outline of redder skin across the top of his forehead where some hair must have once grown. He wondered if the job had caused him to lose his hair, or whether it was something in his genes. Whatever it was, it had had the opposite effect on his arms: thick curls of white hair sprouted from under his rolled-up sleeves like the stuffing from a slashed mattress, covering his forearms and the back of his hands right up to the second knuckle. There was a watch in there somewhere, too, but it looked like it had been a while since the sergeant had last used it to tell the time, putting it on more out of habit than usefulness.

With a long-suffering sigh, the sergeant signed off on a woman complaining about the kids kicking a football about outside her house, and then looked over to where Barney was sitting on a bench at the far side of the reception area.

"Okay, son," said the sergeant, beckoning him over with a curl of his forefinger. "Come and tell me what's on your mind."

Barney climbed to his feet and walked over to the counter, glancing out of the front door as he went. "It's about my mother," he said. "I think she might have killed someone."

"She might have done what?" replied the sergeant, startled.

"I think she might have killed someone."

"This is a joke, right?" said the sergeant, the muscles along his jawline twitching. "Tell me this is a joke."

"It's not a joke," said Barney, feeling fragile.

"Okay, so it's not a joke," said the sergeant, deciding to humour the kid for the moment. He picked up his pen and leaned over the pad on the counter. "In that case, why don't you start by telling me who your mother is supposed to have killed."

"Paul Ballard," Barney told him. "He was pushed from the top of our building on the Castle Estate last month."

The sergeant felt all his good humour and goodwill evaporate. Standing upright, he shook his head in despair. Then turned and took a moment to look out of the front door in order to compose himself, hoping for someone to walk through the door and rescue him from the life that some cruel joker had built for him when he had not been looking.

"Did you have a fight with your mum this morning?" he said. "Has she been on at you about your homework or something?"

Barney narrowed his eyes at the sergeant.

"This is about the reward, isn't it?" said the sergeant.

"No, it's not about the reward. . . . Are you saying you don't believe me?"

"It's not that I don't believe you, son," said the sergeant, leaning on the counter again and looking him in the face. "But ever since that lad's parents stumped up for a reward, the phone here's never stopped ringing. I've had seven kinds of fruitcake on that line, all wanting to shop their mothers or their fathers, their friends or their neighbours, a dealer that ripped them off, anyone but the person who actually killed Paul Ballard, and every one of them talking out of their behinds. And if I sent up to CID every person who came through that door telling me they had some fresh information . . ." He trailed off then and hung his head low, shaking it wearily.

"But it's the truth," cried Barney, his voice cracking open the last word. "What's the point in me telling you lies?"

The sergeant picked up on the escalating desperation in his voice. He shook his head and let out another sigh. "All right, son. Do you want to start by telling me your name and address?"

Barney told him his name and address.

"And you live there with your parents?"

"No, it's just me and my mum," replied Barney. "My dad lives up in Golders Green with his girlfriend."

The sergeant wrote down this information. "Okay," he said. "Do you want to tell me what happened?"

"There's not that much to tell," said Barney. "Just that I overheard my mum talking to Lucille Hook about—"

"Whoa, hold on there a minute," interrupted the sergeant. "You say your mum was talking to a woman called Lucille Hook?"

"That's right," said Barney, nodding.

"The same Lucille Hook that lives on the Castle Estate?"

"Yeah, that's her. She lives in our building."

"And you say that she's a friend of your mum's?"

"That's what I'm trying to tell you," said Barney.

"All right, I'm sorry," said the sergeant. "Go on, son."

"Well, I stopped over at my dad's place last night," said Barney, his eyes locking on something beyond the physical as he tried to recall the detail of the scene he had overheard minutes earlier. "And when I got home this morning, I heard Mum and Lucille Hook talking about Paul Ballard. I was starving, so I went straight into the kitchen to make a sandwich. They were in the front room, but I don't think they could hear me. . . . They didn't say anything, anyway, like tell me to come through or anything like that. Lucille Hook was telling Mum that it was best for her not to go to the police so you'd think that it was part of a gang war, Paul Ballard being pushed from the roof and killed like that, I mean, and then you'd have to arrest all the drug dealers on the estate and make it safer for the rest of us again. But Mum said it was self-defence and she shouldn't have to go to prison, anyway, so what did it matter? And then Lucille Hook said it had been a month now, so why hadn't she been to see the police before? If she went now they'd only think she was trying to hide something, they'd never believe her. But it was self-defence, Mum said, of course they'll believe me. I just followed him up onto the roof and—"

"Whoa, whoa there," interrupted the sergeant again, holding up his hand as if he was directing traffic. "You'd better stop right there, son. I think I'd better get one of the detectives to come down here and have a word with you."

Barney stared at the sergeant.

"Just take a seat over there for now," said the sergeant, reaching for the phone with one hand and pointing to the cracked plastic seats on the far side of the room with the other. "There'll be someone down to see you in a minute." He punched a four digit number into the grid on the phone, and then as he waited for it to be picked up on the other end, he stared at the kid in the corner with a look of bemused acceptance on his face.

"I think you'd better come down here," he said at last into the phone. "There's someone who wants to talk to you about the Ballard case, and what they've got to say I think you need to hear with your own ears."

Ten minutes after he took the call from Dobie, Spencer was on the phone to Marnie.

"Where are you, Boss?"

"I thought I told you where I was going," replied Marnie, sounding a little out of breath.

"I know you're on the Castle Estate, Boss, but what I meant was have you been to see Sarah Price yet?"

"I'm in the stairwell right now. Why, what's happened?"

"Her son Barney, he just walked into the station and told us that his mother killed Paul Ballard."

"Jesus no," said Marnie, feeling like she had just been punched in the chest. Her feet hesitated for a second, but then she kept on walking until she reached the second floor landing. She took a couple of steps along the walkway, and then stopped to lean on the balcony and look out across the estate. Cool air drifted up from below and tightened the skin around her mouth.

"You still there, Boss?" said Spencer.

"You think he's serious?" said Marnie. On the far side of the estate she saw a man in a dark suit and a pair of red shoes kicking the side of a car.

"You mean do I think his mother killed Ballard?"

"Did he ask about the reward?"

"Dobie told me that he mentioned it to him, but I think the kid was more interested in having someone listen to him."

"You think he's telling the truth?"

"I think he believes he's telling the truth."

"So where is he now?"

"I asked Kern to take him down to one of the interview rooms," said Spencer, naming one of the more recent female police officers allocated to the station.

"What about his father? Is he still around?"

"I just called him up in Golders Green, he said he'll be down here as quick as he can."

"Okay, thanks," said Marnie. "I'll be back there in about five minutes. Don't let anyone talk to him until I get there."

"Yeah, hello," said Roscoe, picking up the phone. He had just climbed out of the shower and was dripping water on the carpet.

"Is that Inspector Roscoe?" said a female voice in a clipped London accent. He imagined a little pinched mouth and her hair pulled back in a bun, the tendons in her neck stretched tight like guide ropes holding her head on in a storm.

"Yeah, this is Roscoe."

"Rosie Sheehan from Park Cars on Dartmouth Park Road. You wanted some information about some of our bookings?"

"That's right," said Roscoe. He had not heard from either Charlie or Rhiannon again that morning, and so the calls he had made to local cab firms the previous afternoon had been all but forgotten. He wiped a towel across his face, and then hung the towel around his neck.

"For just one particular night last May?"

"That's right," said Roscoe again, and gave her the date. "For somewhere on Brecknock Road between about nine and ten."

There was the sound of pages being turned, background static, the mutter of foreign-accented voices.

"Well, from what I can make out, it looks like there were just two bookings made for addresses on Brecknock Road that

252

night," said Rosie Sheehan at last. "The first one was for nine on the dot to a flat in Hilldrop House."

Roscoe tried to picture Hilldrop House on Brecknock Road, but it remained out of focus. He stepped over to the bookshelf and picked out the *A-Z*. He flipped through to the well-thumbed volume to the right page and held it up close for a better look.

"Inspector?"

"I'm just checking it on the *A-Z*," said Roscoe.

"It's a part of the Hilldrop Estate, right down at the Camden Road end of the street," said Rosie Sheehan.

"I'm looking," said Roscoe, squinting at the point just above the tip of his finger as he tracked it across the page. And then he could make out Hilldrop Road and Hilldrop Crescent but no Hilldrop House. He assumed it must be down there in the jumble of little streets somewhere. "All right, found it," he said at last. "And what was the name of the fare on this one?"

"It looks like Thorne or Thomas, something like that . . ."

"Right, thanks," said Roscoe again, making a mental note of the details, even though he was almost certain that this was not the one he was looking for. "How about the other one?"

There was a rustling of paper, and the clunking of the phone being put down and then picked up again, and then Rosie Sheehan came back on the line. "The second booking was for quarter past nine for the middle bell at 173 Brecknock Road . . ."

"173," repeated Roscoe.

"That's right down at the other end," she said, picking up the unasked question, and Roscoe felt his heart step up a beat. "About ten houses up from Tufnell Park tube station."

"And that was in the name of?"

"It looks like Frank . . . or Francis."

"John Francis," said Roscoe under his breath, and knew for certain then that Dillon was crooked.

36

Since his little chat with Spencer earlier that morning, Dillon had changed his mind about heading out and waiting for Spencer to call him. He decided instead to remain down in the basement for as long as he could. He reasoned that if the name of a suspect in the Ballard case did come up, then he was best placed to hear about it right there in the station and not out on the street. And if Spencer did ask him what was happening with the two kids, then he would tell him he was going out to look for them later when there was more chance of them being around.

For the rest of the morning he worked in the basement, sorting and loading files into crates and keeping to himself. The routine of the work calmed him, and it felt good to get the blood flowing again without some kind of stimulant—coke, adrenaline, or the fear of others—and he felt his shirt sticking to his back, the chill air around his neck. Since the accident most people had kept well out of his orbit for fear of being tainted with the same suspicions, and even though he had now been cleared of reckless driving and all other charges, he knew that it would take some time for them to come back to him. Not that it bothered him all that much; for the time being he had far more pressing matters to attend to.

Ten minutes short of noon, Steve Knott, a man with hair like copper wire, and another of the helpers in the basement that morning, came in from having a cigarette out in the car park.

"You know, sometimes I think that the greatest weapon we

have against crime is greed. Dangle enough money in front of someone's face and there's nothing they won't do. I was talking to Dobie just now, he was telling me about this kid that walked into the station this morning and shopped his own mother."

"Someone shopped their own mother?" said Lorna Kaiser, a tall thick-hipped Jewish woman who had joined the force after a spell helping out at a hostel for the homeless in King's Cross.

"I know, unbelievable," said Knott, grinning.

"What's she supposed to have done, anyway?"

"Kid said she was the one that pushed that dealer off the roof of the Castle Estate."

"The one where the parents've just put up a reward?"

"Like I said—greed will get them all in the end."

"For something like ten thousand quid . . ."

"Something like that," agreed Knott, shrugging.

"So after all that she's done for him, that's all that he thinks she's worth," said Kaiser, her voice fading out as she realised that in some homes around here, giving birth was about all that some mothers would ever do for their kids.

"If you want to look at it like that, then it's also the same ten thousand quid that the victim's family put up for him."

"Yeah, but that was probably all that they could get together," argued Kaiser. "It's not like they were saying that's all he was worth, like this kid is doing with his mother."

Dillon had been working at the far end of the basement, and came forward now coughing and smacking clouds of dust out of his clothes. "Jesus Christ, it's like Tutankhamen's tomb back there."

"If it's buried treasure you're looking for, you'd be far better off out there on the street," said Kaiser.

Dillon glanced at Knott and then turned to look at Kaiser, a look of questioning creased his forehead.

"Ah, it was just something that Dobie said," said Kaiser.

"Yeah, what was that then?"

"Just something about this kid who came in this morning and shopped his mother."

"Kids're just mean," said Dillon, grunting.

"I don't think this one was just being mean," said Kaiser.

"No, this one was just in it for the money," said Knott.

"You mean the reward?" said Dillon, his ears pricking up.

"That's right," said Knott.

"What's she supposed to have done?"

"Kid told Dobie she was the one who pushed that dealer off the top of the Castle Estate . . ."

"What, she killed Paul Ballard?" said Dillon, feeling that familiar spark in his blood once more.

"That's what Dobie told me," said Knott, shrugging again.

"So when did all this happen?"

"Sometime this morning, I suppose."

"So where's the kid now?"

"In one of the interview rooms, I think."

"What, he's talking to Spencer?"

"No, I think he's waiting for DS Stone to get back, and the kid's father to get here too, of course."

"So his mother's still out there wandering free?"

"I suppose so," said Knott, but Dillon was gone, stalking up the corridor and taking the stairs two at a time.

He pushed open the door to the reception area and found Dobie in his usual place at the front desk. He walked up to him keeping his face and his limbs as cool and as loose as possible.

"Dobie," he said, glancing at the closed door that hid the stairs up to the CID offices and hoping it remained closed for the time being. "I'm supposed to be helping out Spencer tonight, tracking down this kid from the other night who offered to tell me who killed Paul Ballard in exchange for not getting busted. It wasn't worth a bust, and at the time I thought he was joking, but Spencer thinks it might be worth talking to him anyway. But then I just heard that some kid walked into the station this morning and gave up his mother for the crime."

"That's right," replied Dobie, leaning over his paperwork.

"You think it might be the same kid?"

"I don't know. I don't know what your kid looks like."

"Well, what's the kid that came in look like?"

"I don't know," said Dobie, looking up from his paperwork. With his head tilted like that, his double chin disappeared. "Just like a kid, I suppose. He looked just like a kid."

"You're wasted behind that desk, Dobie. You should be up those stairs in CID."

"I had my chances," said Dobie, a ghost of a smile on his face.

"At least can you remember his name?"

"Barney Price," said Dobie. "His name's Barney Price, and he lives in the same building where Ballard was killed."

"Thanks," said Dillon, and then turned and pushed out through the door. But instead of going back down to the basement, he turned right and headed out to the car park.

There were a couple of people out smoking cigarettes and chatting, and so he kept right on walking over to where his car was parked. Unlocking the door, he slid in behind the wheel, and then leaned across the passenger seat and clicked open the glove compartment as if he was looking for something. He rummaged around in there for a couple of seconds, and then sat back up again and pulled out his mobile phone.

He punched in a number he had memorised and been told to use for just this sole purpose, and then rattled his fingers on the wheel as he waited for the call to be picked up.

"Yeah," came the response, hard and cool. Dillon recognised the voice at once: Jem Tobin, one of Bar Code's top men.

"It's Dillon," he said under his breath, as if he was afraid of being overheard. "And I better make this quick, because I'm just on a break out in the car park at the moment."

"Go on then," replied Tobin.

"Well . . . it looks like our little plan worked after all," said Dillon, glancing over towards the smokers. "I just heard we're going to pick up someone for the Ballard murder."

"And about fuckin' time, too."

"But there's a catch . . ."

"Yeah, and what's that?"

"Well, the thing is. . . . The thing is I don't know her name, the suspect."

"I thought you said you were just about to arrest someone," snapped Tobin. "What is this, some kind of fuckin' joke?"

"It's not a joke, but you will need to do a bit of work on this one yourself," said Dillon.

Tobin took a deep breath and wondered what Bar Code would do. "Yeah, all right, let's hear it, then . . ."

"Right, listen up: the woman going to be charged was shopped by her teenage son. Apparently, he just came into the station this morning and gave her up. I don't know why. Maybe he just thought she was going to go down for it anyway, he might as well get the reward. I tried to get her name but. . . . Fuck it, it's too long a tale to tell here. All you need to know is that her son is called Barney Price, and that the pair of them live on the Castle Estate in the same building that Ballard was pushed from."

"How can we be sure that it was her?"

"People've been coming in here with stories all weekend, so why would they choose to listen to this one in particular? The kid must've broken the code or something, told them something about the murder that hasn't been released to the press."

Tobin thought about this for a moment. "Yeah, all right . . ."

"Anyway, she shouldn't be too difficult to find, but you'd

better get onto it quick. No one's spoken to the kid officially yet, they're still waiting for his old man to arrive, and for the DS to get back to the station, but I don't think it'll be too long before the word's put out to pick her up."

"I'll get someone onto it right now," said Tobin.

37

Roscoe found Burns sitting at the bar in the Linton Tree, a pint of bitter and a glass of scotch on the scarred wooden bar in front of him. There were just two other customers in the place, a pair of old women drinking stout for the iron. Roscoe heard the radio in the kitchen, playing one of those avuncular lunchtime Radio 2 DJs, lilting and mocking.

Roscoe hitched himself up onto a stool beside Burns. He folded his arms on the bar and looked straight ahead. Burns took a second and then glanced across at him. He showed no sign of having recognised his old friend, save for a brief flicker of blue light on his pupils. The landlord Roscoe had spoken to earlier was nowhere to be seen, but after a couple of minutes a barmaid in a tight denim skirt and a black T-shirt came out from the kitchen and raised her chin at Roscoe in question. She rested her hands on her hips, and he saw the cold loose flesh of her upper arms and the tattoo of a cross on the back of her wrist.

"Bottle of Miller, please," said Roscoe.

The barmaid took a bottle from the fridge, uncapped it and set it on the bar in front of him. She picked up the three pound coins he had stacked on the bar, crossed to the till and rang up the sale, and then put his change, a handful of silver and copper shrapnel, down on the bar beside the bottle.

"You're not going to buy me a drink?" said Burns.

"You've already got two drinks on the go," replied Roscoe,

nodding at the drinks on the bar.

"You're right, another one'd be far too greedy," said Burns.

Roscoe gave him a slow smile in return, and then took a drink from his bottle. "Something like that," he said.

The pair sat in static silence for a moment, with just the radio and the chink of bottle on bottle for background noise as the barmaid restacked the fridge. After a while the two old women finished their drinks and then slowly got up and left, like shadows being wiped out by the sun angling around a corner.

"Me and Rhee often used to talk about what kind of a world we had brought Karl into," said Burns at last, his thoughts becoming vocal, sad and low. "What with all the war and terrorism on the map, and the drugs and crime on our streets. But that's all been going on forever, there's nothing new about that. No, it was all the other things that bothered us the most: the gradual erosion of morals and respect, and all that other old-fashioned stuff our parents used to remind us about. I don't know, it's like global warming's affecting the soul or something. And you know what, most of it seems to be fired by greed. From film stars selling the pictures of their wedding for a million dollars, to women listing their hobbies as shopping and collecting shoes, and the street kids that will steal another kid's mobile phone not because they want another one, but because they don't want their victim to have one. Back when we were kids greed was a bad thing, but now it's become almost a virtue." He paused to take a drink, and seemed to drift into another dimension for a moment. "You think it's wrong of me to want revenge for Karl?"

"I don't know," replied Roscoe. "But wasn't it Gandhi who said that an eye for an eye will make the whole world blind?"

"Okay, so I'm a mess of contradictions," laughed Burns. "But that just goes to prove that I'm a regular human being."

Roscoe smiled and sipped his beer, and the pair fell into a static silence once more. The barmaid finished restacking the fridge and carried the empty crates through into the kitchen. Burns watched her go, and then keeping his eyes on the space she had left behind, said, "You're going to tell me now that you just found out for certain that Dillon was trying to hit someone in the crowd, and that Karl just got in the way."

"I'm afraid that's what it looks like," said Roscoe, feeling the words catch like barbs in his throat. He took a sip of beer, swallowed hard. "I'm really sorry, Charlie."

Burns tilted his head back and pressed his thumb and forefinger to his eyelids, but the tears still came, like blood drained of all its colour and strength, rolling down his cheeks.

Sarah took another bite of the falafel in pita bread, and then tossed the remainder into a bin in disgust. It tasted like cardboard, or like it had been sitting around in a damp cupboard for weeks. She spat the mouthful out into her hand and dropped it in the bin with the rest of the food, and then wiped her hand with a napkin. She rummaged around in her rucksack and took out a bottle of water, and washed the taste out of her mouth. Then she dipped into her rucksack again and took out a pack of cigarettes and a book of matches, and fired one up.

In front of her, a group of tourists were looking through a street stall that sold drug paraphernalia: cannabis leaf-shaped candles, giant rolling papers, hash pipes, roach clips, bongs, and flags, posters, towels, shirts, and baseball caps with a range of slogans and motifs. In the group of three men and two women who were no older than eighteen or nineteen, with Danish flags on their backpacks, one girl was trying to decide which of two hash pipes she should buy, holding them in her mouth and making a face like she was stoned in front of her friends. All of a sudden Sarah felt a huge ball of anger well up inside her chest. She felt the anger knot the muscles in her shoulders, tighten the muscles in her legs, and pin her to the ground. Her mind raced to keep up with the loose thoughts of different ages of her life ricocheting through her head, and each time she managed to bring it under control for a second it was on the same thought: that she hated all the things that had brought her to this place, and all the things that this place had become.

From the battered copies of Jack Kerouac to the beggars under the cashpoint machines.

From the Freak Brothers look-alikes selling dope in the Students Union to the smack dealers on the Castle Estate.

From *Go Ask Alice* to children on street corners drinking alcopops.

From the amphetamine rush of punk rock to the Chemical Generation.

From trying to break a butterfly on a wheel to giving the butterfly its own gilded kingdom.

From the margins to the mainstream . . .

. . . to a government in the pocket of the big food chains . . .

. . . to vertical drinking . . .

. . . to the one hundred thousand drug tourists that flooded the area each weekend . . .

. . . to the local council for promoting Camden Town as a leisure centre for hedonists . . .

. . . to the media folk with offices in Camden who thought their coke habits were not a part of the greater drug problem . . .

. . . ditto the after-dinner joint smokers . . .

. . . to the liberals who let it all happen . . .

. . . to John Price for getting her pregnant . . .

. . . to the kid who sold the drugs that killed her son . . .

. . . to her son for thinking it was cool to take drugs in the first place . . .

. . . to Paul Ballard for being in the wrong place at the wrong time . . .

. . . to Lucille Hook for thinking that she had all the answers . . .

. . . and most of all to Sarah herself for taking more than two decades to realise what was happening.

Sarah watched the Danish tourist put the hash pipes back on the stall and then walk off, laughing with her friends. She watched them stroll up the street, peering up at the giant model boots and aeroplanes and Red Indian statues pinned up high on the front of the buildings, and staring at the people with Camden Town hair, as Luke had called people with pink or blue hair back when he was small and still innocent. They disappeared into the KFC restaurant in the middle of the parade. Sarah finished her water and dropped the bottle into the bin. She glanced up and down the street, and then crossed the street and started walking towards home.

She walked down Buck Street and turned into Kentish Town Road. Across the street she heard the rattle of trolleys in Sainsbury's car park, the junkies and winos checking the slots for forgotten pound coins. Past the independent video store that carried DVDs of some good French films she remembered seeing back in college, the Students Union Film Club, but she had no DVD player so what was the point in even looking? Over the short bridge that spanned the canal, the water brown and rimmed with some kind of froth. A pair of ducks circled and bobbed in the water, and up past the bridge at Camden Lock where she saw the roof of a boat in the lock, fresh paint glistening in the sun.

As she crossed into the Castle Estate, she recognised a couple of drug dealers sitting on the kids' swings, smoking and kicking their feet in the earth. The sight of the dealers brought it all back. She still did not know what she was going to do, but if she knew one thing then she knew that it was going to be her decision. She would not let herself be bullied by the likes of Lucille Hook anymore. It was time she stood up for herself. She dropped her head to her chest and hurried on. In the distance someone was singing along to the radio, note for perfect note, what sounded like The Chi Lites' "Oh Girl".

Sarah stepped across the tarmac path that ran behind the swings, turned into her building, and started up the stairs. It was cold in the stairwell, and she could see her breath in front of her face. Pushing her hands in her pockets she climbed on. As she rounded the first corner, she bumped into someone coming down the stairs and felt a sudden pain in her chest, hot and cold at the same time. She fell back a step, and tried to step aside to let them through, but her legs had turned to molten lead and she could not move. Black curtains fluttered in front of her face, and the scrape of retreating footsteps filled her ears like the sound of surf on a deserted beach. The pain in her chest increased and she realised she was alone on the stairs, alone and afraid. She felt faint, and clutching her hands to her chest, found a hot stickiness there. A cold wind chilled her skin and she reached out to the wall for balance, but her hand slipped and she fell back and tumbled down the stairs. Her head banged on the stone steps as she rolled, tied up in limbs, and blood pumped from the wound in her chest. The world rippled in front of her face, flickered in black and white. The last thing she saw was a fresh graffiti tag on the pitted concrete wall, red and green, some words she could not understand.

38

She came to rest with her head on the ground floor, her legs raised and stretched across the lower stairs. A crisp packet had swirled in on the cool air and settled against her cheek, and chewing gum was stuck in her hair. Blood had collected in her face and neck and turned the skin a deep purple, spangling her pupils with broken red threads. Her bloated tongue lolled out of her mouth and rested on her lips like the head of a snake creeping out of her stomach. She looked like she had been dead for centuries. It was hard to believe she had ever been alive.

Marnie regarded the corpse on the stairs and felt a familiar heaviness in her bones. Despite all her time on the force she had never gotten used to seeing a fresh corpse. She had no problem with morgues and autopsies; it was just seeing people in the place where life had left them that somehow disturbed her. She sensed that it had something to do with the mundane becoming the immortal, the fact that despite a lifetime of hopes and dreams, of happiness and regret, of parents and siblings and children, it all came down to something like this: the bottom of a stairwell on a council estate in North London.

". . . and she's sure that this is Sarah Price?" she said to one of the PCs standing guard. He had been the first officer to arrive on the scene after a neighbour had called 999, having stumbled across the corpse on her trip home from the shops. Scenes of Crime had strung up blue-and-white incident tape, but neighbours stretched and pushed at the tape for a better look, and a number of PCs had been positioned to keep them back.

"She said she recognised her straight off," said the PC.

"So she knew her quite well, then," said Marnie.

"I think she said that she lives three doors down from her on the same landing, and that she saw her around all the time."

"And so she knew her name," said Marnie.

"I think she got her son to call it in, and he told the desk that it was Sarah Price."

"All right, thanks," said Marnie. "I'll talk to her later."

Scenes of Crime personnel in their white jumpsuits moved through the scene like ghosts, silent and precise.

"So what have we got?" asked Spencer, standing beside Marnie with his notebook in his hand.

"Well, for starters, I think that it would be too much of a coincidence if this turned out to be nothing more than a mugging that went wrong," said Marnie, resting her hands on her hips. "Some kid walks into the local nick to give up his mother for murder, and less than an hour later she gets killed herself."

"So there must be a connection," agreed Spencer.

"It might be the kid told someone else what he heard before coming to speak to us," said Marnie.

Spencer shrugged in response, then looked over to where a man in the crowd was pointing towards a small group of dealers huddled around the phone booths; the man was staring across at the area with cruel fascination. He could tell from the twist of his mouth that the man was blaming the dealers for the murder. "I'll make sure the uniforms ask the right questions during the canvas," he said.

"From what the kid told Dobie, it sounds like he came straight in after he heard his mother talking with Lucille Hook."

"Perhaps he stopped to talk to one of his friends, or call his father. I don't know, but we'll soon find out."

"This doesn't look like a domestic," said Marnie, shaking her head. "What about the reward, where are we with that?"

"You mean on the Ballard case?"

Marnie rested her hands on her lips, looked into his face. "Like for starters, who put it up in the first place?"

"James Wilkinson," said Spencer, squinting at Marnie like she had lost her marbles. "I thought we talked about this . . ."

"And he did this because?"

"Because . . ." echoed Spencer, shaking his head.

"Wilkinson put up the reward because?"

"Because his son was mugged and killed and the killer has never been caught. He thought if he helped someone else in the same situation it might help to ease his own grief."

Marnie raised a palm and cut him off.

"Paul Ballard was a lowlife drug dealer," she said. "If James Wilkinson's son was killed during a mugging, ten to one it had something to do with drugs, and he would know this. Why would he put up a reward to catch the killer of another drug dealer?"

"I can see that," said Spencer, nodding his head.

"But what if the dealer worked for you, and you thought his murder had punctured your armour, made you look weak in front of your rivals. I don't know, maybe someone was looking to muscle in on your action, maybe take over your business. How would you fight back, what would you do?"

"Find the killer and teach them a lesson, send a message to anyone else thinking of trying the same thing."

"And what's one of the easiest ways to find a killer?"

Spencer shrugged his shoulders, pursed his lips.

"After us of course," said Marnie from behind a grim smile.

"You could put up a reward," said Spencer at last, uncertain.

"Right," said Marnie. "Put up a reward, wait for the killer to be thrown into the square, and then put a nail in him."

"But I checked the records," said Spencer. "Wilkinson's son was killed just like Ballard told me."

"He spoke to Wilkinson? Ballard spoke to Wilkinson?"

"Yeah, a couple of times I think."

"And he was sure that it was Wilkinson he spoke to? How did he know it was Wilkinson? Had he ever spoken to him before?"

"I don't know," said Spencer, starting to feel as if he had been caught out, starting to feel uncomfortable.

"You spoke to Wilkinson, though."

Spencer shook his head, no.

"I thought we'd covered this," said Marnie, her face creasing in frustration. "I thought we'd gone through all this before, and now . . . Jesus, Spencer. . . . Go and do it now, please."

Spencer flushed crimson with embarrassment, glanced around at a couple of the PCs, caught grins, and then hid his face as he ducked under the tape. He took out his mobile phone and walked to a spot far from the noise of the crowd.

Marnie turned back to the corpse. The Scenes of Crime personnel were hard at work, dusting surfaces, bagging bits of trash from the floor, and measuring and photographing the scene with infinite precision. But Marnie knew that it would all amount to nothing unless someone decided to talk. She stared at the wound on Sarah Price's chest, the blood around it black and starting to harden. Blood had also pooled on the floor, and some had spilled between the cracks in the concrete as if Sarah Price's body was already attempting to return to the earth.

Ten minutes later Spencer ducked back under the tape and walked into the damp stairwell. "You were right," he said, holding his mobile phone in his hand. "I just spoke to James Wilkinson, and he told me that he's never heard of Paul Ballard."

39

It was quiet inside the interview room, with just the muffled sound of footsteps in the corridor outside breaking the silence, and so when Barney's stomach started to rumble, it sounded to his ears like a firecracker going off. Glancing across at the WPC beside the door, embarrassed at the behaviour of his own body, he was relieved to see that she appeared not to have heard, instead looking more like she was adrift somewhere on her own thoughts.

Despite the peanut butter sandwich he had eaten earlier, he had not eaten much else in the last couple of days and he was feeling pretty hungry. The WPC had fetched him a can of Sprite when he had first been shown into the interview room, and offered to fetch him something to eat too, but he had declined the offer. But that was almost two hours ago now, and he was starting to regret his decision. He supposed that he could ask her again, but then he got the impression that she felt like she had better things to do than look after him, and so asking her might make her mad. Apart from asking him about the food, she had not so much as glanced at him in two hours.

What he really fancied eating he didn't think they would have in the police canteen, anyway. No, what he really fancied was a cheese, peanut butter, and beetroot sandwich, just like his mother used to make for him when he was home sick from school. Years ago he had asked her to make him something to eat one afternoon after waking up from a fevered sleep, and she had presented him with this strange offering. But he had devoured it in great bites, and it had soon become his favourite comfort food. His mother had told him once that she had eaten nothing but cheese, peanut butter, and beetroot sandwiches when she had been pregnant with him, and that the taste for them must have passed from her blood into his. He could not remember the last time he had eaten one, but it was what he really fancied right now.

The man on the seat opposite him had his legs crossed at the knee, and the rumble of the train kept jiggling his foot around, causing it to tap John Price's shin. Not hard, just enough to be noticeable. But hidden behind the *Guardian,* the man did not appear to have noticed, and that made Price more mad than the tapping itself. Price kept huffing and puffing and shuffling his feet around on the floor, but it made no difference, the man was immune, and in the end Price climbed to his feet and stood beside the doors.

Price looked over at the man and shook his head, telling himself that it served him right for thinking that it would be all right to sit down. Most trips he stood near the doors, and he had been caught enough times to know that the chances of choosing a seat near someone irritating or dangerous were too high, so he had no idea what had made him think that it would be different this time. Still shaking his head, he turned and stared out into the blackness rattling past.

The incident had done nothing to lighten his mood. He had woken still a little drunk from the night before, and the sketch with the kids being caught in the same bed had been an amusing diversion, but after a couple of hours the alcohol had dried out and a killer headache had snapped across his skull. He had taken some aspirin, and drunk a couple of pints of water and tried to keep off the coffee, but all that had done was make him feel bloated and more tired. And now he had to travel into Kentish Town on the tube and pick up Barney from the police station. Fuck knows what that was all about, the message had just said to get there as soon as possible but that Barney was all right.

"Yeah, Stone here."

"Hey, Marnie, it's Frank."

"Hey, Frank," said Marnie, watching a couple of paramedics loading the stretchered corpse of Sarah Price into an ambulance.

"You remember we were talking about Dillon going after—"

"Frank, there's something—"

"—someone in the crowd, and the new witness I found telling me about the two men near a minicab having to—"

"Frank—"

". . . jump out of his path—"

"Frank, just shut the fuck up and listen to me," snapped Marnie, causing Spencer to glance across at her with a look of caustic surprise on his face, as if she had been talking to him.

The line went silent for a second, and then Marnie heard a faint grumble on the other end. "Sorry, Marnie," said Roscoe, apologetic. "You were telling me?"

"Sarah Price was killed less than an hour ago," said Marnie. "I'm at the scene right now, on the Castle Estate. The paramedics have just finished loading her into an ambulance."

"Jesus Christ," said Roscoe, disbelief curling his tongue. "What happened?"

"We don't know yet," said Marnie. "On first glance it looks like she was mugged, but I think there's more to it than that. Her son came into the station this morning and told us that she was the one who pushed Paul Ballard to his death."

"That must be some kind of joke. Was he after the reward?"

"I don't think so," replied Marnie. "I haven't had a chance to talk to him yet, but from what Dobie told me, it looks like he just heard his mother talking about it with Lucille Hook this morning and then decided to come in and tell us about it."

"The people's friend," said Roscoe, deadpan.

"That's her," said Marnie, allowing herself a brief smile. For a moment she thought that she might have alienated Roscoe with snapping at him like that, but she should have known that he would have the balls and the humour to take it, not like some of the men she had known in the past. "Anyway, the kid said he heard his mother telling Lucille Hook that it was self-defence, and that she now wanted to turn herself in, after panicking at the time. But I think Lucille Hook was telling her to forget all about it and just look out for herself and her son. Ballard was nothing but a drug dealer and no one was going to miss him. The kid must have taken it upon himself to speak out for her."

"So there's more to it than a mugging that turned sour?"

"Well, it's a bit of a coincidence, don't you think?"

"Yeah, I think you're right," said Roscoe.

"And the reward was a fake, too," said Marnie, disgust curdling her words.

"What do you mean the reward was a fake?"

"The man who was supposed to have put up the reward has never heard of Paul Ballard, or his father."

"So the offer of a reward was just a ruse to draw out the killer," said Roscoe.

"We don't even know if she was the killer," said Marnie.

"I don't know," said Roscoe. "I think whoever did this must have had at least some idea who the killer was, and all that business with the reward was just a means of confirming that. But then again, perhaps it didn't matter to them who killed Ballard just so long as someone was seen to be punished for it."

"That's just animal," said Marnie, swallowing a lump in her throat.

"That's the way it happens out here," said Roscoe.

"I know, I know," said Marnie, soft and hurting a little.

Both of them fell silent for a moment, contemplating the lethal mindset of a man prepared to sacrifice an innocent woman just to protect his reputation and his business.

"You think Bar Code was behind all this?" said Marnie after a short time.

"It is bang in the middle of his territories, so I think we can take it as read that Ballard was working for him."

"And so it was nothing but a warning to his rivals . . ."

"It's beginning to look like that," agreed Roscoe.

"If Bar Code was behind all this, his alibi'll be so tight I reckon his fingerprints might as well have been burned off for all the solid connections we're going to find."

"You're right," agreed Roscoe. "His alibi'll have him on the other side of the world or something."

"I'd like to bury him so fucking deep that it might as well be on the other side of the world," said Marnie, caustic and frustrated. She took a deep breath and let it out in one great long sigh. "Anyway, what's all this you were saying about a cab?"

Roscoe told her about the call from the cab office that morning, about John Francis being the fare on Brecknock Road.

"I always knew Dillon was dirty," said Marnie, shaking her head. "So what are you going to do now? You want me to help?"

At that point Spencer glanced across at Marnie again, a frown creasing his forehead.

"What was that about Dillon?" said Spencer.

"Hold on a minute, Frank," said Marnie, dropping the phone to her side. "What is it, Spencer?"

"Is that Sean Dillon you were talking about, the uniform?"

"Yes."

"Well, I don't know if it means anything, but he was up in the CID room this morning asking about the Ballard case. Some bullshit about a kid he rousted last night offering him the name of the person who pushed Paul Ballard to his death. Asking me if I wanted him to keep an eye out for the kid tonight, and asking me to let him know if we came up with a suspect in the meantime."

"You told him about the Price kid coming in?"

"No, but it was all over the canteen at lunchtime."

"Fucking Dobie," said Marnie, shaking her head. "Him and his big mouth have just gone and got Sarah Price killed."

There was a hard rasping sound coming from the phone, almost a rattle, and Marnie raised it back up to her ear.

"Did I just hear you say Dillon is involved in the Ballard case?" said Roscoe, breathless and sounding like he had been shouting to get heard.

"That's what it looks like," replied Marnie. "Frank, where are you right now?"

"I'm in the Linton Tree with Charlie."

"Right, hold on for me there. I just need to go and have a word with John Price, and then I'll be over in about an hour."

"Make it the flat," said Roscoe, and cut the call.

40

Dropping the phone into his pocket, Roscoe turned back to the bar. He picked up his bottle of Miller and drained it. Hunched at the bar Charlie glanced him and said, "What was all that about?"

"Dillon," said Roscoe. "It sounds like he's got his fingers in more rotten pies than we thought."

"That's no great surprise," said Charlie, disgusted.

"I'm meeting Marnie at the flat later," said Roscoe. "Don't worry, we'll figure out some way to bring him down."

"You just said he was dirty," said Charlie, pain and confusion etched across his face. "What's left to figure out?"

"Sure, we might know it in here," said Roscoe, clutching a fist to his stomach. "But proving it is another thing altogether, and at the moment all we have are circumstantials."

"So what's going to happen, then?" asked Charlie, blinking as if struggling to keep focused on something falling out of reach.

"That's what I hope to figure out this afternoon."

"You and the Hitchcock blonde," said Charlie, allowing himself a brief humourless smile.

"Me and the Hitchcock blonde," said Roscoe, echoing the phrase and the brittle smile. "Anyway, what are you going to do now? You can't go back to Brighton like this. You need to sober up a bit first. You want to come back to the flat and take a shower, or have something to eat?"

"Thanks, but I think I'll head over to Rhee's for a while. Maybe we can go and take Karl some flowers or something."

"Come on, then, let's get out of here," said Roscoe, and put his arm around his old friend and led him out of the pub.

Two in the afternoon and Mel was bored out of her skull. Archie had gone out to a record fair first thing and left her in charge, but it had been quiet in the store and she had not spoken to more than a handful of people all morning. She had closed the place for ten minutes while she had fetched some lunch from the deli up the street, and now she sat on a stool behind the counter munching on a Greek salad in a plastic container. There were three customers in the store, all middle-aged men in leather jackets pecking through the racks of old plastic. Mel snorted and shook her head. She thought the Internet was supposed to have taken people like this off the streets. She could not remember the last time someone of her own age had been in the store, but on second thought she reckoned that that would just make things worse.

All her life she had felt too old for her age, and as a result she had found it difficult to make friends. Of late, and for all their talk of wanting to be different, she had found her contemporaries signing up to the same old tired list of influences and attitudes that had been handed down from generation to generation. She could even recognise large chunks of her mother in some of the girls in her class. Such people angered her. Depending on their level of intelligence, most of them were more concerned with being seen as either cool or hard than being their own person, and there were just a few brave souls prepared to go against the grain and follow their own compass. Mel had no idea where she fell in this argument, or how others saw her; all she knew was that she still found it difficult to make friends.

She considered Barney to be his own person, although she

was under no illusion that he was aware of how the world turned. But she was also sure that he had no second skin he put on before facing the world. No, he had his own presence, both innocent and tragic, and in her mind that made him real. It had taken her some time to come around to his charms, but now at last she felt that she had made a deep and lasting connection. She squirmed around on her stool, and crumbs of Feta cheese fell onto her lap as her lips spread into a wide smile as she remembered the night before.

Back at the station Marnie and Spencer headed straight for the interview rooms in the basement. Near the bottom of the stairs Marnie touched Spencer on the arm and held him back.

"I think we'd better talk to the kid about the reason he came in this morning before we tell him about his mother," said Marnie. "If we wait until afterwards he might be too distraught to remember much about what happened. Let me have a couple of minutes with him before we go and talk to his father."

"We should let Price know about his wife first," protested Spencer.

"I know, I know, but if we don't talk to the kid right now then we might lose out on what he knows," said Marnie.

"Two minutes," said Spencer, holding up two fingers.

"Go and get a coffee or something," said Marnie.

"Looks like I've got no choice," said Spencer, and then turned and headed back up the stairs.

Marnie waited for him to disappear around the corner and listened to his footsteps on the cracked lino in the corridor upstairs. Then she took a deep breath and stepped across to the interview room and let herself in.

She stood for a moment with her back to the door, looking across at the boy on the far side of the room. She had been told that he was fifteen, but he looked so small sitting there with his hands folded in his lap, a look on his face that reminded her of a child whose mother had forgotten to pick him up from school. He had come into the station of his own accord, so she knew he was not like all the other teenagers she had to deal with on a regular basis. But also because of this she felt her throat thicken with guilt at the thought of not telling him about his mother until she had found out what she needed to know.

"Hello, Barney," she said, pulling out a chair and sitting down across the table from him. She rested her hands on the table in front of her. "I'm Detective Sergeant Stone. I'm sorry to have kept you waiting for so long. How are you doing, anyway? Are you being looked after okay?"

The boy blinked and looked across the table. "I'm all right," he said, rubbing the back of his hand across his chin.

"Would you like a drink?" said Marnie, and then turned at once to the WPC standing against the wall. "You mind fetching us a couple of cans of Coke from the canteen, please?"

"Sure," said the WPC, nodding, and then left the room.

"So, Barney," said Marnie on a great sigh, leaning into the table and folding her hands together. "You want to tell me what happened this morning. . . . I understand that you spent last night over at your dad's place, is that right?"

"Yeah, that's right," said Barney, nodding.

"Okay, let's start over at your dad's place, then," said Marnie. "You remember what time you left there this morning?"

"Not really, no," said Barney, remembering the scuffling and pushing it straight out of his mind again.

"You must have some idea. Eight, nine, ten?"

"I think Mel had to be at work in Camden Town for ten."

"Mel?"

"She's sort of my stepsister," said Barney, pursing his lips.

"And she lives with your father and stepmother?"

"They're not married, but yeah, she lives with them."

"Tell me where he lives again? Your father?"

"Golders Green, near the crematorium."

"You travelled into Camden Town with Mel this morning?"

"Yeah, on the tube."

"And then you went with her to where she works?"

"Yeah, more or less," said Barney, remembering the kiss and feeling his cheeks getting warm.

"And where's that, where does she work?"

"In a record store on Inverness Street. In the middle of the market there. Shake Records, I think it's called."

"I think I know the place," said Marnie. "I might even have bought a couple of CDs from there. Must be one of the few independent record stores left. Sells a lot of old vinyl, right?"

"I think most of it's secondhand," said Barney.

"Yeah, that's the place," said Marnie. "So the pair of you got there about ten, and then what, you went straight home . . ."

"Yeah, I went straight home after that."

"Five, ten minutes walk?"

"Something like that," said Barney, shrugging.

"Okay," said Marnie, swallowing her conscience. "Before we talk about what happened in the flat this morning, I want you to tell me about what happened afterward, after you left the flat."

"Like what?"

"Like where did you go, who did you speak to . . ."

"I came straight here," said Barney, confusion creasing his forehead. "I didn't stop anywhere, or talk to anyone."

"You came straight here," said Marnie. "You didn't stop and talk to a friend, or a neighbour, someone from the estate?"

"No, I came straight here," shaking his head, emphatic.

"You're sure about that?"

"I wanted to tell someone before I changed my mind."

"That's very brave of you, Barney," said Marnie, and then bit her tongue as she found herself wanting to add something about his mother being proud of him. "Anyway," she pushed on, placing the flat of her hands on the table, elbows raised. "I need to go and talk to my boss now, but I'll be back as soon as I can to talk about what you heard in the flat this morning."

"When's my dad going to be here?"

"I . . . I don't know," said Marnie, standing and turning her back to him, feeling the heat in her throat. "I'll go and find out what's happening, get someone to come and talk to you."

"Thanks," said Barney.

Marnie bumped into Spencer out in the corridor, closed the door tight behind her.

"How did it go?" said Spencer.

"He just asked me where his father is," said Marnie.

"And you didn't tell him he was in another interview room just down the corridor?" said Spencer, grinning.

"Piss off, Spencer," said Marnie, half joking. She lifted the cup of coffee from his hand and took a sip, handed it back. "Anyway, as far as Barney's concerned, it doesn't look like he spoke to anyone on his way in to see us this morning, so I better go and warn Belmont about what's happening."

"I thought we were going to talk to Price now?"

"The chain of command," said Marnie, mock frowning. She glanced up and down the corridor. "I think I just heard someone say he was in one of the rooms down here somewhere . . ."

"You want me to talk to him on my own?"

"I just told you, I have to go and talk to Belmont," said Marnie. She turned and headed for the stairs, left him there. She had just put her foot on the second step when she heard the roar of John Price as Spencer opened the door of the interview room at the end of the corridor: "And about fucking time, too. Now at last can someone please tell me what the fuck's going on? First you tell me to get down here as soon as I can, and then you keep me waiting for over an hour. I mean what the fuck's that all about? And what's Barney supposed to have done in the first place, anyway?"

"Mr. Price, please," replied Spencer, and then the door closed and all she could hear was the muffled thump of words.

Marnie shook her head and headed up to the CID room. She crossed to her desk, picked up the phone, crooked it in the shrug of a shoulder, and flipped through her phone book to find Belmont's home number. That's when she caught sight of Charlie Burns in the street outside. Leaning against a car parked in the side street opposite the station. Replacing the phone in its cradle, Marnie stepped up close to the window to make sure she was not mistaken.

It was him all right. He even had on the same clothes from the night before.

Still at the window, Marnie took out her mobile and scrolled through the incoming call numbers until she came to the one from Roscoe, and then pressed the return call button.

"Hey, Marnie," said Roscoe. "You finished so soon?"

"Frank, where's Charlie at the moment?"

"He told me he was going over to Rhiannon's, why?"

"He said he was going straight there?"

"Yeah, why? What's going on?"

"I'm in the office right now, and I can see him standing across the street. It looks like he's waiting for someone."

"Oh shit . . ."

"I think you'd better get over here as fast as you can," said Marnie.

41

From where he was standing, Charlie could see the front of Dillon's car on the far side of the police station car park. He could not see the back entrance to the station, the staff entrance, or the spot in the car park where he had confronted Dillon earlier that morning, but on second thought he reckoned that to be a good thing. If Dillon did spot him coming out of the building then that would just put the policeman on his guard and make it that much more difficult for Charlie to do what he had to do. Not that he had a clear picture in his mind of what it was he had to do. But he trusted his own instincts to let him know when the time was right. His own car was parked on a meter down the street from the station, close enough for him to be able to fetch it and be on Dillon's tail before the policeman had made it out onto Kentish Town Road.

Marnie's call cut across the opening bars of "Greetings to the New Brunette," and Roscoe rolled off the sofa and hit the pause button on the stereo before picking up the phone. His foot had been throbbing and fit to burst when he got home, so he had taken a handful of painkillers, dug out some old copies of *Uncut,* stuck on some music, made himself a mug of strong black coffee, and then stretched out on the sofa to wait for her call.

He was surprised she called so soon, but when she mentioned seeing Charlie outside the station he understood what was happening and cursed himself for thinking that Charlie had calmed down from the night before. Now he could see that his friend had just been keeping quiet because he knew that if he showed his true feelings, Roscoe would just attempt to talk him down from the ledge again. Not to mention the fact that he had been too full of Marnie and his own inflated role in the situation to see what was happening with his friend.

After putting down the phone, he hit the pause button on the stereo again, bringing the track back into life, and then searched around the flat for the boots he had taken off minutes earlier. He found one in the kitchen and one in the hall, and then carried them through into the front room where he sat on the sofa while he pulled them on. He swallowed hot coffee and waited for the track to finish, all the time thinking about Charlie and Karl and what he would do in the same circumstance. If he was being truthful with himself, he did not know for sure. He clicked off the stereo and headed for the door.

"That's it, I'm out of here," said Dillon, taking a last look at the picture of Uma Thurman taped to the inside of his locker door before slamming it shut. He left the locker room without looking back, offers of a quick drink in the pub bouncing off deaf ears, and headed straight for the car park. He had heard about the killing of Sarah Price an hour earlier and had felt a muted sense of elation and fear. Time had since dragged, and now he just wanted to be out of the station as soon as possible.

He pushed on through the back door and took long hurried strides across the cracked tarmac. He unlocked the car and lowered himself into the driver's seat. Fired up the engine and put the car in gear. He rolled across the car park and checked the street, then pulled out and cruised the short distance to the junction with Kentish Town Road. Moments later a break appeared in the traffic and he joined the flow heading north. He did not notice the car that joined the flow two spots behind him.

42

"Come on, Frank, get in the car," shouted Marnie through the open window, the Saab idling at the kerb on Holmes Road. The police station loomed in the background, monochrome and unwelcoming. Blank faces appeared like ghosts at the windows and then disappeared again. Roscoe had just arrived in a black cab and was handing the cabbie a tenner, telling him to keep the change. "Get a fucking move on, Frank. We're going to lose them at this rate."

Roscoe ran around to the passenger side where Marnie had opened the door for him. He just had time to climb in and slam the door shut behind him before she hit the accelerator. "What's the rush?" he said, breathless and blinking at perspiration.

"Dillon left the station about two minutes ago," said Marnie, at the end of the street now and edging the Saab out into traffic. "You must've just passed him. He went up Kentish Town Road with Charlie about ten seconds behind him."

"Shit, what the fuck's he up to?" said Roscoe, under his breath.

"I don't know," said Marnie, steering around a white Astra estate parked in the bus lane with its warning lights flashing. A fat man with a handlebar moustache and thick black hair on the back of his hands was unloading cases of beer from the boot and stacking them on the pavement. "But, whatever it is, we need to stop him before he goes and does something stupid."

"I should have spotted this before," said Roscoe, shaking his head. "I was just talking to him for a couple of hours."

"You really think he might try and hurt Dillon?"

"I don't know what he might do," said Roscoe. "I thought I knew him, but I guess you never really know how someone will react when it comes down to their kids. I mean look at Sarah Price, look at what she did."

"I bet her friends never thought she'd do something like that, either," said Marnie, glancing across the seats.

Roscoe caught the glance and accepted the meaning.

At the top of Kentish Town Road, Roscoe saw Charlie's white Metro turn onto Fortess Road. In front of him were a green Fiat Punto, a blue transit van, and a red Honda Civic. "The red Honda," he said, pointing. "That must be Dillon's car, right?"

"The red Honda," agreed Marnie, nodding. The police radio crackled beneath the dashboard, and there were a number of tapes and discarded paper coffee cups on the floor that Roscoe had to push aside with his feet to get comfortable.

"You want to cut him off and let me have a talk with him?"

"I don't know," replied Marnie, pulling up at a red light near Tufnell Park tube station. She frowned and then looked deep in thought for a couple of seconds. Dillon was at the head of the line of traffic, pushing at the lights. "It's an idea, but now that we have Dillon in our sights, I don't think we should tip our hand if it turns out that Charlie is just riding out his anger. Did he have much to drink this afternoon?"

"Three or four beers," said Roscoe, shrugging. "Scotch."

"So you think he might be feeling reckless, then?"

"I don't know," said Roscoe, looking out at the street, the blurred buildings sliding past him like fast-melting icebergs.

Marnie glanced across at Roscoe for a second and caught the side of his face, the muscles along his jawline tense. She turned face front and drove in silence for a couple of minutes, her hands turning white on the top of the wheel.

"I should have told Belmont about Dillon before we left," she said at last.

"You haven't told him?" said Roscoe, surprised.

"I haven't had the chance," said Marnie, watching the lights and pushing the Saab forward to make sure she made the cut. "I'd just got through speaking with Barney Price and gone upstairs when I saw Charlie hanging around outside."

"So what happened with the Price kid?"

"Not much," said Marnie, and then proceeded to tell him about her talk with Barney minutes earlier. "But for what it's worth, I believe him. I think it happened just like he tells it."

"You've told him about what happened to his mother?"

The lights changed and Marnie moved forward.

"I sent Spencer in to talk to his father," she said. "I just wanted to speak to Barney before he heard about his mother and clammed up on us. I let Spencer deal with all the rest of it. I'm no good with emotions, the female side of things."

The traffic started to thin out on Junction Road, but as they reached the wide roundabout at Archway, another wave of motorists from the Holloway Road fleshed out the line heading north and Marnie had to jump around a couple of stragglers to keep Charlie and Dillon in her sights. Dusk had started to fall, and one or two cars had put on their lights, Dillon included, little flecks of red and white sparking in the air. The three cars headed up Archway Road towards Suicide Bridge and Highgate. Four hundred metres further on, the Boogaloo, the place where Dillon had supposedly found Francis beaten up, was a solid reminder of what they were up against.

"Where d'you think he's going?" said Roscoe.

"I don't know," said Marnie, shaking her head. "I thought he lived over in Kilburn or Cricklewood, somewhere like that."

"Doesn't look like he's going home, then," said Roscoe.

"I don't think he's the kind of man to sit in front of the TV or a computer screen all night," said Marnie.

Just past Highgate tube station, Dillon hung a right into Muswell Hill Road and headed up through the woods towards Muswell Hill. There were just a few vehicles on the road now, and Charlie was hanging back, nothing but a couple of buses and buckled macadam between the Metro and Dillon. A black cab with a couple of men in suits inside buffeted Roscoe and Marnie from the others.

Before he reached the roundabout on the outskirts of Muswell Hill village, Dillon signalled right and headed down a long residential street. Identical brick houses stretched down the hill on both sides of the street, with hanging baskets and different coloured doors offering unique public faces.

Two hundred metres along the street, Dillon pulled up at the kerb in front of a house with a dark blue door. Charlie drove straight past without so much as a sidelong glance. Marnie pulled up on the opposite side of the street behind a black Fiat Uno, far enough back to get a clean look but not close enough to be seen herself. Dillon got out of the car and walked up the path and rang the doorbell. The door opened and he slipped inside.

"You think Charlie might have changed his mind and gone home?" said Roscoe, peering down the street for a sign of the Metro.

"I wouldn't have thought so," replied Marnie, pointing to the glove compartment. "There should be a camera in there."

"What's that?" said Roscoe, distracted. He was hoping that Charlie had changed his mind and decided to go home. Or perhaps Charlie had just seen Roscoe and Marnie in his mirror and for the time being decided against doing whatever he was planning on doing.

"A camera," repeated Marnie. "In the glove compartment."

"Oh, sure," said Roscoe. He rummaged around in the glove

compartment, lifted out the camera and held it out for Marnie.

"Thanks," said Marnie, taking it from him. She checked that there was film and then held it in her lap, her hands positioned to use it. Seconds later she leaned into the windscreen a fraction, squinting. "It looks like Charlie was just turning around," she said. "He's coming back up towards us now."

Roscoe watched as Charlie drove towards them and pulled into the kerb a couple of car spaces behind Dillon.

A peculiar silence fell on the scene, taut with an unspoken threat. People strolled past the Saab, innocent and talkative.

Three minutes later the door of the house opened again and Dillon appeared in the frame, another man at his shoulder. Dillon had a black holdall in his hand, a Reebok logo on the side. He spoke to his companion for a moment, and then turned and headed back down the path to his car. The other man stood on the threshold of his home for a second, squinting and looking up and down the street as if he was waiting for someone else to turn up, and then went back inside without acknowledging Dillon again.

"That's Jem Tobin," said Roscoe, startled.

"The one who works for Bar Code?"

"His red right hand," Roscoe confirmed, nodding. "As long as Bar Code chooses to keep a profile lower than the mud in the Regent's Park canal, then it'll be Jem Tobin that'll be the unacceptable face of his organisation."

"This is getting interesting," said Marnie, snapping the slow action with the camera.

"What's he got in the bag?"

"If he's working for Bar Code, then it's bound to be either drugs or cash," said Marnie.

"This time of the weekend it'll be drugs," said Roscoe. "Saturday night's his biggest market, so he's going to need all hands on deck to get the product out on to the street."

"In that case we'd better see where he's taking the bag," said Marnie, passing the camera across to Roscoe as she started up the car again. "And make sure we get it all on film."

"What are we going to do about Charlie?" said Roscoe, taking the camera from her and acquainting himself with the workings.

"I don't know," admitted Marnie, biting her lower lip. "If all he's interested in doing is tailing Dillon and working out his frustration and anger that way, then I think we can just let him get on with it. But if he decides to confront Dillon, or if Dillon spots him and decides to do something about it, then we'll just have to jump in and pull him out. We might not nail Dillon this time, but I'm not having another civilian get hurt."

"I don't think we should leave it to chance."

"Let's just see where Dillon's going first," said Marnie, reaching for the ignition. "Come on, he's on the move again."

"Yeah, all right," said Roscoe, reluctant.

The pair watched Dillon do a three-point turn and start back up towards the main road. Moments later Charlie pulled out from the kerb and followed him. Roscoe and Marnie turned their heads aside until both vehicles had passed, and then Marnie turned the Saab around, flicked on her lights, and headed after them.

At the junction with Muswell Hill Road, Marnie looked to her left and saw the cars heading back the way they had come.

She followed them towards Highgate, turning left at the lights and passing under Suicide Bridge once more. She kept Dillon in her sights, the red Honda a beacon on her radar. Charlie was a couple of steps behind, clipping at the heels of a black cab decorated in the colours of a budget airline.

"Looks like Charlie's getting a bit too close," she said.

"He must be getting impatient," replied Roscoe.

Dillon headed back into Archway, but instead of going back

to Tufnell Park and Kentish Town, he circled the roundabout and drove up Highgate Hill. Just past the Whittington Hospital he took a sharp left and made for the council flats that backed on to Highgate Cemetery, the final resting place of Karl Marx.

Reaching the end of the street, Marnie saw Charlie parked ten metres down and across from her, on the corner of a short street of brick maisonettes. She edged the Saab around the corner and pulled in tight to the kerb behind a battered green Cortina.

"Down there," said Roscoe, pointing across the street past Charlie to where Dillon had parked outside one of the maisonettes on the estate. He had his head bent over the passenger seat and looked as if he was fiddling with something. He ducked out of sight for a couple of seconds, pushing something under the passenger seat, perhaps, and then sat up again and climbed out of the car. He had a blue plastic carrier bag in his hand; there seemed to be something heavy in it by the way it was hanging. Roscoe adjusted the focus on the camera and ran off another couple of snaps as Dillon walked around the car and rang the bell of the ground floor flat. He turned his back to the door and looked around as he waited for it to open. Moments later a black man in a white tracksuit with blue piping around the collar and cuffs appeared at the door. He had a cigarette in his mouth that shook out smoke signals as he spoke.

"You recognise him as well?"

"Not this one, no," said Roscoe, snapping the two men at the door.

"And it has to be drugs," questioned Marnie.

"He's not delivering pizza, that's for sure," said Roscoe.

Dillon spoke with the black man for a brief moment, both of them checking their watches and glancing around all the time, and then handed across the carrier bag. The other man at once ducked back inside, closing the door and leaving a startled Dillon on the doorstep. He tried to appear as if he knew that that was going to happen, and then took one final quick look around before scuttling back to his car. Seconds later, he was on his way.

"I think you're right," said Marnie. "It looks like he's dropping off tonight's supplies. I better call for some back up."

Dillon signalled to make a left as he steered the Honda out from the kerb, and drove the short distance to the end of the street in first. Charlie followed him as he started to make the turn.

"They're going round the block," said Roscoe. "We can pick them up again further on down Dartmouth Park Road."

Marnie put the Saab in gear and pulled out, picking up the others fifteen metres further on down the road as predicted.

"I hope he's not going along Brecknock Road," said Roscoe. The street where Dillon had mowed down Karl Burns was across the junction at the foot of the hill.

"If that doesn't provoke Charlie into doing something, I don't know what will," said Marnie.

Approaching the lights at the foot of Dartmouth Park Road, Dillon accelerated to get through the green light on its final call. Charlie tried to follow him but a black Taurus waiting to come out of Fortess Road was too quick off the mark and Charlie had to pull up sharp on the edge of the grid to avoid a collision.

Marnie reached the lights four cars back.

Roscoe saw Charlie leaning into the wheel as he waited for the lights to change, thumbs tapping hard, and spotted his chance.

He checked the bike lane over his shoulder, and then opened the door and stepped out onto the road.

"Hey, what d'you think you're doing?"

"Just keep following him," said Roscoe, and then slammed

the door. He hurried up the line of cars, keeping low, until he reached the white Metro. Within a fraction of a second he had opened the passenger side door and slipped into the seat.

As he hit the leather, Charlie snapped his head around, startled. "What the fuck," he said, his pupils darkened with shock.

"The lights have changed," said Roscoe, cool, pulling the door shut and pointing at the fresh green light up ahead. From behind them in the queue a car sounded its horn. Roscoe did not need to turn around to know that it had been Marnie.

Charlie stared at Roscoe for a second, and then let out a short laugh and shook his head. He stuck the Metro in gear, but then managed to stall it as he tried to pull out. He tried again, and this time managed to get out from under the red and edge the Metro into the centre of the grid. As he waited for the oncoming traffic to pass, he glanced in the mirror and recognised Marnie.

"How long have you been following me?"

"We should be able to catch Dillon at the next lights," said Roscoe, pointing down Fortress Road. The oncoming traffic had cleared and, after shooting Roscoe a look loaded with both pride and frustration, Charlie turned the wheel and started back towards Kentish Town.

"Marnie called me from the station," said Roscoe. "She saw you waiting outside and thought you might be going to do something stupid. What were you planning on doing, anyway?"

Charlie said nothing, just slid Roscoe a sidelong glance that was full of the claustrophobic sense of his terrible predicament.

"At least we know what Dillon's been up to now," said Roscoe.

"He's nothing but a fucking bag man," said Charlie.

"Marnie's calling for back up," said Roscoe. "So we should be able to pick him up before he finishes his rounds. Get us out from under this terrible fucking business once and for all."

"Nothing but a fucking gofer," Charlie went on, shaking his head.

"Just concentrate on keeping him in our sights," said Roscoe, pointing up ahead. "We don't want to lose him now."

Dillon towed them back through Kentish Town, past Holmes Road and the police station without so much as a glance, and then hung a right into Prince of Wales Road. He cruised around the double parked cars and the people wandering in the middle of the road, little kids trailing their mothers and old men trailing their wives, and then turned into Malden Road. He drove a further hundred metres before pulling up across from the Denton Estate.

Roscoe touched Charlie on the arm and signalled for him to steer into the kerb a good distance back. Seconds later Marnie pulled in behind them. Up ahead Roscoe saw Dillon glance across the street and then bend across the passenger seat once more.

"So now we just sit and wait," said Charlie, turning to Roscoe.

"Sit and wait for the cavalry to arrive," said Roscoe, and then noticed Charlie's eyes move to a point above his left shoulder.

"It's the Hitchcock blonde," said Charlie, pointing behind him.

Roscoe turned to see Marnie beside the car, crouching low on her toes. She motioned for him to wind down the window.

"We better go after him now," she said as soon as Roscoe had opened the window a fraction.

"I thought we were waiting for back up?" said Roscoe, feeling the hairs on the back of his neck stand up.

"There isn't time," replied Marnie, her eyes darting from Roscoe to Dillon and back again. "You saw how much stuff he took from Tobin's place. Another couple of visits and he's going to be cleaned out. We have to do it now, Frank. It's now or never. Come on, Frank, he's on the move again," she implored, tracking Dillon as he climbed out of his car and started across the street.

Roscoe felt panic flood his heart and jangle his senses. He knew that he had been getting closer to going back to work, but he hadn't wanted it to be thrust upon him like this. He watched Marnie stand up and walk down the street, nothing but confidence in her stride, and made the decision in his mind: he could not let Marnie think that he had lost his nerve. He felt a brief shock of fear shake his belief and glanced at Charlie for confirmation.

"Go and nail the fucking bastard," said Charlie, cold and hard.

"You wait here," said Roscoe, grabbing the door handle and climbing out of the car. He hurried down the street to where Marnie was squatting behind an overloaded skip. There were cracked needles and used condoms buried in the builders' rubble. Roscoe slowed and crouched down beside her, and at once felt a sharp pain snap around his ankle and shoot up his leg. "Jesus wept," he managed to crunch out through clenched teeth before falling onto his side, his hands clutching at his ankle.

Marnie jerked her head around. "What is it, Frank? What happened to your leg?"

"It's my ankle," replied Roscoe, easing himself onto his back and stretching out his leg in front of him.

"Are you going to be all right?"

Roscoe grimaced and rubbed hard at his ankle, keeping quiet.

"Just give me a couple of seconds," he said at last, his breathing almost back to normal. He was clutching his thigh in both hands and holding his leg in the air, rotating his foot in a slow circle to help ease the pain. "I shouldn't squat down like that," he said. "It puts too much tension on the tendon. Stretches it tight like an old elastic band about to break."

"You sure you're going to be all right?"

"You need to keep your eye on Dillon," replied Roscoe, and gestured for her to turn around with a wild flap of his hand. She offered him a brief smile of commiseration, and then turned her attention back to the street and Dillon.

The Denton Estate consisted of four three-storey buildings with front-facing open walkways arranged in a loose arc around a patch of threadbare grass. The grass was scarred with worn makeshift paths from the front entrance of each building to the street, and scatterings of trash, torn scraps of newspaper and crisp packets, fluttered a few inches off the ground like seagulls with broken wings. In the centre of each building was an open arch that led to a staircase to the upper floors. Dillon was walking through the arch of the building second from the left.

"We'll just wait and see which flat he's going to, and then we can go in after him," said Marnie, her eyes climbing the stairwell as if she could see Dillon through the concrete.

"You're in charge," said Roscoe, attempting a smile.

Moments later Dillon appeared on the second floor. He stopped for a moment to catch his breath, and took the moment to scan the immediate area. From the top of the new buildings up near the Lock on his right, to the pedestrians and traffic on the Prince of Wales Road to his left and all points in between. Starting up again, he walked to the door at the far end of the walkway, took a final look out across the street, and then turned and knocked on the door with the back of his hand.

"Let's go to work," said Marnie, and ducked out from behind the skip. With a quick glance in both directions, she hurried across the street, running low across the patch of grass, and into the dark stairwell that Dillon had vacated moments earlier.

Roscoe took a deep breath and, with his heart in his throat, went after her. The pain in his ankle had eased a little, it was

now no more than a nagging ache deep in the muscle, a tight-
ness around the bottom of the calf, the tendon, but once more
he had been made aware of his own limitations and it both
frightened and angered him. But he knew he had no time to
entertain such thoughts now, and pushed them aside as he followed Marnie across the grass and into the stairwell.

On the second floor landing Marnie was waiting for him.
"He's just gone inside," she said, and then noticed the crumple
of frustration on his face. "Is the ankle going to be all right?"

"It'll be fine," replied Roscoe, a half truth.

Marnie nodded. "So," she grinned. "Think you can remember
what to do in a situation like this?"

"Like riding a bike," said Roscoe, grinning back.

"Let's get on with it, then," said Marnie. She touched the
back of his hand, and then hurried along the walkway. On reaching the far end, she turned and waited for Roscoe to take up his
position on the near side of the door. She raised her brows and
asked him if he was set, and then knocked hard on the door.

There was no response and she knocked again.

"Yeah, who is it?"

Marnie waited, and then knocked again.

Footsteps behind the door. "I said who the fuck is it?"

Marnie waited a beat, and then knocked again.

Seconds later the door was ripped open and a man appeared
in the frame. He had cropped black hair that matched the
stubble on his chin, one ring through his nose and another
couple along the ridge of his left ear. "Yo, Big Bad Wolf, stop
banging on the fuckin' door or I'll—"

"Or you'll what?" snapped Marnie, grabbing hold of his shirt
and tugging him out onto the walkway. The man stumbled and
fell forward, his arms spiralling out in front of him, chasing balance. Roscoe put a hand on his shoulder and pushed him to the
ground. His face hit the deck and Roscoe dropped into the cen-

tre of his back on one knee. Marnie handed Roscoe a pair of handcuffs and, before the man knew what was happening, Roscoe had threaded his hands through the railings and secured his wrists together.

"Yo, Stevie, what the fuck's going on out there?" shouted Dillon from deep inside the flat.

Roscoe and Marnie looked at each other.

"The front room," whispered Marnie.

Roscoe nodded in agreement.

The flat's blueprint was familiar to them from numerous trips to other flats on the estate: a short hall ending at the living room with two doors leading off the hall to the left, the kitchen and bathroom, and two doors leading off the hall to the right, the main bedroom and a second smaller bedroom.

"You take the rooms off the hall, I'll go and see Dillon," said Marnie, then stepped into the hall.

Roscoe nodded and followed her across the threshold. There was no carpet and their feet sounded loud on the concrete floor. He pushed open the kitchen door with his foot, no one there, and the bathroom was also clear. He opened the first bedroom door, the smaller of the two. It looked like a kid's room, with posters of Linkin Park and the Foo Fighters tacked to the wall, and he found that clear too. He took a quick glance at Marnie striding up the hall, a swagger in her step, and found himself smiling as he kicked open the door to the main bedroom. He stepped inside and swept the room with his eyes, checking the wardrobe and under the bed. There were fresh clothes scattered across the floor like stepping stones, and a games console rigged up to a widescreen TV at the foot of the bed was switched on, the game on pause, but there was no sign of human occupation.

In the front room Dillon was standing beside a scarred wooden table, looking out of the window. The stereo pumped out some kind of urban music, thick and low, and the smell of stale marijuana smoke and fried chicken hung in the air.

"What the fuck's going on," said Dillon as he saw Marnie enter the room, a look of bald surprise on his face.

Spread out on the table in front of him were a couple of shrink-wrapped bricks of white powder, and a precise set of paraphernalia for cutting the powder—a tall plastic container of another, pale yellow, powder, scales, blades, a mirror—and parcelling it up into ten quid wraps for the street.

"The job not paying you enough, Dillon?" said Marnie.

"This is not what it looks like," Dillon snapped back.

"So tell me, what's wrong with the picture?"

"Stevie's one of my snitches," replied Dillon, breathing through his mouth as if he was chewing gum. His hands had rolled into loose fists in front of his thighs, and his cold eyes darted around the room, out of the window and back again.

Roscoe stepped into the room beside Marnie. She gave him the briefest of smiles, and then walked over towards Dillon.

"And you're paying him with drugs," said Marnie, sweeping a hand towards the table.

"I didn't know he was into all of this," said Dillon. "I thought he was just another piece of street scum."

"That's no way to talk about your friends," said Marnie.

"We've been following you since you left the station," said Roscoe.

"Who the fuck are you, anyway?" said Dillon, leaning forward and jabbing a blunt finger over Marnie's shoulder.

"Detective Inspector Frank Roscoe," said Roscoe.

"He's been on sick leave," said Marnie.

"You're the one who was shot in that drive-by down in Chalk Farm," smirked Dillon. "Yeah, I heard about that."

"Been off work for seven months now," said Marnie. "Waiting until the time was right to come back."

"And when I heard that a bad cop had killed the only child of one of my oldest friends, I knew then that the time was right. You remember Karl Burns, Dillon?"

Dillon stared at him, rode it out.

"How about Sarah Price, then?"

Dillon's face went cold, and his fists unrolled at his sides. He looked at the drugs on the table, then back out the window where he could see a group of kids skateboarding in the car park at the back of the estate, the garages with broken doors spilling entrails of plastic and rusted iron, and then back into the room. For a split second his focus was drawn to a point behind Marnie and Roscoe. Roscoe caught the shift in attention and turned to see the kid outside, Stevie, struggling to turn around and sit up. The kid saw Roscoe looking at him and stopped struggling for a moment, a fighting look of resentment crossing his face. Roscoe turned back to Marnie and Dillon.

Seconds later there was a surge of noise and cold air from the open front door, and Roscoe spun around to see a man in a black hooded top coming at him, a blue steel bar raised in his fist. Roscoe froze for a split second, and flashbacked to the pale blue car coming at him, the flash of gun metal raised in the open window, but it was enough time for the Hood to get up close to him.

"Frank, what the fuck're you wai—"

The steel bar sliced through the air, and Roscoe had just enough time to raise his right arm in defence before the bar caught him near the wrist and a bolt of pain shot up to his shoulder. The blow also managed to knock him off balance, his feet twisting at the ankles and causing him to turn his back on his assailant.

The Hood raised the steel bar and hit Roscoe across the right shoulder, a glancing blow that caused the Hood to stumble a little and lose his momentum. A blanket of pain spread across

Roscoe's back and then was gone, replaced with a chill numbness. Roscoe gritted his teeth and clenched his fists as he fought to keep on his feet. His assailant was standing off to his side, the steel bar still clenched in his fist. On the edge of his radar he saw Marnie approaching Dillon, the palms of her hands held up in front of her and telling him to remain where he was.

For a moment it looked as if Dillon was going to listen to her, but then in one swift movement he grabbed a chair from near the table and swung it around in a high arc, hitting Marnie across the shoulders just as she turned her back on him to shield herself. She fell to her knees with a solid thump, shocked and shaken to the bone, but she still had the presence of mind to roll onto her back and cross her hands and feet in front of her like a wounded animal before Dillon came at her again with the chair. His breath escaped in short hard bursts as he hit her again and again, her hands getting caught in the tangle of chair legs, her fingers cracking, her torso bruising. Then he tossed the chair aside and started to kick her in the ribs and in the legs. Marnie rolled up into a foetal ball. But he soon tired of that and, taking a quick glance at the drugs on the table, rushed across to where Roscoe and the man in the hood were fighting.

Marnie remained conscious, the room around her blurred, but the terrible pain in her chest felt like one of her ribs was broken. She could still breathe, but each strained breath had to be bought on credit. Her shoulder throbbed like someone was jumping up and down on it, and she thought that at least one of her fingers was broken, too.

Roscoe had managed to remain on his feet after the second blow, and after lurching at the Hood with as much strength as he could muster, he was struggling to wrestle the steel bar from him. The Hood kicked with wild feet like there was a dog snapping at his ankles. Their torsos arched back and forth with the effort, limbs flapping like the loose ends of a knot unravelling, great beats of air escaping from their mouths, and then a kick caught Roscoe on his damaged tendon and his hands snapped loose from the steel bar and went to his ankle. He found himself losing his balance and fought to right himself, but the Hood punched him in the side of the head with the full thrust of the steel bar in his hand and Roscoe fell to the floor like a rock, blood splattering the floorboards like a Jackson Pollock painting.

Dillon inched around the damaged figure stretched out on the floor, ran out of the flat and kept on running. The Hood watched him go, then climbed to his feet and scoped out the room. The flat had been his home for fifteen months with Stevie, but now that it had been stained it was of no further use to him. The lease was in some poor hump's name that Stevie had chased off back when he was looking for somewhere for them to live, so there was no link back to him there. Stalking across to the table, he snatched up the product, stuffed it back inside the blue carrier bag, and rushed out of the flat.

"Yo, he'p me, man," pleaded Stevie. "Get me out o' these fuckin' irons."

But his flatmate just blanked him and kept on walking.

Roscoe rolled onto his back, groaning. He blinked at the light, once, twice, and then closed his lids tight. His heart seemed to be pumping from four corners of his frame: in his ankle, at his temple, his shoulder, and deep and fast in the pit of his stomach. Black clouds ghosted across his sight, and as he realised what had just happened, a terrible feeling of guilt flooded his senses. It had been his mistake that allowed the third man to come at them from behind. His mistake that got Marnie hurt. He let his head fall to the side to look across to where Marnie was curled up on her side facing him, her right hand cradled to her chest like she was nursing a frightened child. She had a look of tired anger on her face, and Roscoe felt as if a cold hand was twisting his heart in his chest.

Charlie saw Dillon step out of the flat and knew at once that something was wrong.

He watched Dillon stumble along the walkway, glancing back at the flat and the kid that Roscoe had cuffed to the railings, and then fade into the darkness of the stairwell. He tracked Dillon down the stairs, got ahead of himself. There were a couple of kids sitting on the bottom step, under the arch, smoking, and from somewhere on the estate, he could hear the clattering mesh of rap and pop music that sounded like a stoned teenager beating up his kid brother. Charlie returned his focus to the flat, still hoping to see Roscoe come chasing out of the door after Dillon, but there was still no sign of either Roscoe or Marnie. He felt his heart step up a beat and his hands tighten on the top of the wheel. Firing up the engine, he put the car in gear, preparing to follow Dillon once more.

Ten seconds later Dillon emerged from the stairwell, blinking at a sudden flash of headlights as if he had been underground. As he stepped onto the grass he stumbled across one of the kids' trainers, and the kids yelled after him, barraging him with obscenities. Dillon ignored it all, and half-walked, half-ran across the grass, glancing back up at the walkway every couple of steps. Seeing no one following him, he took a moment to catch his breath, leaning forward and resting his hands on his knees. Charlie let out the clutch and pointed the Metro at the centre of the road, easing out across the tarmac a little. He depressed the clutch and let the car idle. Dillon took a deep breath, arched his back and stood up. He glanced down the street, waited for a green Megane to pass, then stepped out onto the road, the curl of a relieved smile on his face.

At the sight of the smile, all the sorrow and grief that had been building up inside Charlie since Karl had been killed erupted across his senses in a searing burst of rage. Blood red thoughts swirled around in his head, but before the thoughts could clear, he had stamped his foot down hard on the accelerator and let up the clutch.

The Metro screamed and tore out from the kerb, squealing and ripping down the centre of the road. Dillon had a split second to realise where the noise was coming from if he wanted to rescue himself, but when he saw the Metro bearing down on him, shaking on its wheels, his feet were stuck to the tarmac and all he could do was raise his hands in front of his chest in a futile attempt to defend himself.

Clamping his lids shut tight, Charlie locked his arms at the elbows and held his course. His knuckles whitened on the rim of the wheel, and his leg was shaking with the sheer effort he was putting into pressing down on the accelerator.

The Metro hit Dillon high on his right thigh and flipped him across the front of the car. His head thumped into the centre of the bonnet with a gruesome crunch, his arms and legs flailing around like whips in a storm, and his torso crashed and bounced off the windscreen, cracking the glass like thin ice, before he was tossed onto the roof. He spun across the roof in one quick roll, and hit the boot with his left shoulder before crashing back to earth, his skin burning and tearing on the tarmac, before coming to rest with his head in the gutter. Seconds later, a slow pool of blood spread out from the back of his head, like a splintered map of all the places he would now never see.

As the sounds of Sean Dillon crashing to his death were absorbed into the surrounding landscape, Charlie Burns eased his foot up off the accelerator, changed into second gear, and kept on driving straight ahead.

He did not look back.

LATER

Two weeks later Roscoe arranged to meet Marnie at the café on Parliament Hill. It was a bright morning, the sun clear and high, but autumn had turned to winter, and at noon a brittle white frost was still etched in the shadows. The café was full of nannies with their little charges, and Roscoe took his coffee to a table on the grass outside as he waited for Marnie to arrive.

He had been waiting for ten minutes when he saw her walking towards him along the path past the tennis courts. She was wearing faded blue jeans with the cuffs turned up, scuffed black boots, a black polo neck jumper, and a battered three-quarter-length black leather coat that looked as if she had picked it up in Camden Market. Her hair was a little longer than he remembered it, curling around the upturned collar of her coat, but then he had not seen her since the incident on the Denton Estate.

Before the smoke had cleared out on the street, four police cars had appeared out of nowhere and the area had been sealed. The officer in charge, a corpulent DCI out of Camden Town station knocking on his pension door, soon had the man chained to the railings pointed out to him, and on going to investigate, he had found Roscoe and Marnie bloodied but not broken in the flat. After first checking and receiving assurances that there were no immediate life-threatening injuries, he told them what had happened outside and asked if either of them could elucidate. Shocked but not surprised, Roscoe told him about

Charlie and then furnished him with a description and the registration number of the Metro. Within fifteen minutes of the call going out on the air, Charlie had been apprehended crossing Waterloo Bridge.

A couple of CID men had spoken to Roscoe and Marnie, both together and alone, and then an ambulance had taken Marnie to the Whittington Hospital while a taciturn PC had escorted Roscoe to see his regular doctor, Ellen Jenkins. After the damage to his face and his shoulder had been treated, Ellen checked his ankle over. There had been no further damage to the tendon, but Ellen had warned him to take it easier for a couple of weeks.

The Chief Constable at first wanted to charge Charlie with first degree murder, make a public statement about how the force reacts to cop killers. But when the full list of Dillon's criminal activities had been laid before him, he performed a quick about-face and come down hard on the ghost of Sean Dillon instead. In the end, Charlie was charged with manslaughter, but his solicitor, an old acquaintance Roscoe had recommended to Rhiannon, thought that under the circumstances he just might get a suspended sentence. The press had been all over the case, delighting in jumping on Dillon, spouting righteous anger and indignation, seeing a stronger tale in the bent cop and the grief-stricken father. For once, thought Roscoe, their hearts were in the right place.

The morning after the incident, Roscoe had still been feeling too low and embarrassed to call Marnie direct, and so he had spoken to Spencer instead to ask how she was. Spencer had told him that there was no serious damage, just a few cuts and a blanket of bruises spread across her torso and legs, but the doctor had still ordered her to take a complete rest for three weeks. Roscoe had thanked him and left a message asking her to call, but he had not heard from her until earlier that morning.

"Thanks for coming," said Roscoe.

"It was me who called you," Marnie reminded him, smiling.

"Yeah, I know, but . . ." Roscoe started, embarrassed, then shrugged off the end of the sentence.

"You want to take a walk?" asked Marnie, starting towards the path again without waiting for a response.

"You don't want a coffee, then," said Roscoe, rising.

"No, come on, let's walk," said Marnie.

The pair walked along the path towards the running track in silence, the sun on their faces. The last leaves of autumn rolled down the hill and scuttled across the path like a desiccated stream. Just before reaching the pavilion, Marnie walked across the path and leaned on the iron railings. She looked out across the track towards the lido at Gospel Oak. Roscoe joined her, pushing his hands deep inside his pockets.

"So, how are you getting on?" asked Marnie.

"Well, the foot's all right," replied Roscoe. "I just need to rest it a while longer, that's all. Doctor's orders."

"That's good to hear. What about the rest of you?"

Roscoe touched a tender hand to his temple where the iron bar had connected. Most of the swelling had subsided, and there was just a slight discolouration left in the skin. But he knew that was not what she meant. "Yeah, fine," he said, dismissing the thought. "What about yourself, Marnie? Spencer told me there were no broken bones. You healing all right?"

"I'm getting there," replied Marnie. "There's just a little rainbow skin left of the bruises, that's all."

"That's good," said Roscoe, almost a whisper. He turned and looked back towards the café for a second, clearing his throat. "Look, Marnie, I'm really sorry about what happened back there in that flat. I can't apologise enough. I fucked up. None of that stuff should've happened. I should've been keeping a look out, known what was going on behind us. I don't know, after all this time off the job, I must've lost my instincts or something . . ."

"Don't worry about it," said Marnie. "It's me who should be apologising. I shouldn't have put you in a situation like that in the first place. I'm sorry, I didn't know your foot was still as bad as that. Not to mention your head."

"What about my head," said Roscoe, attempting a grin.

"Come on, Frank," said Marnie, reflecting his grin. "I've only been off work for two weeks, and I'm already starting to climb the walls. Seven months. . . . Jesus, what do you do all day?"

"I do loads of things," protested Roscoe.

"But don't you find that it gets to a point where time just starts to drift?" said Marnie. "You just start to drift?"

"Sometimes, I suppose," agreed Roscoe, the grin fading.

"And that just makes you feel lost and alone," said Marnie, turning to face him. "I don't know . . . abandoned, I suppose." She smiled and shook her head, the lines around her eyes crinkling. "It doesn't take long before your head starts to go soft."

"You think your head's starting to go soft?"

"I think it was heading that way," said Marnie, smiling. "That's why I've decided to go back to work on Monday."

"You sure you're ready? I thought you had another week."

Marnie fell silent for a moment, corralling her thoughts.

"I'm not fooling myself, Frank," she said, calm and measured. "I know that something like this could happen again, and I'll admit that a big part of me is scared about that. But I don't want that fear to control me, and the longer I leave it, the longer it'll take me to go back."

"I hear what you're saying," said Roscoe, looking off towards the lido. He fell silent for a moment, aware of Marnie at his side. "And I know that it's something I have to face, too, and sooner rather than later. But I need to find out who shot me first, otherwise my mind will never be fully on the job."

"I understand," said Marnie, touching his arm. "And if there's anything I can do to help, just let me know, all right?"

"Sure, thanks," said Roscoe.

"Come on, then, let's go to the Magdala," said Marnie, turning from the railings. "I'll buy you a drink, and then you can tell me some more about the bloody history of Camden Town."

Roscoe smiled and shook his head, let Marnie hook her arm through his and lead him out of the park.

ABOUT THE AUTHOR

Jerry Sykes was born in Yorkshire in 1960. His short stories have appeared in numerous publications in the UK, the USA, Italy, and Japan, and are regularly included in Year's Best anthologies. He is a two-time winner of the Crime Writers' Association's Short Story Dagger. This is his first novel.

Crestwood Public
Library District
4955 W. 135th Street
Crestwood, IL 60445